Hidden Magic

HARPER SHADOW ACADEMY: BOOK ONE

LUNA PIERCE

Alt Book Cover Design by EmCat Designs
Book Cover Design by Mibl Art
Editing by https://studioenp.com
Developmental Editing by Cruel Ink Editing
Editing by Cruel Ink Editing
Proofing by Tiffany Hernandez
Formatted by EmCat Designs
First Edition 2020
ISBN 978-1-7332322-3-4 (paperback)
ISBN 978-1-957238-12-8 (alt paperback)
ASIN B0899K9XHY (ebook)

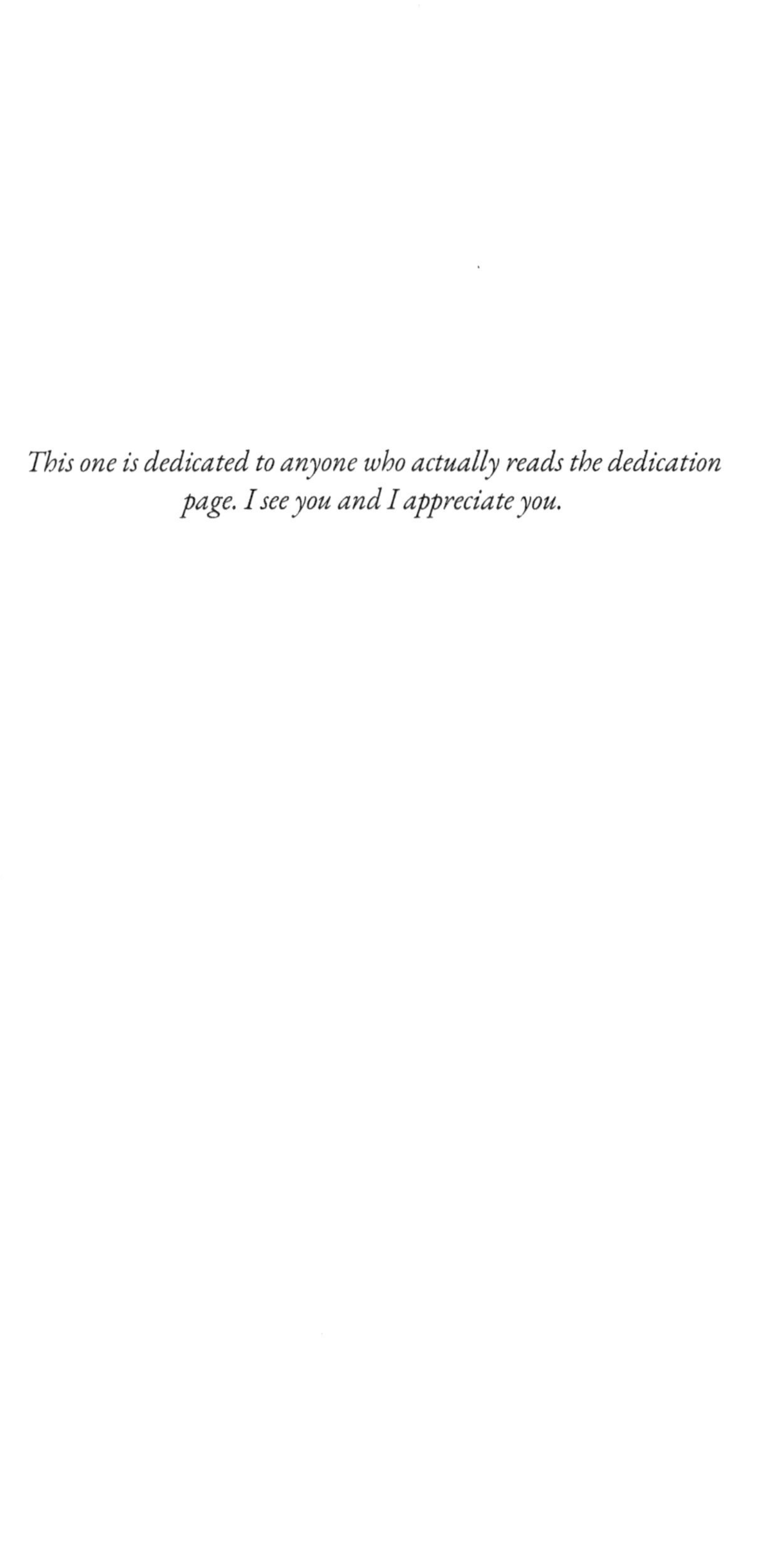

This one is dedicated to anyone who actually reads the dedication page. I see you and I appreciate you.

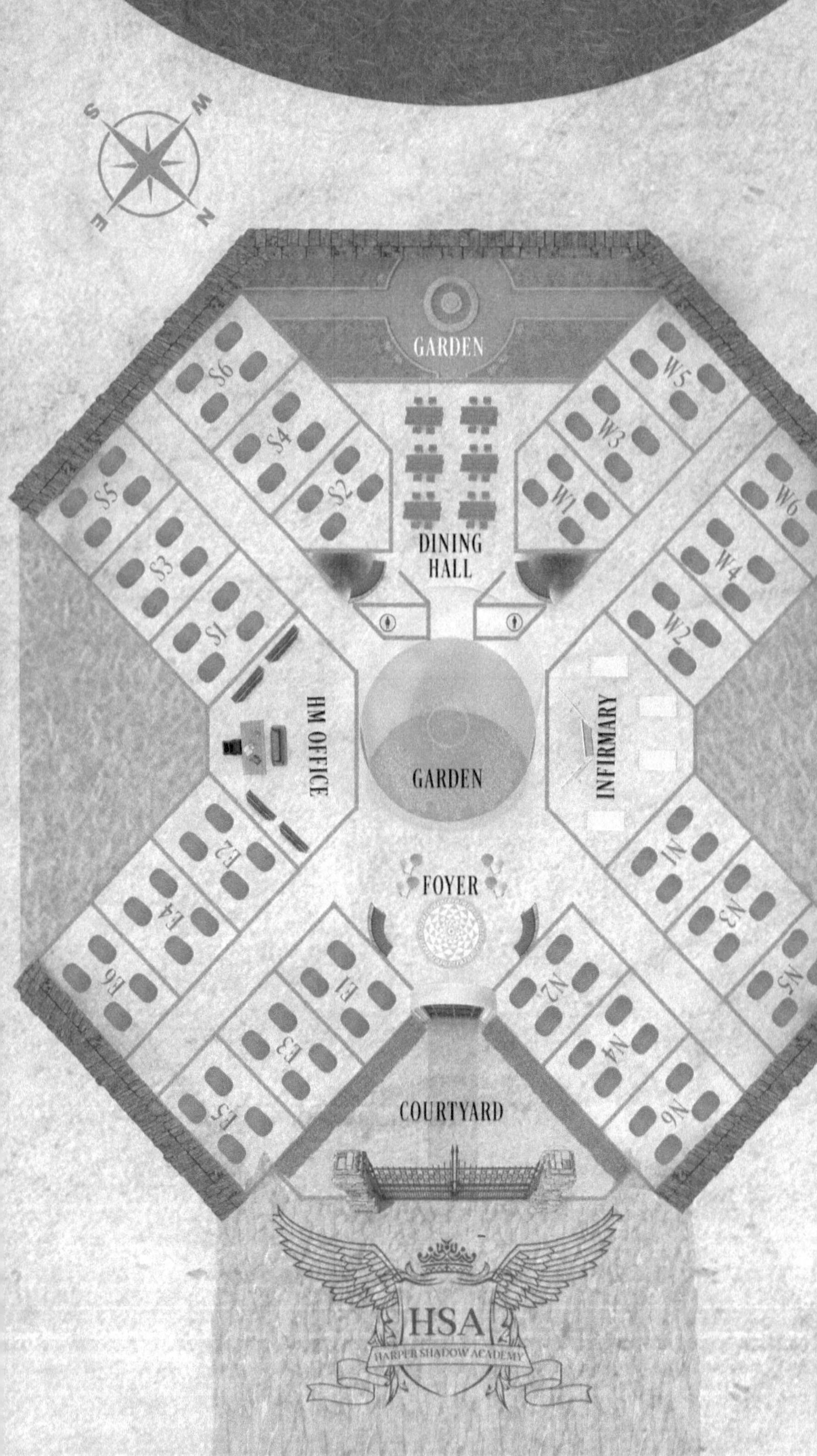

S
W
E
N
GARDEN
S6
S4
S2
S5
S3
S1
W5
W3
W1
W6
W4
W2
DINING HALL
HM OFFICE
GARDEN
INFIRMARY
N1
N3
N5
E2
E4
E6
E1
E3
E5
FOYER
N2
N4
N6
COURTYARD
HSA
HARPER SHADOW ACADEMY

BASEMENT/ LIBRARY

CHAPTER 1

My mother is a witch.

And by extension, that means I am, too.

But I know better. And the rumor whispered not so quietly in our small town is truer than her incoherent mumblings.

My mother is crazy.

For years now, she's acted strange—distant and scatter-brained, like she lost herself somewhere deep in her mind, never to return. She wasn't always this way, but with each passing day, I grew to realize she might not ever be the mother I distantly remember from my childhood.

At some point, I don't really know when, the roles seemed to reverse themselves. I became the nurturing, responsible party who began taking care of her. That's how it's been for a while. It isn't what a teenager expects from their adolescence, but it's what I've grown to understand and accept. One might even say I *liked* stepping into that position. The ability to count on myself was something I found comfort in.

Hungry? Make dinner. Bored? Do a puzzle or read a book. Need some new clothes? Get a job at the corner coffee shop and buy them. I quickly learned you're more prone to disappointment anytime you rely on someone else. The easiest and most effective way to fix that problem is to simply figure out how to do things without involving others.

Although, sometimes, it's possible to disappoint yourself, too.

For example, standing in front of the oversized antique mirror in my bedroom, the stench of dissatisfaction is heavy. A sigh nearly forces its way out, my shoulders following suit and hanging low.

"I, uh, thought you were going with black?" Brooke questions with a hint of sarcasm.

"I did, I totally did." I shout, "Look," and throw the empty box of hair dye at her playfully and turn my hands over twice. "My freaking hands are stained. Do you see this?"

"Uh-huh." She nods slowly. "And you dyed *your* hair?"

"Yes, you idiot. The color didn't take at all." I face the mirror and settle my gaze over my towel-dried, not-black-whatsoever hair.

"Listen, Will, your water must have been too hot or something. That's the exact stuff I use on my hair." She stands, stepping from my bed toward me, holding a thick lock of her shiny jet-black hair in her hand for my examination.

"I nearly froze to death using cold water, like you told me to do." I narrow my eyes.

"I can grab another box tonight. I get off work at eight, and we can try again tomorrow," she offers in an attempt to cheer me up. "I'll help this time."

"Why am I even surprised? How very anticlimactic. I had to wait until graduation to dye my hair, and guess what, it didn't work anyways." I always was a rule-follower. And despite my mom pretty much mentally checking out, I still clung to the few things I remembered her having an opinion about. Maybe it was my way of hanging onto that maternal role and pretending our dynamic wasn't entirely screwed up.

I didn't sneak out, not for the reasons teenagers in movies usually did. I might climb onto the roof to stargaze in the middle of the night, but I wasn't up there smoking pot or sipping from my mother's not-so-secret whiskey stash. I got pretty okay grades, homeschooling myself all the way through. It wasn't without challenges, but I figured it out. That's what you do when you have a problem—you solve it.

I saw no point in rebelling, because I'd be the one to face those consequences alone.

Why would I choose to make my own life more difficult?

"You're being dramatic." Brooke steadies herself behind me to look into the mirror. "I'm still baffled that you wanted to. You realize people kill for that weird silver thing you have going on."

She's not wrong. My hair has always been a focal point people gravitate toward, which is exactly why I wanted to change it. I want to blend in, not stand out, especially in a few days when I start at Harper Academy. A fresh beginning, becoming someone other than Willow Oliver—the girl who grew up too quick, the girl with the crazy mother—is exactly what I'm after. It's not that I'm unhappy with who I am, I just want to upgrade to another version. One where I'm living for myself and enjoying life a bit more. For the first time in my almost nineteen years, I want to know what it's like to exist the way other kids my age do. Even if I remain a wallflower to watch it unfold.

I slump onto the bed next to Brooke, my best friend since pretty much forever. "Fine."

She leans into me with her shoulder and gives me a push. "I'm still mad at you, though. Don't think I've given in yet."

"Oh, whatever." I push her back. "You're going to forget about me in like twelve seconds flat." I let out a small laugh, however, on the inside I'm equally bummed that we're going to two different schools.

"You're ashamed of me. That's it, isn't it? I finally figured it out." Brooke juts out her bottom lip in her best attempt to lay the guilt on thick.

"Ashamed? Of you? You're the one who told me Harper Academy is for the county rejects!" I scoot around the scattered pile of books on my bed and rest against the headboard.

Brooke dodges the books and positions herself between the headboard and one of my many pillows. "I said I was sorry, what more do you want from me? How was I supposed to know my best friend was going to go there?"

My house might be situated down a long-forgotten lane, but that never stopped the oh-so-curious Brooke from skipping down our gravel drive and insisting on being my friend. She never judged me for my weird hair color the same way the other kids in town did, and she never questioned my mother's strange behavior. It's like there was some unspoken agreement between us that superseded all the weirdness. I was grateful for her friendship—the one thing I could rely on throughout those very lonely years of my adolescence.

Brooke once asked why I didn't go to school like all the other kids, but I explained to her that I did my classwork at home, and she responded, "That's cool; my cousin Mary is homeschooled, too. She lives in Utah." It never came up again, and I was glad for it.

Over time, the older we got, the more I knew she could see the things we'd never spoken about, but still, she never asked the questions I feared she would.

"You know, if things were different, I would have been right there with you. Even with Danny taking over with Mom, this is the farthest I could manage." I pause for a second. "I'm lucky I got in anywhere." I lean my head back, inhaling deeply and closing my eyes.

The energy in the room shifts ever so slightly.

"This can't be it, okay?" Brooke says, almost in a whisper.

"What do you mean?" I open only one eye to peek at her.

"This whole *go to college and grow apart from each other*. The same thing that happens to everyone else at this point in their life."

If I didn't know better, I'd think Brooke was about to cry, but I do know better, and Brooke is incapable of crying. Quite literally, too. She's admitted to thinking she has some type of eye duct disability, especially once we tried to force her into crying by cutting up a bunch of onions and straight-up making her bite into them like apples. We were easily entertained kids, what can I say?

"It won't." The words exit my mouth, but the uncertainty lingers on my tongue. Do I want to grow apart from Brooke? Hell no. We've been through pretty much everything together. Training wheels, pimples, periods, and hardships galore, like when her dad decided to leave her mom for some bimbo from his work. Not to mention the whole, *my mom has been gradually losing her mind for the last six years*.

Mom mumbles often, specifically about being a witch. That she's a witch and I'm a witch and Grandma was a witch and our families are cursed. At first, I was freaked out. I was twelve years old, and my mom was suddenly rambling about coming into magic, reigniting some long-lived curse on our family. That I would be next, and I had to resist the urges. Little did she know, I was a kid, but I wasn't too stupid to find her whiskey stash she'd been nursing for breakfast, lunch, and dinner.

A quick house visit from the local doctor was just the thing to secure the medication she needed to calm her nerves and put a limit on the outbursts where she yelled out, "I'm an Oliver witch."

Time passed, and I found that it was easier to console her and say, "Yes, Mom, you're a witch." It beat arguing. It certainly beat telling her the truth that she was, in fact, not a witch, but instead was going through an unexplainable rough patch.

Uncle Danny helps from time to time, but because I didn't want to leave Harper, the town I was born and raised in, and move to the city with him, I had to step into the role of caretaker. I knew the risks I would be taking at a young age—to stay put in a town I was familiar with—but it was something I was willing to do to keep the few certain things I had.

I guess Danny's feeling sympathetic because I'm graduating this year. He said something about wanting to help me come into my own. He relocated his accounting business to mostly online so he could move back to Harper and care for my mom so I can go to college. And when I say *go to college*, I mean go to the local academy that's only a ten-minute drive from home. I'll be living there, but it's nothing like the way Brooke gets to escape this place.

During one of Danny's bi-annual visits to check in on me and Mom, he had checked the mail.

"This looks important," he had said while tossing the thick envelope at me.

I caught it seconds before it fell into the pan of sauce I was stirring. "Thanks, jerk."

Danny was always more of an annoying older brother than an uncle to me, but I didn't mind. It was nice having someone other than my mom or Brooke around.

I barely glanced at the piece of mail, instead, I discarded it onto the counter and continued adding salt and pepper to the sauce.

"If you're not going to open it, I'm going to." Danny reached for it without waiting for me to protest.

I rolled my eyes and sighed. "Opening someone else's mail is a federal offense, you know."

Danny let out a laugh. "Who are you going to call, Bill? He's probably drunk down at the station. Man should arrest himself." He slid his finger under the seal of the envelope and ripped it open.

Continuing to focus on our dinner, I ignored the strange

uncertainty that formed in my chest. The envelope seemed official in some capacity, but I hadn't been expecting anything to arrive. Not then, or ever. My life was like that. Boring and predictable.

Still, my heart picked up its pace as I pretended to not count the seconds it took his eyes to gaze over the text before he opened his mouth.

"You got a scholarship to Harper Academy," he said without looking up from the paper.

"I..." Blinking a few times, I tried to understand how that could be possible. "I didn't apply."

Danny shrugged and turned the document toward me. "Says here you're eligible for room and board tuition. I think that means it includes your food, too."

I snatched the paper out of his grasp and scanned the printed black text that confirmed he wasn't making the whole thing up. It was a two-year program, including all the bells and whistles. It had to have been too good to be true, and like all things, it was. Because when my sights settled on the one major deal-breaker, I knew I couldn't entertain this fever dream of a possibility.

I was expected to live on campus, and first year students were only allowed to leave once per semester.

The pot that once had my attention started bursting red bubbles onto the off-white backsplash, a reminder that I needed to get back to reality and stop living in the fairytale I imagined in the twelve seconds I allowed myself to think of what it might be like to get out of here.

"Not going to happen." I tossed the paper aside and took the pan off the burner, my hidden gaze glistening as I stirred the sauce into the pasta.

Danny had sighed, dramatically if I remembered it correctly, and marched over to the paper once again. "What's the issue? This sounds like a really great opportunity for you."

I ignored him and pulled three plates out of the cabinet, setting them gently on the counter and not allowing my emotions to bubble over like the sauce had and give away the immense sadness coursing through me.

I wasn't sure which was more overpowering, the disappointment or the guilt of having actually entertained the idea of leaving.

That's when Danny did something completely uncharacteristic. Instead of poking fun at me, he came over and set the paper onto one of the plates. He pushed his finger onto it like he was trying to get me to understand the severity of whatever it was he was about to say. "We'll make this work."

"Danny—"

But he cut me off. "Will." He kept his voice low. "I know I give you a hard time but opportunities like this don't come often, and I won't sit back and not push you to take it."

I shook my head slowly. "It won't work."

He nodded. "Yes, it will. I have my laptop and my phone. You guys just got better internet installed a few months ago. It won't be perfect, but it won't be permanent either. What's two years when you've given your entire life to caring for your mom? Let me help, please. I know that's hard for you, to accept help, but I refuse to take no for an answer. You're doing this. End of discussion."

And after going back and forth about it for the next month or so, working out all the details to make it happen, it was decided.

It wasn't an ivy league, and the credits probably wouldn't even transfer to any of the state universities, but it might mean that my future held more than working in the back of a coffee shop for minimum wage. The owner was kind enough to give me an under-the-table job before it was legally allowed, but I couldn't rely on that forever. Not when my mom only seemed to get worse instead of better and what was left of our savings had almost dwindled completely away.

Maybe with a half-assed degree, I could get a better job to support my mother, and while I was at it, I could get a glimpse of what it was like to act my age.

I would be attending the incredibly small and not even accredited college in this quaint small town.

Harper: Population six hundred and thirteen.

And after Brooke leaves, there will be one less person in this living ghost town.

Formerly a booming mining city has been resolved to boarded-up homes and a barely functioning economy. It's as though everything that remains has been frozen in time and thanks to the new state routes, unless your GPS is set to come here, not a single person would ever accidentally stumble upon us.

Brooke once joked and said that Harper Academy is full of rejects, but what she really meant was it's for those who can't seem to escape Harper County. There's nothing wrong with anyone who comes here, they're just notorious for never leaving this sad excuse of a town.

And maybe going to Harper Academy is a mistake, maybe I'll be doomed to the same fate of being stuck in this town, but how will I know if I don't try? If Harper Academy is the best I can do given the circumstances, I'm sure as hell willing to find out. And in three long days, I'll be doing exactly that.

What's the worst that could happen?

CHAPTER 2

The thudding between my ears manages to stay consistent throughout the day while I pack the few belongings I'm taking to Harper Academy. Call me a minimalist, but less to pack means less to unpack, and less I'll have to bring back upon finishing my schooling.

Clothing is a given and pretty much the extent of what I'm taking with me. Various shades of black, gray, and dark blues litter my suitcase. Not much variation, especially considering the goal is to blend in. I did a damn good job of it until now—clocking in and out of the café in the dark hours and doing the bi-weekly grocery shopping early when it was just me and the forgetful elderly people. I avoided people my age because I had zero desire to explain who I was, or why I was different than them. Especially when I couldn't make sense of it myself. I check the contents of my small makeup bag—concealer, powder, blush, and mascara—and throw it on top.

I strategically place my black boots on opposite ends and shove a couple notebooks where I can manage them. I was told Harper had a decent library so I take the risk of not packing any books in hopes I can read what they have there.

I really hope that's not a mistake.

I sink onto the ground next to my bed and lean against my nightstand, staring blankly at the bag in front of me while I rack my brain to think of anything I'm forgetting. I'm not sure why I'm so concerned, given that I'm not exactly going that far away from home.

My cell phone buzzes loudly on the hardwood floor, nearly scaring the shit out of me. A text from Uncle Danny.

Danny: Almost to town, need anything?

Me: Just don't forget to stop by the apothecary and grab Mom's meds.

Danny: 10-4, good buddy.

I let out a small chuckle. Who knew accountants could be funny?

Placing my phone on the bed, and off the floor so I don't smash it, I catch a faint sound of footsteps coming up the stairs. They're light and I immediately recognize that they're hers.

The bedroom door creaks open.

"Hey, Mom," I mutter.

She smiles bleakly. "Can I come in?" Her gaze trails across the contents of the room.

I pat the spot next to me on the bed. "Of course. Are you feeling okay?"

She adjusts herself exactly where I motioned, and her feeble hands tremble slightly in her lap.

Worry lines my brow, and I reach out to gently place my hand on her shoulder. "Mom?"

It's always a gamble at what she'll say next or how she'll react. Sometimes it's like nothing is wrong at all and she seems totally normal, and other times, her eyes go wild and she mutters incoherent nonsense under her breath.

Her thin lips part, taking in a breath, and she says, "You'll be safe, right?"

I'm startled by the glaze that coats her eyes and the genuine concern snaking its way across her face.

"Yes, Mom." I manage what I can of a comforting smile. "Although I'm more worried about you than I am me. I won't be too far away, okay? If you need me, I can be right here in a flash."

Screw the whole only leaving campus once a semester thing. If I'm needed here, nothing will stop me.

Her regard falls onto her hands, and I follow suit, watching her take her index finger and pick at her thumbnail, one of her many nervous ticks.

Mom speaks, so low it's almost inaudible. "You're special, you need to acknowledge that, Willow."

Feeling the energy in the room shift like a tidal wave, I brace myself for what's to come.

"You don't know the dangers of this world." She looks up to meet my eyes, a fire burning into hers. "They will come for you, and you have to be ready."

The tension rises throughout my body, but I force myself to relax, to focus on being calm, on comforting her. I close my eyes for half a second and take a deep breath, and on the exhale, I visualize the stress being erased. I can't get worked up because then *she* gets worked up. This was one of those lessons I learned the hard way early on.

Pick your battles.

I take her cool hand into mine and cup it between my palms. "Okay, Mom. I'll keep an eye out."

Perhaps she accepts my response. Her expression loosens, and the bewilderment once consuming her dies down.

Once I'm, what I think to be fully packed, Uncle Danny carries my bags downstairs.

"You sure this is it, kid?"

"You're making me second-guess myself, Danny."

"You're going *so far away* to college that I'm not sure I'll be able to spare the few minutes to bring you anything you forgot." He chuckles and nudges me with his elbow.

I roll my eyes and grab my backpack from the floor. "Come on, I don't want to be late."

The drive to the school with Mom and Danny is short and quiet, but the view is great. Long, windy roads surrounded by overgrown greenery. Just when I think the ride has finally settled my nerves, the car slows to a creep and turns onto a gravel lane. The change in terrain further unravels my anxiety, and I swallow the lump forming in my throat.

Knowing someone at Harper Academy would have put me at ease, but considering I homeschooled myself so I could tend to my mom and work part-time at the coffee shop, the chances of seeing a familiar face would be slim to none. That was my plan all along, to go unnoticed, so I shouldn't be upset I succeeded in becoming a nobody.

The journey comes to a crawl and then to an abrupt stop the moment we reach the parking area in front of the school. My heart thuds at a million times its normal rate, and I force myself to remember I'm doing this for me, that I deserve this.

I step out of the car, and a few warm raindrops greet me. I tug the hood from my sweatshirt up in response. The three of us making our way to the front gate, I keep my eyes to the ground, avoiding any notice from onlookers. I quickly pull my phone from my pocket and read the instructions again.

Make your way to the headmaster's office upon arrival.
Please arrive between 3:00-6:00 p.m.
Rooms will be assigned during admission.

.   .   .

I glance to the top of the page to confirm we have the correct date, and to the clock at the top of my phone that reads 2:57 p.m. I have a thing for being on time. Punctuality is sort of a strong suit of mine.

Prior to leaving the house, I was able to get Mom to take her medication, making our goodbye that much easier, being that she's much calmer while medicated. Making a scene and drawing attention wasn't something that I wanted, but I desperately wanted her around every second I could manage. Although I'm looking forward to this *new* change, I'm equal parts terrified to be leaving home, to be leaving Mom.

Danny has reassured me continuously that he has everything under control, and even with him basically forcing me to go through with this, he made me promise that I would *try* to be a normal college student.

Whatever that means.

Danny and Mom finish hugging me, and I stand for just a moment and watch them walk back to the car. Raindrops pick up their pace, pelting me with a bit more force, like a nudge from Mother Nature to get my ass in gear and get into the school.

I look to the sky and mutter, "Fine, I'm going!"

The universe responds by assaulting me with more of a downpour.

Grabbing the handle to my suitcase, I make a beeline for the entrance to the school. Once my eyes adjust to my surroundings, I have to do a double take on the school insignia to verify I'm in the right place.

Tucked beyond the gate where I said my goodbyes is a beautiful triangular-shaped courtyard with the two massive front ends of the stone building protruding on both far sides. If I wasn't in such a hurry, I'd stop to soak in the amazing architecture. The rain gains momentum, and I bolt for the door.

I step through the threshold in a rush and accidentally bump right into another person. My shoulder slams into theirs, and I nearly knock them down.

"I'm so sorry," I spit out in a panic, my suitcase flinging itself away from me. I reach out to seize the arm of the person I ran into and pull them back onto solid ground.

Topaz-blue eyes radiate into mine, and a rapid flush courses through my body.

"Are you all right?" my victim asks.

"Am I okay? I knocked you down, I'm such an idiot."

I stand here, sort of dumbstruck at what just happened, and quickly realize the time ticking by. Blue eyes glance from me to my rogue bag.

He snatches the handle and places it in front of me. "I'm great now." He grins wide with one of those meets-the-eyes kind of smiles.

When I don't say anything, he continues, "You haven't checked in yet, have you?"

I shake my head, my cheeks flushing, knowing my first inter-action at my fresh new start is an embarrassing one. *At least the view is nice.*

"I'm Cameron." He extends his hand.

I attempt to wipe the rain off my own before meeting his. Warm fingers wrap their way around my palm and grip firmly but gently.

"Willow," I manage to speak.

Cameron's eyes beam. "What a beautiful name."

Holding onto his hand a moment longer, I allow my gaze to fall over him, from his amber wisps of hair to his broad, but not-too-broad shoulders, down to his black-and-white sneakers.

In a flash, another form barrels into him, latching on to his shoulders and breaking our embrace.

"Dude, Cam, c'mon." The intruder's tone changes when he realizes I'm there. "Oops, totally did *not* mean to interrupt."

"The headmaster's office is right over there." Cameron points behind me.

I glance in the direction to see the sign above the door. "Thanks."

"Yeah, no problem, Willow."

My name rolls off his tongue like honey, mending my nerves and erasing the colossal headache I've had all day. *He works better than the strongest pain reliever.*

Avoiding people all my life means I have minimal interactions with the opposite sex. Is it normal to feel immediately drawn to someone or am I just reacting like a typical hormonal teenager?

I make my way across the stunningly decorated foyer, stepping around the oversized comfy-looking loungers. Approaching the door to the headmaster's office, a chipper fire-engine red-haired girl greets me.

"Hi there. First-year?"

"Uh—yes." I nod.

"Name, please?"

"Willow Oliver."

She looks from her clipboard and back to me. "Ahh, here we are. Oh gosh, forgive me, I forgot about the pleasantries. I'm Abigail Spencer, Headmaster Walker's TA this year. Mr. Walker is running a bit late so I'm taking over for him until he gets here."

She extends her hand, and I take it, my mind wandering to a few moments ago when those gorgeous blue eyes met mine, except this time I'm startled by a strange shock that forces its way into my hand and up my arm.

I pull my arm away in a rush. "Crap, sorry, I must have built up static. I do that all the time. I can barely walk through the house without shocking myself with everything I touch."

Her expression changes slightly, and she returns to her bright and bubbly self. "No worries, Willow. Now, if you'll fill out this entrance information. Make sure to note if you have any food allergies. Last semester we had an unexpected peanut allergy that sent a student to the hospital."

I take the clipboard from her, and she motions for me to come into the office and sit. She pulls a rather strange-looking wand from her bag on the table and waves it through the air. The device beeps, and when I glance from the paperwork to her, she frowns for a fraction of a second.

"Wi-Fi issues." She shrugs.

I make quick work of the last few questions, and after glancing over it, she hands me a slip of paper.

"You'll be dorming in the south wing. Room SD four. There will be four to a room, but you're the first one here for this room, so if you get up there quick, you can choose your bed."

"South wing?" I try not to sound as pathetic as I feel.

She smiles warmly. "You'll figure it out quickly. The school is shaped almost like an X but for clarity sake, we have it labeled that each corner is either north, south, east, or west. Girls dorm in the west and south, boys in the north and east. Here." She holds out a sheet of paper with a map and points behind her. "Go left out of the office and then take another left into the hallway. Immediately to your right will be a stairwell. Take that upstairs, and voila, you're in south dorms. Yours will be the second door on your right."

"Okay, yeah, that makes sense." I grab the paper and eye it over. It should be simple enough. North, south, east, west. Upstairs and downstairs. Two lefts and a right. I can do this.

"There will be a small orientation at six fifteen, and you'll report to the East wing in the morning for your class list. The dining hall will begin serving at six thirty so you should have some time to settle in. Hmm, am I forgetting anything?" Without allowing me time to process or respond, she continues, "Nope, I think that's it."

She all but pushes me out of the room and starts in on her next student. Blindly looking at my map and glancing up briefly, I take my first left and run right into someone. *Again. Like an idiot.*

Words haven't even made it out of my mouth when strong hands clamp down on both of my shoulders. "Are you okay?"

My gaze trails from the paper and up to my latest victim, piercing chestnut brown eyes this time, a drastic change from the startling blue earlier. I notice the thick dark hair that covers his brow, and my eyes scan his chiseled jawline. *What the hell kind of school is this?*

"Yeah, I'm fine, sorry. I need to watch where I'm walking."

"Me, too." He laughs. "Although, it looks like you're hiding from someone."

I squint and he points to his head.

"Your hood."

Instinctually, my hand reaches up top. "Oh, right. No, it was raining when I came in. Not hiding from anyone."

"I hate to cut this short, but I have to run. It was nice to bump into you..."

"Willow," I blurt out the moment I realize he was alluding to my name.

"Willow, it's a pleasure to meet you. I'm Deghan." He glances down to the slip in my hand and then points down the hallway to my left. "South dorm is that way, up the stairs around the corner."

"Thanks," I mutter.

He winks and takes off, grazing my shoulder on the way, and those all-too-familiar sparks flow through me. I brush it off without a second thought and head toward the stairs, hoping that I can make it the rest of the way to my dorm without bumping into another person. At least I've managed to embarrass myself in front of two of the hottest guys I've ever laid eyes on. *Good job on not drawing attention to yourself, Will.*

CHAPTER 3

I successfully make it to the south wing dorms with zero additional casualties. Abigail was correct that none of my other dormmates had shown up yet, and the bed in the far back corner with the window nearby is a glorious perk of being on time.

The map she gave me shows that the entire girl dormitory—south and west—share a large bathroom, as do the boys' dorms on the north and east side. The girls and boys each have separate common areas and then a combined common area in the center of the upstairs.

Our dorm room has a sink and a decent-sized mini-fridge, along with four identical beds, dressers, and nightstands. For such a typically frowned-upon school, Harper Academy doesn't seem to cut corners on any of their supplies. Not to mention the building itself is elegant and absolutely incredible—the craftsmanship not faulting whatsoever. So far, nothing about being here is what I expected.

I've put the fitted sheet and blanket onto my bed when a wave of exhaustion hits me. Allowing the nervousness of the last hour to take a breather, I lie back on my twin-sized bed and process the events. Along with punctuality, I'm also great at being an overthinker.

My mind immediately wanders to my mom and whether or not she and Danny are okay. I fish the cell phone out of my pocket and click his name, and the phone takes an annoyingly long time to connect. He finally answers, his voice coming in all scratchy, forcing me to get up from the bed and meander to the window in search of a better signal.

"Danny, are you there?"

"Yeah, I'm here. I hear you a bit better now. Your service isn't that great."

"Must be this building."

Silence.

"Danny?"

More silence. I move to the other side of the window.

"You there, Will?"

"Yeah. How are things going? Is Mom all right?"

Silence falls again, and I grow annoyed. I open the window and, despite my aversion to heights, hang out a bit in an attempt to get better service.

"Danny?" I call out again.

"Mom is fine, and I'm great, thanks for asking." Such a smartass.

"Good, that's nice to hear."

"You realize it's only been like half an hour, right Wills?"

I sigh. "I know. This is hard on me, though. I feel selfish."

He cuts out slightly, and then I make out, "You've been nothing but selfless your whole life, Wills. Cut yourself a break, okay? No kid should have had to take on the responsibilities you have. I'm telling you I have this covered. Please try not to worry, you're going to ruin your time there."

"It's going to take some time to adjust," I murmur.

"I think that's totally understandable."

He continues to speak, but the signal cuts out again, compelling me to lean a bit farther out and reposition my hand somewhat. Just enough for my cell to slip out of it and smash onto the ground below.

"Shit," I cuss under my breath.

"Better your phone than you," a new voice declares.

I nearly fall off the ledge as I focus on the unknown person.

"Didn't mean to scare you." She nods toward my bed. "I see you got the prime location."

"Early bird gets the worm." I smirk despite my nerves. It's really starting to sink in—the whole *roommates* thing.

The newcomer is gorgeous. A total girlie girl with a slim frame, perfect teeth, and an aura that screams she gets along with everyone.

"Touché." She winks. "Mind if I take that one?" She motions to the one directly across from mine along the wall with the window.

"No, not at all." I look down at the hefty bags she carted in. "Do you need some help?"

"Ab-so-lutely." She pauses and then adds, "You should probably salvage your phone first."

"Uh, with my luck, I wouldn't be surprised if it's a goner."

She points to my head. "Listen, we just met, but you totally look like a serial killer."

Having forgotten I still had it up, I yank my hood down and ruffle my matted hair.

My new roommate's eyes widen. "Holy shit, your hair. Who do you go to? Someone around here? It's flawless. Your roots aren't even showing. Did you recently get it done?" She rapid-fires questions while she approaches, reaching out to touch my hair but stopping short, possibly grasping how intrusive that may be.

I let out a small breath, knowing how typical this type of reaction is. Which is exactly why I wanted to dye it black, or anything other than this uncommon silver.

"It's natural, actually. I tried to color it a few days ago, but it didn't stick."

"Color it? Are you insane? People pay big bucks for this kind of thing." She grabs a lock of her own auburn-ish blonde hair. "This cost a small fortune."

"That's what I'm told."

"Anyway, didn't mean to get sidetracked and all up in your personal space. I'm Remi."

"Willow."

"Dope hair, sick name, and super nice? I think we're going to be great friends." Remi winks and carries one of her bags to her new living space. "Hurry back."

Once I'm a few steps outside of our dorm, I realize I left the map behind and don't know my way around the building yet. Instead of wasting more time and going back, I decide to wing it; sometimes, figuring things out the hard way is the most effective. It can't be that difficult, though, can it? Go down the steps and hook a couple lefts until I can find my way outside. Easy-peasy.

I make my way down and toward the center of the building, taking note of the restrooms right next to the stairs, and turn into the dining hall which leads to gigantic floor-to-ceiling windows opening up to an outdoor patio area, making sure to avoid eye contact with everyone.

I clear the threshold to the patio and immediately go in the direction of what I'm hoping is below my dorm window. Luckily, the rain has stopped, but the grass is a bit sloshy under my solid-black Vans. Eyeballing the second story, I follow the trajectory of the window and find myself disappointed at the lack of cell phone on the ground. I take a few steps back, examining the building and locating my window again, the bombshell roommate of mine waving feverishly from our room.

If that's our window, our room, and I dropped the phone

here, why isn't it where it should be? My gaze slides down the wall and onto the first-story window's stone ledge. I walk closer and something shiny catches my eye. I gasp, recognizing my cell phone, sitting there—impossibly—unharmed.

What the...?

Upon inspection, I confirm that the phone is unscathed, and I have two unread texts. One from Danny and one from Brooke. Without reading either of them, I turn around, surveying my surroundings to see if I can uncover the mystery of my absolutely fine phone, which should be shattered or at least covered in mud.

Not many people are on the patio, and none of them seem to show the slightest interest in what I'm doing. I scan the rest of the patio until my gaze meets another, something hauntingly familiar about the guy looking directly at me. His piercing stare sends a shock through me. Frozen in place, I dare to take a step forward at the same time the group of people shift and obstruct my view of the unidentified person. In need of answers, I rush forward, only to be utterly confused when the cluster of people depart, leaving me wholly alone.

First my phone and now this guy vanishing into thin air? What the hell is with today?

The walk back to the dorm is one full of thinking, of trying to rationalize what the heck just happened. Somehow, I autopilot myself back without getting lost.

Once I'm inside, Remi looks up from her spot on the floor. "What's the damage?"

I hold up my phone and respond, "Not a single scratch."

She tilts her head, "How is that even possible?"

"My thought, too." I didn't want to tell her where it was sitting, or about the random guy who appeared and disappeared, out of concern that she would think I was crazy. Unfortunately though, the crease in her brow and her narrowed eyes don't give me much hope—she for sure thinks I'm crazy.

"At least you don't have to buy another one." She shrugs. "Can you grab that bag?"

The next two hours are spent unpacking and arranging our space, and welcoming the last of our roommates, Lillian and Kyra, the former taking the bed next to mine and the latter taking the remaining space next to Remi.

It's safe to say that Remi brought the most stuff. Her side of the room overflows with clothes, shoes, and beauty supplies—a drastic difference from my sparse items. Now I see how she gets those perfect waves...she's got multiple curling wands and excessive hair products.

"We aren't all as lucky as you, Willow," she exclaims in response to my wide eyes at all of her stuff.

"I'm not judging," I reply with my hands in the air. "I'm too lazy for all that, and I prefer sleep over getting ready anytime."

"Fair enough."

First impressions seem to go over well, and the unsettling feeling of not knowing who I would be rooming with disappeared quickly upon meeting everyone. Somehow, I lucked out in the roomie department. Every single girl is uniquely nice and friendly.

Lillian, with her dark hair and plain but beautiful features, is massively soft-spoken and packed about the same amount I did. Our side of the room is meager compared to Remi and Kyra's. Lillian settled in swiftly, shoving the empty bags under her bed and pulling out a book—if only I had done the same instead of relying on a library I've never been to.

Kyra was the last to arrive, hauling in multiple bags, almost outdoing Remi's entrance. Her thick, brown, tight curls bounce against her shoulders as she struggles to heave her heavy bag, her light-brown skin turning red. Kyra is stunning to say the least. All of my new buds are. And so are the random guys I—literally—ran into. Beauty aside, everyone is super pleasant, too.

What universe did I just step into?

Ten minutes prior to the start, we collectively make our way to orientation. We exit our room, and a bright-eyed blonde girl stops short of Remi and nearly bites her head off.

"Watch where you're going," the girl scolds.

Remi's gaze swings from the girl to us and back. "Sorry?"

"You should be. Uh, you're going to make me late. Get out of my way."

The girl storms off, leaving us in a cloud of dust.

"That was...interesting," Kyra adds.

"I guess we found the *mean girl* of the school," I offer.

Rounding the corner on the main level, a large group takes their leave from the dining hall.

"Did we get the time right?" I ask.

"Yep," Remi confirms. "Must have been second years or something."

The people pass, and a loud buzzing weasels its way into my body. Head to toe thrumming, like a generator or something.

"Do you hear that?" I ask Remi.

She glances at me, confused. "Hear what?"

I shake my head. "Never mind."

Something flashes in the corner of my vision, and despite managing to get a hurried peek, I miss whatever it is. I do a complete 360 and catch a glimpse between tree branches of a vaguely familiar face right as they turn and rush up the north wing stairs.

I take notice of the insane floor-to-ceiling glass encasing an outdoor garden in the dead center of the building. *How did I miss this at arrival?*

I'm standing there awestruck, admiring the greenery growing in such a random place, when Remi nudges me. "You okay? You look like you saw a ghost."

"This is..."

"Insane?" She finishes my sentence.

"Yeah, that's a good word for it."

"Look up," she orders, taking her index finger and lifting my chin toward the ceiling.

"Holy shit."

The outdoor garden has a glass top, which is the floor to the second floor. Numerous people walk on the second floor, and I scan their faces. One meets mine and smiles back. Tall, dark, and handsome. *Deghan.*

"Is that hot guy waving at you?" Kyra asks.

"Umm, no, definitely not." I motion toward the dining hall. "Are we ready?"

Kyra rolls her eyes. "Whatever. But you better call dibs before someone else does."

I swallow the lump in my throat. *Dibs?* We've been here less than a day!

CHAPTER 4

The orientation goes well, considering it was put on by Abigail, given the headmaster is still missing in action. She assures us he will be arriving soon, but here we are, reporting to our respective wings bright and early to receive our class lists and direction with no sight of him.

A round-faced older woman with gray hair greets us near the entrance to the east wing.

"Good morning, girls. I'm Professor Strong."

What a contradiction that is.

"Good morning," we mutter in return.

"Go ahead and gather in room E five, I'll be down there short-ly." She smiles, showing us her yellowed teeth.

Adding in the lines and lines of wrinkles around her mouth, I can only assume both are caused by years of smoking.

"Yes, ma'am," I reply.

Looking at the small signs near the doors, we find E five situated at the end of the tiled hall on the left. The room is large with a rounded window letting in massive amounts of natural light. One thing this school did not skimp on is windows.

"Willow," a voice boasts.

I turn to the sound, scanning the room, and land on those stunning blue eyes. *Cameron.*

He waves excitedly until I give him my attention. The girls mutually side-eye me but follow me to the table Cameron's sitting at.

"Hey." I sit in the chair opposite of him.

Remi pulls up the chair to my right, Lillian to my left, and Kyra goes around to sit next to Cameron. She winks at me from across the table.

"Not going to lie," he says. "I totally did not expect *that* under your hood."

"Yeah, yeah, I get it. My hair is always a big surprise. It's just hair." I huff.

"You could have been bald for all I know, it's"—he seems to get lost in thought for a second—"it really brings out the blue in your eyes. Or is that green? I see both."

"Could be both. They sort of do their own thing. But, uh... thanks?"

He teases. "You're not the best at taking compliments, are you?"

At that, Mrs. Strong strides into the room.

"Good morning again, students." She coughs and continues, "I'll be passing out your class itinerary shortly. The rest of today will allow you to get familiar with the campus and find your classes, with tomorrow being the official first day. I strongly urge you to pair up and explore today."

Remi gives my chair a delicate kick, and when my eyes falter from Mrs. Strong, Cameron gives me a questioning glance and shoots his hand into the air.

"Why, our first question, and so soon. Yes, young sir?"

"Do we get to pick our partner?" he queries.

"I suppose so. It was merely a suggestion more than a requirement."

Cameron cuts her off, blurting out, "I choose Willow."

My cheeks burn with a flush, and I sink into my seat, thinking that maybe I can melt into my chair and stop the watchful eyes from being drawn to me.

Remi sighs and kicks Cameron's chair, not delicately like she had done mine. She gives him a death stare, and he grins immensely at her.

Mrs. Strong hands out our papers and dismisses us. Our table hangs back to let the rest of the students disperse while we study our schedules.

"Who does everyone have for first?" Kyra questions. "I've got Strong."

"Weller," I respond, meeting the eyes of our little group, hoping someone has the same.

"Strong." Cameron sighs.

"Same," Lillian whispers at the same time Remi replies.

Cameron pokes at my paper. "We have creative writing together...and psych 101."

"You two ought to go find them since you're *partners* and all," Remi jokes.

"She said it wasn't required. You realize we can all go together, right?" I add.

"I'm just screwing with you. I have to run and grab my phone, though, I forgot it this morning." She focuses on Lillian and Kyra. "Coming with me or hanging with them?"

"You two go ahead." Kyra smirks at me. She lowers her voice, "Dibs and all."

"We can wait, I really don't mind." I look to Cameron. "Do you?"

He swipes a lock of hair from his brow, his sparkling sky-deep eyes meeting mine, and verifies, "Not at all."

"We'll meet you in the foyer in ten," Remi confirms.

A few seconds pass following the girls leaving us alone, and I become fidgety. I scan the wall for a clock and make a mental note of the time.

"So...what brings you to Harper Academy, Miss Willow?" Cameron leads us from the classroom.

I spy the numbers outside of the rooms, even numbers on one side, odd on the other. One through six.

"An education, you?"

"I guess you could say the same. I couldn't really afford to go anywhere else, and this was the most cost-effective. And that's with me paying what my grant didn't cover."

I don't verbally respond so he resumes. "I got a grant for living in Harper. Are you from out of town?"

At this, I laugh. "Born and raised here, actually."

"In Harper? You're kidding me. How have I never seen you around?"

He places his hand on the small of my back and leads me toward the foyer seating area. His touch is equally comforting and alarming. I've known him a whole twelve seconds, and he's touching me, and I don't hate it.

"Sorry," he apologizes. "I shouldn't have done that." He stops in front of me, a mere distance from my face, drawing me to a stop, too. A handful of inches taller, he looks down at me, surveying my every movement. His hand moves from his side, motioning toward the couch next to us. "Want to have a seat while we wait?"

I sit on the dark and thoroughly comfortable couch, facing what I think is the north wing. Cameron sits too, turning toward me and sitting sideways, one elbow on the back of the couch, almost like he's waiting eagerly for me to share my deepest darkest secrets.

"I was homeschooled," I finally respond.

"Oh, how rad. That's awesome."

"Not really. It wasn't a great time."

"Yeah, but you probably got to sleep in and stay in your pajamas all day?"

"I started working part-time at fourteen."

At the change in my tone, he concedes, "I didn't mean to bring up anything bad." Cameron tenderly puts his hand on mine. "I'm not trying to pry. Or maybe I am. I don't know. But I'm sorry if it comes across that way. I'm incredibly intrigued, Willow. Like a moth to a flame."

Despite my nervous energy, I sense his genuine nature spill through, setting me at ease.

"I'm not really used to talking about myself," I admit. "There's never really any time for it."

"Whatever you're running from, whatever's been stealing your light, I hope you can escape it here."

Vague as it may seem, his words speak volumes. Without giving him much of me at all, he can somehow see through me and onto the struggles I force down and face myself.

I've always thought of myself as a reserved and guarded person, and here I am, not even a full twenty-four hours of being here, and surprised by how unexpected this entire experience has been. I imagined it would be *different* than my everyday life, but not like this. Am I foolish for wanting to just go with the flow and see what happens, despite it going against who I've been my entire life? Isn't that what I wanted—a fresh start, a chance to be someone other than Willow Oliver, her crazy mother's caretaker?

He pulls his hand away. "Wow, I'm coming across much creepier than I intend." He shifts to face away from me, settling his back against the couch and planting both feet on the ground.

He startles faintly when I touch his shoulder.

"I don't think you're creepy, Cameron. I think you're far nicer than I deserve."

His growing smile fuels my soul.

A commotion from across the room surprises me and grabs my attention. Three guys and a girl barrel down the east wing stairs and around the corner down the hallway. A weird haze, almost like a floating black-and-purple shadow clouds my vision, and they disappear into it.

I shift my gaze back to Cameron, who is seemingly unfazed by the shadow. He might not have noticed it, maybe he wasn't looking in that direction.

"Hey, lovers," Remi announces, walking toward us. "You two get a room yet?"

"I know we just met yesterday, but I'm totally going to smother you in your sleep."

"Simmer down, killer. Dead bodies creep me out." Kyra laughs. "Let's get to exploring."

"Where to first?" Lillian asks.

"We're good with east, right? Let's check out the south wing first," Remi suggests.

"Ladies first." Cameron grins, clearly pleased he gets to sightsee with four good-looking gals.

The south wing is nearly identical to the east. Room number five has the same picturesque, rounded window, leaving me to assume rooms W five and N five will, too. I have psych 101 in S three in the afternoon with Cameron. *Second room on the left*, I memorize.

Past the bathroom I noted prior, by the south wing stairs, and beyond the dining hall entrance, is the boys' bathroom, which is next to the west wing stairs. I enter the west wing, and a strange energy shift hits me and brings me quite literally to a stop.

Cameron halts a moment after me, and with concern lining his brow asks, "Are you okay?"

The sudden burning of eyes impales me from an unknown source, but I feel too exposed to survey my surroundings. *Stop drawing attention to yourself, Will.*

"Yeah, I'm good." I shake my head and try to rid myself of the strange feeling flowing through me.

"You two coming?" Remi calls from halfway down the hall.

That purple-and-black shadow appears to her left and catches my eye, but when I try to focus on it, it disappears. I force a breath and resume walking.

"Yeah, right behind ya."

Cameron hangs back and slows to meet my pace. He doesn't say anything else, but I'm grateful for his welcome and calming presence.

Pushing away the creepiness of whatever visions I keep having, I endure the rest of the exploration. I was correct in my assessment that the wings would be similar, all of the odd rooms on the left, even on the right, and the fifth room having the oversized, rounded window. I make another mental note for room six in the west wing, where I'll have accounting during last period.

Abigail had mentioned that the building is shaped like an X, and now that I've seen it for myself, that makes total sense. On the mirror opposite side of the building from the headmaster's office, placed neatly between the west and north wing, is the infirmary.

We pause for a second, looking over the pieces of paper in our hands, comparing schedules. The humming coursing through me lessens until we continue toward the north wing.

The air seems to thicken, the energy pulsing in bursts.

"Are you sure you're good?" Cameron asks, concern lining his brow.

I force a smile. "I just have a headache. I get them often."

"I can get you something. Tylenol? Water? What do you need?"

I uncross my arms, only now realizing I had been hugging them together, and touch his shoulder. "I'm okay. Thank you, though. That's very kind of you. Let's get this over with. I could use some fresh air."

My first class with Professor Weller is in N five, tucked away with another gorgeously massive window. Ethics, which is following lunch, is in N six. Both classes are without either of my new friends, and I dread both of them. I barely know any of them, but it's still favorable to have them around on this exciting and terrifying journey.

The shadow only appears once during our time in the north wing, but it disturbs me all the same.

Without waiting for the rest of the group, I locate my two north wing classes and bolt from the area, across the foyer, past the unbelievable indoor garden, through the enormous dining hall, and onto the outdoor patio. Crossing the threshold to the exterior, I suck in a much-needed breath of refreshing air.

My feet seem to have a mind of their own, marching me beyond the terrace and into the wooded area behind the school. I don't look back, walking farther away from the dense energy of the shadows lurking within the school.

I'm not really sure how long it takes me to calm down. Ten minutes, maybe thirty, an hour or more? But by the time I finally do, I grasp that I am completely and foolishly lost. The burning sensation—like eyes watching—vibrates and sends chills racing down my spine. Fear sinks its teeth into me, and it's everything I can do to stay calm.

I stop. Close my eyes. Breathe deeply. Listen intently to my surroundings. Consume all that is near.

Birds chirping. The aroma of rain-soaked earth. A sweet hint of honeysuckle. A branch creaking. The wind blows a dusting of leaves against the terrain.

I open my eyes and feel much calmer, grounded. I will myself to find a way out, to get back to the school.

"How do I get out of here?" I mutter to no one but myself.

At that, the tree to my left slowly illuminates at the bottom, and light pink-and-white flowers surrounding the trunk radiate a soft glowing aura. The rational part of me knows I should question what's happening yet it appeals to me in the gentlest of ways, whispering nothing my brain can comprehend. I'm drawn to it, and with my step forward, the giant oak tree a few feet away from the first lights up at the base, too, calling me forward.

Each stride brightens the path, and despite it being irrational, I follow—uncertain of where it might take me, yet being completely content with whatever the outcome may be.

I wake the next morning rested and relieved that I'm not feeling like a bag of crap, having stayed up most of the night trying to decipher the freaky shadows and somehow enchanted flowers that led me back to the school. I finally convinced myself I was having a psychotic break, and maybe whatever was wrong with my mom was hereditary and I was basically following along in the familial footsteps. At the time, I didn't doubt the flowers at all, but in hindsight, I realize how absolutely insane that is. What if it was a trap? What if it put me in danger? What if my new 'friends' saw me losing my mind?

I guess I'm crazy, too. Thanks, Oliver gene.

I throw my hair back into a loose braid and pull on a thick black sweater to fight the draft of the lavish but outdated school. I don't bother with makeup, not that first impressions don't matter, I just prefer to appear like the same person the entire school year and not exclusively in the beginning when I'm putting forth extra effort.

"I'm starting to hate you," Remi declares.

"Me?" I point to myself and look to the other girls for answers, then back to Remi.

"Yes, you. You have that whole 'I woke up like this' thing going on. It's totally not fair."

I shrug. "I told you, I prefer sleep."

At that, she throws something at me. I catch it in my left hand. Mascara.

"Rude!" I toss it back.

"You're rude!" she teases. "We've been here a day, and you already have two hot guys eyeballing you. Leave some for the rest of us."

"You're out of your mind." I glance down at my phone that's sitting on my nightstand. "And you're going to be late if you don't finish. I'm heading to class. I'll see you at lunch." I walk past her on my way out of the room and poke her in the side, her partially curled hair flopping in her attempt to avoid me.

It's strange how at home I feel with these people, considering I've been a loner all my life. I should question it, but instead, I ride the fresh euphoria of not being alone. *Here's to the new and improved Willow Oliver.*

I grab the granola bar I stuffed into my pocket and tear into it on my way to homeroom, hoping the little bit of sustenance calms my first-day jitters. Yesterday was like dipping my toes in the water, but today is when classes actually begin. I preemptively took a headache reliever and brought a bottle of water in my back-pack just to be safe. *Don't need to be getting weird on day one.*

I get to my first class, and I'm pleased to find it empty. *Another worm for the early bird.* I find a seat in the corner, making sure there's a clear path to the door—you know, in case of emergencies and such.

A rush passes over me, and I'm not sure whether it's the worries of the day taking hold or more weird north wing vibes.

I force a breath, closing my eyes and whispering to myself, "You are okay, everything is going to be okay."

"No freaking way," a thick voice breaks my pep talk.

I open up to find dark, sultry eyes staring daggers into me. He flops into the seat right next to mine and lets out a long sigh.

"I can't believe you left me hanging like that yesterday, Wills."

I should cringe at hearing him use a name reserved for friends and family, but I can't help but internally smile at the sound of it coming from him.

"Deghan," I reply, turning a bit to face him.

"I'm hurt," he says while caressing his heart with his hand.

"Such dramatics *this* early?"

"I have a way you can make it up to me." He beams brightly.

"For the record, I had no idea you were waving at *me*. But if you insist, how can I make it up to you, you poor, poor soul?"

"Who else would I have been waving at?" he replies and then shakes his head. "Never mind that, promise me I'll see you at the party tomorrow night."

"Party?"

"Yeah, it's an annual Harper Academy thing. First Friday of every new term."

"Oh... I, um..."

"Oh, c'mon!" Deghan holds his hand tighter on his chest and leans back, laying the drama on copiously. "You wouldn't hurt me again, would you?"

My gaze locks on him, lowering to his navy-blue T-shirt that's clinging in all the right ways. I force myself to look away, a smile tugging at my lips when his bottom lip juts out, pulling at my heartstrings.

"Fine but stop doing that! It's not fair."

"Ahh, she does have a heart," Deghan declares.

"You're ruthless."

"Or I just know how to get what I want." He winks.

It sends my heart fluttering.

Is he flirting with me? Was Cameron flirting with me? What the hell is happening?

A little birdy pops into my head and says *better call dibs*, but I whoosh it away, knowing there's no way in hell I could choose between the two, at least not this early.

Students pile into the room, claiming seat after seat until finally, our professor strolls in.

"Good morning, class," he marvels. "My name is Professor Bradshaw, and I'll be your math teacher this term." He sets his shoulder bag onto the large wooden desk at the front and opens it to retrieve a stack of papers. "You." He points to the girl sitting closest to his desk. "Pass one of these out to each student, please."

She takes the papers without a word and makes her way around the room.

"What you're receiving right now is your course syllabus. We'll spend the morning going over it, answering any questions anyone may have, and beginning our material if the time presents itself. Today should be rather straightforward and simple, but I still expect you to pay attention and give me your all, now, and the remainder of your time here at Harper. I won't lie to you and say I'm a harsh professor because I'm probably the most lenient of them all, but I won't tolerate people who don't put forth an effort, so please, try to give your best."

He glances around, almost like he's waiting for some type of response. He doesn't get one, so he speaks again. "Now, let's get the first-day awkwardness out of the way with a little icebreaker."

Oh god.

"Everyone introduce yourself and tell us something about you." He points again to the girl who passed out the papers. "You can start."

"I'm Sophie and I love playing the piano."

"Great, good job. Next." He points to another student.

"My name's Brock. I—uh... have two sets of twin siblings."

The next person goes, and then the next. My blood temperature seems to rise the closer it gets to me. *What the hell am I going to say? Oh god, oh god. Maybe I could bolt out the door before they get to me?*

Another student, and another. I'm in such a panic I don't really recall what they said.

My mind stumbles to a stop watching Deghan adjust in his seat.

He bumps his nose with his hand and inhales, speaking with confidence. "Hey, everyone, I'm Deghan James, and for as long as I can remember, I've made it a point to look at the sunset every single night."

"That's quite impressive," Weller admits. He then points to me, signaling that it's now my turn.

You got this.

"Hi, I'm Willow Oliver and..." *I'm crazy...* "I really like brownies." Brownies? Really? Did I just say that? I guess it's better than my first thought.

The heat in my face passes, and I glance over to catch Deghan grinning my way.

"I can agree with that one, Willow," Professor remarks. "It's great to meet everyone. Now, if you'll turn your attention to the syllabus, we'll go ahead and get started."

***

The rest of the class goes fairly smoothly, aside from the couple of strange occurrences of the buzzing between my brows. My headache must be fighting the medicine I took this morning, forging a battle it's not ready to give up.

Weller dismisses us and we all stand and pack our things. I take a step away from my desk but I'm stopped by Deghan's hand on my elbow, pulling me back.

"What's up?" I ask him.

"What's next?"

"Umm...what do you mean?" I adjust the straps to my backpack.

"Your classes. What do you have next?"

"Oh, right. Duh. Creative writing. E... five, you?"

"I'm in S one next." He frowns. "Can I walk you to class?"

"Seriously?" I blurt out.

"Yeah, is that bad? Am I being too forward? Oh, wait, do you have a boyfriend? You totally have a boyfriend. I shouldn't have asked. Of course you do."

Watching him unravel, I can't help but laugh.

"No. No, it's perfectly okay for you to walk me." I blush. "I don't have a boyfriend."

His chocolatey eyes darken and widen at the same time. "You don't? Well, that's great then."

We step out of the classroom, and I look down the hall as the purple haze settles over the entrance to the north wing. I stop completely and observe the shadow form and then disappear. Trying not to draw any unwanted concern to myself, I blink away my insanity and continue on.

Deghan side-eyes me. "Are you dorming in the west wing?"

"South," I answer. "You?"

"North."

Without me really thinking about it, my mouth forms words. "Was that true what you said during your introduction?"

He nudges me and smirks. "You calling me a liar, Wills?"

"No, not at all. That's...incredible. Good for you."

"I remember being a kid. I would sit out on the front porch in the evening and wait for my parents to come home, and it never failed that I would see the sun setting on the horizon. It just kind of stuck, ya know?" He sidesteps another student and then approaches me again. "Now I'm not sure I could get through the day without it. It's like the one good thing I can always count on and look forward to."

"That's wonderfully poetic."

"And on that note, you owe me some deep dark secret, because *wow*, I did *not* expect things to get so intense right there."

"Maybe Friday?" I volunteer.

"I would be honored, Willow Oliver."

I look up to realize that we've reached my next classroom: E five. I hate to admit that I'm let down that the walk to class was this brief. I would have been happy with another minute with Deghan.

"Is that your schedule?" He peers over my shoulder and questions.

"Yep." I lean in closer, letting him study it over, his chest pressed up against my shoulder to get a better vantage point. The heat from his body radiates onto mine, sending a shiver through me. The scent of earth and cedar takes hold.

"Bummer," he admits. "We don't have anything else together. If we don't run into each other between classes, hopefully I'll see you this evening. And if not, you better save me a seat in first."

"Ditto. Thanks for walking me to class, Deghan."

"The pleasure was all mine." He bows and takes hold of my hand, sending invisible sparks flying before raising it to his lips for a gentle kiss.

He takes off down the hall, toward his next class, and I stand there dumbfounded for a moment.

A loud throat-clearing grabs my interest, and I turn. Remi stands a few feet into my next class. Her eyes are wide, and she shakes her head in a *give me the details* kind of way.

I take a seat in the back with Remi, Cameron, and Lillian, opening my mouth to speak, but I'm cut off by the professor starting class.

"Morning. I'm Professor Elliot, welcome to creative writing." She has a kind, young face despite the raspy, gritty tone of her voice. She must be a smoker, like Strong, too.

Luckily, Elliot doesn't torture us with ice-breaking awkwardness and moves on with our syllabus once she does a brief introduction. She informs us that all majors are required to take creative writing, along with all of the other first-year classes, and that we won't be getting into the "meat and potatoes" of our major for a little bit.

Harper Academy doesn't offer many degrees to choose from. Business, Economics, English, Psychology, and Communications. It keeps things simple and probably doesn't require much overhead, considering we have such a little town and inadequate funding for the school. For us local folks, though, we get a small grant for going to Harper Academy; it's a way to keep people living around here, and an incentive for students to choose Harper for higher education. It's not the typical college experience, but it serves its purpose being a college, and somehow the term "academy" has stuck since the early days. Not like most of us could afford anything else, anyways.

The remainder of our time in class doesn't really allow any room to chat. Elliot keeps things flowing, pushing through the syllabus before starting in on our first assignment. She passes out notebooks to each of us and tells us that we will be keeping a daily journal. Each day we are to fill one page. The words will not be graded, but we are to show her our pages for verification that we are putting words on the paper. She encourages us to think of ourselves as onions, peeling back a layer at a time and processing our thoughts and emotions, diving into deeper layers hidden within.

It sounds terrifying to me. I'd rather just keep things to myself and process them on my own, not flesh them out on paper for someone to possibly read.

My stomach growls, and on cue, Elliot thanks us for our cooperation and dismisses us for the day.

I begin packing up my things, and Cameron stands next to my desk.

"I thought that was never going to end," he says.

"It wasn't too bad, but I'm not thrilled about these." I hold out my notebook and shove it into my bag.

"You're telling me," Lillian chimes in.

Grabbing her bag from her seat and swinging it across her shoulder, Remi frowns.

I roll my eyes at her and walk away, knowing the Deghan thing is driving her crazy.

She catches up to me in the hallway in a flash. "Tell me everything," she demands.

CHAPTER 6

"He walked you to class? How is that *nothing*?" Remi exclaims quietly. "Wait until I tell Kyra about this."

"Can you please not? It's really not a big deal, he was just being nice," I explain, walking the path to the dining hall for lunch.

With another step, a familiar feeling settles over me. *Someone is watching.* I peer over my shoulder, not trying to draw attention to myself, and notice a memorable face. The one from the patio the time I went to retrieve my cell. His dark eyes bore into mine for an intense moment, and when I blink, he disappears. *That was weird. What's with that guy?*

A warm sensation courses through me, and my heart pitter-patters.

Like he can sense the slightest shift in my being, Cameron offers me a warm smile.

We reach the dining hall and head straight to the food selections. Surprisingly enough, the choices don't seem that bad. Pre-made salads. Grab-n-go sandwiches. Pizza. And thankfully, there's a dessert area with—you guessed it—*brownies*. The drinks are near the end of the line, in glass dispensers with glass jars, a great effort for reducing plastic waste.

I choose a grilled chicken salad, pour a glass of unsweet tea, and follow behind Remi to whatever table she deems fit.

The mean girl from next door eyes me suspiciously and whispers something to her friend.

I meet the friend's stare and make out the word, "Freak," leaving her mouth.

I brush it off, not wanting to make enemies, and pretend like nothing happened despite the insecurity that festers within me. Cameron takes the seat next to me, and Lillian and Remi sit across the table.

"Where's Kyra?" I ask, scanning the dining area.

"Right here!" she calls from behind me. "Did you miss me already?" She relaxes in next to me with her slice of cheese pizza and continues, "So, what did I miss?"

My gaze darts across the table at Remi, me pleading her not to say anything to Kyra. It's not that I don't want her to know Deghan walked me to class, I just really hate being in the limelight and don't want all of the gossip to be about me.

"I forgot a fork, that's what you missed," I blurt out in an attempt to change the subject.

I start to stand, but then Cameron cuts me off.

"I'll get it," he announces cheerfully.

I smile up at him. "Are you sure?"

He nods and is off before I can protest.

"Oohhhh, he *likesss* you," Kyra boasts.

"He's not the only one," Remi betrays.

Kyra's eyes go wide in response.

I'm going to drop out of school, right here, right now.

I throw a cherry tomato from my salad at Remi, and it bounces off of her and lands on her sandwich.

"Gross," she whines.

"I have more." I point to my salad. "And I'm not afraid to use them," I threaten.

Cameron sits back down and hands me a fork, ever the gentleman.

"Thanks." I smile.

"No problem."

The girls decide to be kind and not bring up the boy talk anymore. Part of me thinks it's because they don't want to hurt Cameron's feelings by talking about another man in front of him when he might have a thing for me.

I won't lie and say I don't have a thing for him, too. Because I'm drawn to him, a sort of comfort I didn't know was possible to have with someone. But, if I had to choose between him and Deghan right now, it would be an impossible decision I'm not capable of making. I expected to go to Harper, get an education, and focus on myself for a while. Never in my wildest dreams did I imagine I'd have two of the most gorgeous people at this school fawning over me in the first week. And there's the very real possibility that I'm reading way too into this and Cameron only sees me as a friend. Navigating these types of situations aren't exactly my specialty.

"Hey, did you guys hear about that party?" I ask curiously.

"The tradition one?" Kyra mutters between bites.

Remi's eyebrows raise. "Party? I am absolutely in."

Lillian shrugs and adds, "Whatever."

I'm not really sure if that means she's down to go or not, her simple face not giving any insight either way.

"You want to go, Willow?" Cameron questions.

"I think it might be fun. What about you?"

"I'm there if you are. When is it?"

"Tomorrow night. I don't really have any other details. I'm sure it'll spread around campus by then, though."

It's then that it hits me that Deghan made me promise I would go to the party, and now Cameron is telling me that he'll go if I do. I'm in trouble. But do I have to be? They're both my friends, and I haven't had to call dibs yet. I could go to the party and spend time with both of them. That's possible, right?

We finish lunch and say our goodbyes, most of the group having their next class in the south wing while mine is in the dreaded north. Cameron hangs around for an extended second like he's wanting a moment alone.

"I have to get to class," I tell him.

"Yeah." He nods his head. "Of course."

"We'll catch up later," I say in an attempt to soothe the awkwardness rising.

"Definitely." A subtle grin forms on his handsome face.

It's not that I don't want a second alone with him, too, but I'm a weirdo when it comes to being on time, and I really don't want to be late, especially to this class.

A memory of the purple haze flashes in my mind, but I quickly push it away. *Don't go crazy, Willow.* None of my new friends are in this next class, so I'm not really sure what to expect. I'd secretly wished that Deghan would be, given he got me through my anxious north wing time this morning. I'll have to make do with myself and focus on not losing my mind. At least I'm halfway through the first day of classes.

On cue, the moment I make my way toward the entrance of the north wing, the purple shadow appears and then dissipates in front of my eyes. It has to be the lighting in this building. That's the one thing that potentially makes sense. Maybe I need to get my eyes checked. I should make it a point to stop at the infirmary in the future and see if the nurse can give me an eye exam. Or maybe my headaches are getting more intense, and this is some weird precursor to my next unbearable migraine. There has to be some logical explanation for what I've been seeing. But then again, how do I explain the illuminating flowers leading me back to the school when I didn't know how to get back?

I'm going crazy, that has to be it. My gut twists at the idea of my mom and how she's adjusting without me there. I hope I haven't made things worse for her by leaving her. Maybe she was right all along, and there really is an Oliver curse, but instead of being witches it just involves us going crazy.

Focused on my thoughts, I walk the long corridor to the last room on the right, N six. Only a few students have arrived, so I make quick work of finding a seat near the back with a clear exit path. Typically, I'm not one to choose a seat next to someone if I can avoid it, but the person seems so entranced in whatever they're doing that they might not bother me. Facedown in a book seems like the exact kind of person I want to be around.

I make an attempt to peek at the cover of their book, but his nearly onyx hair-covered head blocks it from my line of sight. Whatever it might be has his undivided attention. He doesn't bother to stir while I claim the seat next to his.

I open a notebook and flip it to a clean section, placing a pen on top in preparation for what's to come. This class is a bit shorter than the rest, so it should help propel me well into the last two classes of the day. Ethics, then psych 101 with Cam, and accounting with Lillian. Pretty boring lineup of courses, but it is what it is—an education. It'll do the job just fine.

My nearby seat partner starts when the teacher clears their throat. Well, it's more...hacking up a lung and practically dying in front of us. What's with all of the teachers sounding like they smoke thirteen packs of cigarettes a day? This time it's a gray-haired man who looks to be nearing his seventies and has thick bi-focal glasses.

The mysterious dark-haired guy shoves his book into his bookbag without allowing me a glimpse at what was so consuming. He plops a notebook onto his desk and shuffles around inside his bag for an extra few seconds, shaking his head and letting out a sigh. He looks to his right, at an empty seat, and then turns my direction.

His emerald eyes meet mine, and his lips part. "Do you have a pen I could borrow?" He exudes kindness and purity, mixed with secrets and longing.

How do I know that?

"Yeah, absolutely." I reach into my bag to pull out a spare. Of course I have an extra pen. A couple of pencils, highlighters, permanent markers, and sticky notes, too, along with pretty much anything else I could possibly need.

I hold out the pen, and he graciously takes it, but upon him grabbing it from my hand, I swear to everything actual fire kisses my fingers. It's both a gentle and fierce sensation all at once.

His brows furrow. "Are you from the west wing?"

What a weirdly timed question. Maybe he thought he recognized me from there.

"No," I respond, a bit caught off guard.

"Huh," is all he mutters, turning around.

What the hell is his problem?

He moves toward me again. "Did you go to admission with Abigail?"

Another odd question? "Yes..."

"Was the Wi-Fi working?"

Really, he's asking me about Wi-Fi right now? "She waved some wand thing and told me the Wi-Fi wasn't working. Why?"

His intense gaze falls to the floor in thought. "No reason. Err, well, I was just wondering." He holds out the pen. "Thank you."

"Yeah, no problem," I drone while being utterly confused about what just happened.

"I'm Sydney, by the way." He extends his hand, like he's challenging me in some way, a mischievous grin plastered on his face.

"Willow." I accept the dare and take his hand into mine, firmly grasping it—the fire from a moment ago burning all over again with his touch.

His eyes meet mine in a showdown, every circuit in my body

firing and urging me to let go and hold on at the same time. The color of his eyes shifts to a brilliant aquamarine, his jaw clenching in pain and pleasure. Whatever this is, it's fucking magical.

He breaks our encounter, sucking in a breath and staring down at his hand, only inches from where mine still lingers.

"Did you feel that? I whisper.

Sydney studies me, tracing his eyes over me fanatically, his demeanor changing. "Feel what?" he answers, shaking his head. He faces forward in his seat, his posture alert and rigid, doing everything he can to get away from me while staying in his seat.

I come to the conclusion that I am absolutely going batshit crazy. There is no other way to explain anything that is going on. The visions, the shadows, the illuminating flowers, the fireworks while touching. My mom had an unexplainable psychotic break, and now here I am, having one too.

Aside from seeing and feeling things that others don't, I'm also convinced I can feel energies, too. Like when someone is about to break bad news. Before they manage to change their expression, the air becomes thick and heavy. It's always been that way, I've just never really paid much attention to it. It's not always exclusively bad news, either. I can feel good energy and busy energy and sad energy and fearful energy. But that's not possible, right? It must be a figment of my imagination...along with everything else.

Sometimes I'm certain I can control other's emotions, too, or maybe that's wishful thinking. There were plenty of times my mom lost her temper while I was growing up, and if I tried hard enough, if I willed it, I could help bring her back to the brink of calmness. I did this quite often in the past, sometimes completely unaware until I processed it later on. It drained my own energy, and made my headaches worse than normal, to the point I had to sleep for hours on end. It was almost like I had to recharge myself.

I shake my head to clear my muddy, nonsensical thoughts. This is all just in my head. I can't truly do any of these things and I know it. It's impossible.

I shift my brain to autopilot, not even remotely listening to the teacher as he begins his lecture. He introduces the class and goes over the syllabus while I scribble half-ass notes—never fully letting the words register in my mind. I focus on praying for the seconds to tick by quicker so I can be done with this day and have a moment to myself, a true moment alone—without apparitions and utter fucking drivel.

I refuse to be the freak that people say I am.

I refuse to be another crazy Oliver woman.

CHAPTER 7

The moment my ethics class is dismissed, I bolt from the room. I packed my bag up ten minutes early and made it out of the room before anyone else. I disregard the stupid deep-purple shadow that appears near N three's entrance, reminding myself that I'm just fucking seeing things.

I almost decide to skip my next class but quickly push that thought aside, knowing what a horrible impression that would give my teacher. Plus, this one is in the south wing. It's one of the only areas in the school that doesn't make me feel *off*. Not to mention, Cameron will be in attendance, which I'm counting on to settle my nerves.

I pay minimal attention on my way to psych 101, making my way past the indoor garden located in the center of the building and down the south wing hallway. The room is the second on the left, and upon my entry, Cameron waves me over to where he's already claimed a seat.

"Hey, you." His lips curve into a smile, and my heart picks up pace in an entirely different way than before...when I was thinking I was losing my mind.

"Hey," I breathe.

"What a day, am I right?"

"You're telling me." I settle into the seat on his left and lean my head back, closing my eyes and letting out a sigh.

"You good?" he asks.

I shake my head gently, tilting myself forward and putting my head in my hands on my desk. "I..."

Cameron scoots his desk closer, and it squeaks off the floor in protest. His hand finds contact with my shoulder, and I tense at the first connection, then ease into his touch.

I pull myself from my own embrace and stare deep into his sapphire eyes.

I feel like I'm losing my mind, Cameron. I feel like everyone thinks I'm crazy, and I'm not really sure they're wrong. I feel like nothing will ever be normal, that I'll never be normal. I'll always be a freak, an Oliver freak. That I'll be the girl whose dad disappeared when she was too young to remember and whose mom eventually went insane. The girl who grew up too quickly and can't wrap her head around how to trust or let anyone in because everyone leaves, *but sure has a spare pen to borrow, or can bake a cake from scratch because she learned to do it on her thirteenth birthday—by herself.*

But instead of saying any of those things, instead of maybe scratching the surface at what I'm screaming to tell someone, anyone really, I say, "I just have another headache."

"Damn, Willow. Another one? God, you poor thing." He rubs my back in slow, tender circles.

"I'll be okay," I manage, because I will be. I always seem to master that whole suck-it-up-buttercup thing and get by. I shove the feelings deep inside, somewhere never to be seen again, and force a smile. If I simply play pretend, I can convince myself everything will be okay.

Who am I kidding, though? Why am I here? I haven't even made it through a full day of classes yet, and I'm teetering on the edge of a breakdown around every corner. I should be at home, caring for my mom, and working part-time at the Harper Café. Maybe I could even ask for a full-time position. Sure, there's no progression, however, it's the constant I could count on.

But I was lucky enough to get this opportunity; why would I waste it? Wouldn't going back to what's comfortable be a selfish choice in the end?

Professor Strong walks in and announces that our psych teacher will be out the first few days, so she's going to be filling in for her. *Another missing-in-action authority figure?*

I grab my notebook, find a blank page, and start taking notes, filling the pages without much thought. Only this class and the next stand in the way of getting out of here. Will every day be this difficult to get through? I freaking hope not.

Throughout the class, Cameron gives me a sympathetic yet reassuring glance. Near the end, he passes me a note.

What is this, grade school? The gesture has me smiling, nonetheless.

Scribbled on a piece of scratch paper is: **Want to get a bite after your next class?**

No matter how tempting his invite, I really do need to be alone for a little while. I fold the paper and write on a blank side: **Maybe another time? I need darkness for this headache.**

I catch him frown faintly, and he responds: **Deal. I hope you feel better. Let me know if you want some company.**

The rest of the class goes by fairly fast, and somehow, I find myself not rushing out of it like I did in ethics. Maybe it was finding comfort in Cameron, or being out of the north wing, but I feel a bit more myself, not so overwhelmed with blasting energy and peculiar deliriums.

The west wing managed to throw me off during our exploration, but I'm determined to swallow down whatever I think is happening and get this last period over with. At least I have Lillian to sit with, and I'm really looking forward to her chill personality. I'll anchor myself to her and ride out this gnarly wave of an official first day. Who would have known I would have found comfort in two strangers when I've spent my whole life dealing with things on my own?

A quick goodbye to Cameron and a pit-stop at the bathroom still manages to make me nearly late to my accounting class. I relax into the seat behind Lillian and take out the usual—a notebook and pen.

My head buzzes, and I instinctively put it in my hands, rubbing my temples with my index fingers. That uncomfortable feeling of someone watching me grabs on to me, and I squirm in my seat. Out of the corner of my eye, I latch on to something memorable yet unfamiliar. I reposition myself to find the person responsible for the unsettling feeling. The enigmatic guy from the patio, the one who keeps appearing and disappearing in front of me.

His steel-gray eyes that could melt daggers don't budge when I meet his gaze. I force a breath, swallowing deeply, unable to look away. I thought my run-ins with Deghan, Cameron, and Sydney were intense...but that's nothing compared to whatever the hell this is. He hasn't spoken a word, and I don't even know his name, but I can't help thinking, sweet baby Jesus, I'm already in over my head with this one.

———

Accounting goes by slowly, each second dragging on and on. Once the teacher broke the deafening silence and hardcore stare-down I shared with the random guy across the room, I was able to turn forward in my seat and focus on getting through the next hour and a half. Maybe *focus* is a bit of a stretch, seeing as how I spent most of the class fighting off the rising and falling of energy while it coursed through the space.

Lillian doesn't bat an eye when I leave class without saying a word to her. Man am I thankful for her easy-going demeanor. I'd never have gotten off that easily if I shared accounting with Kyra or Remi.

I round the corner and step into the lavish foyer of the building. Not wanting to get caught by any of my new friends, I head straight through the school's front door and out to the courtyard where it all started a couple of days ago.

Once outside, I take a gigantic breath in and out, doing my best to push the day's anxiety away with it. Like it's calling my name, I head around the back of the school, along the paver blocks that are laid intricately at my feet, and into the thick forest. Studying it more, there are paths in the trees that I didn't previously see—three to be exact. One in the middle, left, and right.

For no real reason, I choose the path to the right and walk for a few minutes until I find a small clearing. I take a seat against a large oak tree and pull my backpack to my chest. Moments continue to pass, and I sit there, doing absolutely nothing other than attempt to calm my aching nerves. Solitude is my friend, and I have missed it dearly. Why was I naïve enough to assume being around so many people wouldn't be overkill to my system? I can pretend to be a different person but the old Willow remains.

The crumbling of leaves draws my attention from myself to my surroundings. My posture stiffens, and I strain to focus my hearing. A shape appears in the distance, but then is gone as quick as it emerged.

"Hello," I whisper. "Is someone out there?" My gaze shifts around the clearing to no avail. "It's probably just an animal," I tell myself.

A branch cracks, and I stumble to my feet in a hurry. I've never known myself to be petrified of the woods like this, but with the day already unsettling me, I'm not sure of anything anymore.

"You shouldn't be out here," a soothing yet deep voice commands.

I shift toward it but can't locate the source.

"It's not safe."

"Who's out there?" I hastily reply. "Come forward."

About six feet to my left, the figure appears from the darkness, stepping into a light-covered area. Blinking to get my eyes to adjust, I finally make out the character.

"It's you," I breathe.

"You shouldn't be out here," he repeats.

"You said that already." I swallow.

"It's not safe…"

"You said that, too." I take a hesitant step toward him. "Why isn't it safe?"

His jaw clenches, and he matches my step by taking one back.

My eyes meet his, and my heart slows and speeds up all at once. With a mind of their own, my feet take another cautious stride.

He doesn't move so I take one more.

A strange burst of energy bolts through me, and something flutters on the ground, shifting my gaze. The ground between us lights up, this time with radiant red flowers glowing.

He gasps. "How did you do that?"

Wait, what? He can see them, too? That's impossible, I'm merely hallucinating things.

"Do what?" I ask, not betraying anything.

He kneels to the ground, cupping a vibrant rosy bloom under his hand. He flinches and pulls his hand away in a flash like he stuck himself with a thorn.

"That's impossible," he speaks under his breath.

"Can you…can you see them?" I plead.

He stays still for a second and then parts his lips. "What's your name?" His cool-gray eyes turn a bit violet as he scans my face.

I swallow down the lump forming in my throat. "Willow."

"Willow," he echoes.

A blast of hot and cold hits me in the best of ways as he continues examining me with his eyes. I'm rooted in place, unable to look or move away but not sure I would if I could.

"May I come closer?"

I nod, and when I do, the flowers that were bright and vivid between us dull their light and open up a path for him. *What is happening?*

He closes the gap between us at a snail's pace, inching forward thoughtfully until he's so close his breath caresses my forehead. His hand reaches out gently, and I silently beg for him to touch me. *I don't even know this guy, what the hell am I thinking?*

I fight the battle between this feeling unbelievably wrong but oh-so-right.

"What's your name?" I mutter.

His hand rises next to my cheek, but he doesn't give in, despite my desire taking hold.

"Silas."

A wave crashes over me, emotions and energies pushing and pulling their way through every fiber in my body and soul.

Almost like he can see the struggle I fight internally, his brow furrows, and he presses his mouth into a firm line. His porcelain skin and flawless features are otherworldly. I scan the shape of his forehead, his perfectly crafted cheekbones and chin, his just plump enough lips, and perfectly whitened teeth. The viciously pointed incisors that send a shiver down my spine. He swallows, and his Adam's apple bobs up and down, sending my gaze south to his etched collarbone and fitted black T-shirt underneath his black leather jacket.

"Have we met?" I ask, an unforgivable familiarity in his eyes. It's like I've known him my whole life, or maybe in a past life. My body aches to fill some kind of forgotten muscle memory with him.

His expression lightens, and for a second, it's like he might smile. "I've been waiting on you for an eternity."

The words leave his lips, and everything stops. Time halts, the earth's rotation, gravity and everything in between comes to a sudden, abrupt end. The only sound that fills the space is my beating heart. At the same time my body tenses, his face changes, and fear devours me. Like a curtain being drawn on a Broadway stage, my vision goes blank, and I struggle to stay upright.

No matter how much of a fight I put up, I lose the war waging inside of me along with all sense of reality.

CHAPTER 8

I open my eyes to find myself in my dorm room, not quite remembering how I got here. I sit up slightly, and Lillian looks up from her book to give me a vague smile.

"Hey." I rub my shoulder and stretch my neck.

"Hey." She places an old, tattered bookmark in the book, closing it to give me her full attention.

"This may sound weird, but do you have any idea how long I've been out, or...how I got here?"

She nods and lets out a huff. "Creepy guy from accounting carried you in about an hour ago. He said you passed out in the woods, but he didn't really give me any other details." She pauses and straightens. "You're not on drugs, are you? I'm pretty laid back, but I'm not really comfortable with drugs. So, if it's drugs, can you at least tell me, and I can submit a room transfer or like, lock my stuff up so you don't steal it and sell it for crack money."

I shake my head and hold my hand up for her to stop. "No, no, I'm not on drugs. I just get really bad headaches and dizzy spells, and the day was super intense, and I needed a breather. I guess it just consumed me and I fainted. That's never happened before." Embarrassment creeps up my neck.

"Oh," she replies, seeming almost surprised. "Well, I didn't really peg you for the drug type, but you can't be too sure anymore. It's always the unsuspecting ones."

"Yeah, don't worry. Drug and alcohol-free over here. My family has always had a bad experience with even the smallest amounts of alcohol, so I've never been interested whatsoever."

"That's a relief. People always think I'm a snob because I don't drink at parties."

"No peer pressure from me," I admit. I always hated those types of people anyway—why not let people make their own decisions, why force their agenda on others?

"Oh, if you're hungry, the accounting creep came back like super-fast after he dropped you off and brought you some food. Said you should probably eat when you woke up to help your energy levels or something." She points to the mini-fridge across the room.

Food actually sounds pretty good, but I wonder what he brought and how he would even know I'd be hungry. And where my dorm is located...

I open the door to find a paper bag with my name on it. I grab it and head back to my bed, sitting cross-legged and emptying the contents.

A grilled chicken sandwich. *Okay, good guess.*

A glass jar, and upon further inspection, I realize it's filled with... unsweetened tea. *This is getting strange.*

I unwrap a small package to find a decadent brownie. *How did he know?*

There's a note tucked inside that I almost miss, and it says:
I'm sorry I got too close.

The door to our dorm room bursts open, and Remi and Kyra enter, chattering on about something. Their gazes lock on me.

"Where were you?" Remi interrogates loudly.

Taking a second too long to respond, I meet Lillian's eyes.

"She told me in last period she wasn't feeling well and needed a nap, so I brought her dinner when I came back," Lillian offers confidently.

What a sneaky lie! Why would she do that for me? I really was dreading having to talk to Remi and Kyra about *another* guy showing me the slightest bit of interest, but how would Lillian recognize that?

"Oh no," Kyra cries. "You okay? Your crush was asking about you during dinner."

"Yeah, I'm better now." A half-truth.

"You would *not* believe the number of hot guys at this school," she continues on. "Don't get me wrong, there are some duds, but *wow* am I impressed at the selection."

Remi chimes in, "And here I was worried Harper was going to be *boring*."

Kyra throws a pillow at Remi, and they both laugh like lovesick idiots.

Lillian and I exchange a glance, and I try to telepathically communicate that I'm thankful for her keeping my secret. Maybe I underestimated how much I was going to end up valuing Lillian's friendship.

The girls gossip until I fall asleep, and then I dream about forests full of glowing flowers and pathways to wonderful places. One leads me to Cameron, another to Deghan, another to Sydney, and another to Silas. They all bring me some different level of joy, but I feel most complete when we're all together. I know my dream is irrational, but I can't help but revel in the glory of feeling safe and happy for a change, like the world isn't falling apart at the seams and sucking me into nothingness.

Just when I'm finally about to reach all of them—huddled into a beautiful meadow, waiting for me patiently—a thick haze of purple appears, and I accidentally run straight through it. I tumble out on the other side, and I'm forcefully shoved into a brick wall, my shoulder dislocating upon impact. I bite back a scream and shuffle to my feet, frantic to find the opening to get out of the hell I fell into.

A sliver of light appears in the distance, and I run toward it, gripping my injured shoulder. I'm nearly to the portal opening as it slams shut, throwing me back and to the ground. The vision of the guys fades, and blackness consumes the space.

A low, guttural growl permeates the air, and I suddenly realize that something terrible is about to happen. I'm going to be torn to shreds.

I close my eyes and urge every bit of me to find its strength, but opening them, there's nothing but darkness and the approaching doom. I let out a fearful scream, and the next thing I'm aware of is Remi above me, shaking me awake and telling me I'm having a nightmare.

"Willow, girlfriend, wake up," she urges.

I snap wide awake, scooting away from Remi like she's somehow the cause of the madness, a second or two passing until I realize I'm safe and sound. Sweat beads along my spine, and my hands tremble against the bedding I'm clenching in my fists.

"You're okay," she confirms. "It was just a bad dream."

My head shakes, and I try to rid myself of the funk. "What time is it?" I eye her half made-up face, knowing that it must be somewhere close to morning.

"Six fifteen..."

"Christ, Remi, why do you get up so early?"

She raises her hands, trailing them along her head and down her body. "This doesn't come easy, Miss Perfect."

Knowing I won't be able to fall back to sleep after that terrible dream, I throw the covers off me and hop off the bed. "I'm gonna go shower."

"Good luck," she mutters. "I heard crazy's door open a few minutes ago." She motions toward our *lovely* neighbor—the mean girl.

Desperate for a refreshing shower, I take a chance, seizing my bathroom caddy and heading toward the women's shared restroom. Two stalls are occupied near the end, so I go to the far corner and step inside. I undress quickly, turn the faucet, and plunge myself into the semi-cold stream, letting the water wash away my bad visions.

"Yeah, but have you talked to him?" a chipper voice from the opposite end asks.

"No, have you?" the other, more dramatic voice speaks. I recognize the voice immediately. It's the psycho girl from next door.

"Mmhmm...he's a total jock. Like, watch-me-lift-weights kind of guy."

"Gross."

"That's what I thought. Next, please."

"I have my eye on someone else, anyway."

"No way, who?"

"He's dreamy, in like a very serious way. He hasn't really spoken to anyone, but I've caught his eye a few times, and I'm going to make a move at the party tonight."

"You devil, who is it? You're killing me, Allie!"

"Silas Harlow," she boasts.

I drop the bottle of shampoo I'd just grabbed and frantically scramble to pick it up.

Shit, shit, shit.

"Ugh, whatever, we'll talk later, Paige."

I shower in a hurry, only to finish and then turn the water up warmer and stand there for an extra five minutes. I can't believe the evil girl—Allie, I guess—has a thing for Silas. What did she mean he hasn't spoken to anyone? He spoke to me. He carried me back from the forest when I fainted, and he brought me dinner. And he got *too close*, he said. As if that's physically possible.

I get back to my room in enough time to pull out the notebook from creative writing and fill out the daily journal page that I forgot to do yesterday. I write about the décor of the school, the variety of students in attendance, and how everyone—except Allie—seems super nice and welcoming. Harper has been a pleasant surprise. I leave out all the other details, though. The info about my random encounters with cute boys, enchanted flowers, and creepy purple shadows are better left inside my head. *Maybe another time, Mister Journal.*

I finish placing my journal back into my bag while Remi finalizes her outfit. A sapphire-blue shirt, skin-tight shiny black leggings, and heels. I look down at my faded skinny jeans, charcoal T-shirt, and black boots. Nothing fashionable, purely comfort, and blending in at its finest.

"You hungry?" Remi inquires while putting on a coat of bright-pink lip stain.

"I could eat."

"Ugh, you guys aren't going to wait for me?" Kyra urges.

"Maybe if you didn't take so damn long to get ready," Remi jokes.

"Look who's talking," I chime in.

"I'll hang back, you two go ahead," Lillian offers.

"Thanks, Lily, you're the best," Remi purrs. "I'm starved."

I grab my bag, leaving my cell behind. The service never recovered post tumble out of the window, and the Wi-Fi seeming to still be broken makes for a heavy paperweight I don't need to carry around.

If I can just make it through today, I'll be able to relax for a couple days. The real test will be next week, with a full five days to brave. Ideally, I'd love to go home and visit this weekend or next, but since we're only allowed to leave once per semester, I need to be strategic about when I use this opportunity.

And even if I chose this weekend, I'd miss the traditional Harper welcome party, and I'm not sure if that would be a good or a bad thing. I want to go, be social, and do the typical teenage party on the weekend thing, but I also want to stay in and throw on comfy clothes, eat junk food, and read…not to mention, hide away from everyone.

If I stay hidden, no one can find me, no one can weasel their way in and break my heart when they inevitably leave. Even getting close to Lillian, Remi, and Kyra scares me. Brooke has always been a constant and the one person who never judged me or made me feel like the freak I know I am deep down. Not having her around is like a big gaping hole I'm endlessly unsure how to plug, but at a point, like when I had to homeschool myself, I learned to fill that void with strictly myself. Sure, it's a lot lonelier, but it's what I grew to rely on. I found comfort in the solitude.

For now, though, I'm going to let the people at Harper in, keeping them at arm's length, not enough to let them ruin me, but plenty to experience the happiness they bring.

I just have to be extra careful with the guys who threaten to tear down my walls one panel at a time. Especially the one I feel so incredibly fated to, the one bound to ruin me the most. Feelings are bubbling to the surface already, and it's terrifying. We've shared minimal interactions, and it makes no logical sense to feel this way, but then again, when has my life ever made sense?

CHAPTER 9

Deghan greets me with open arms in first period. "I missed you, Will."

I scoff, "You barely know me, what's there to miss?" But I'd be lying if I said I didn't miss him, too.

He narrows his dark gaze. "Trust me, I'm a good judge of character. And who would ever deny that you're one of the best." Deghan wraps his arm around my shoulder and tugs me close to his chest.

It's strange being this near to him, and yet...I don't run away.

"It's only a matter of time until I get to learn more of the mysterious Willow Oliver, brownie connoisseur." He lets out a sigh. "Although, our schedules not matching up is not really doing me any favors. Someone else might slide in and sweep you off your feet."

My thoughts immediately take me back to my interaction with Silas in the thick forest behind the academy where I massively embarrassed myself by passing out.

But I focus on Deghan and allow his presence to distract me from the memory. I even immerse myself in it upon walking through the academy, granting it permission to distract me from the shadows that appear when I catch them in my line of sight.

"I promise I'll be at the party tonight, and we can spend some time together."

He grins, his bubbly personality overflowing and seeping into me in the best of ways. "I'm going to hold you to that, Miss Oliver."

Like a gentleman, Deghan walks me to second period. The second we step over the threshold and into the classroom, he eyes Cameron like he's sizing up his competition. Once he's gotten that out of his system, he passes me off to Cameron and Remi.

Lunch is delicious—another chicken salad, this time with sliced strawberries and walnuts, washed down with unsweetened tea.

"I don't know how you drink that stuff." Remi winces. "Don't get me wrong, I get you're saving a *ton* of calories, but ew, it's like drinking dirty sock water."

"So," I say between bites of salad. "You're telling me you like your dirty sock water sweetened?"

Lillian cracks a smile, and Cameron bursts out laughing like I said the funniest thing in the world. He really is so adorable, and his amusement warms my insides.

"You know what I mean," she replies.

A throat clears. "Can you keep it down over there? You're ruining my lunch."

Allie.

Kyra scowls. "If you have a problem, why don't you come over here?"

Allie stands, and her friend, I'm assuming the girl from the bathroom, Paige, grabs on to her forearm and pulls her back down.

"That's what I thought," Kyra muses.

Allie avoids eye contact, shoving the contents of her half-eaten lunch on her tray, and gets up abruptly, dumping it into the trash and storming out of the dining hall.

A small part of me wants to confess what I overheard in the shower this morning, but that would lead into a whole other line of questioning about Silas, and that's not something I'm ready to discuss with any of them, especially Cameron.

"So, anyway, the party tonight?" Remi says. "I heard it's in the woods behind the school?"

"Yep, that's what I heard, too. There are three paths tucked into the forest, and the party is down one of them. I didn't catch which one," Kyra answers.

"Far right," Lillian whispers.

The one I met Silas on. Where I felt the near warmth of his touch, where the flowers lit up then dimmed to let him through, where I experienced something so intense that I quite literally passed out from it. I can't help but wonder if he'll be there tonight, at the party. But if what Allie said is true, and he doesn't really speak to anyone, why would he go to a social event? Didn't he say the forest wasn't safe? Why would people have a party out there? Maybe it's a safety in numbers type thing.

I already have my hands full with the girls, let alone Cameron *and* Deghan, so I really shouldn't be wishing for Silas to be there, too. That would just be too much. Or maybe it would be enough. I could simply ask him in Accounting and have a for sure answer. Yeah, that's what I'll do.

"Earth to Willow." Kyra throws a wooden fork at me, startling me back to reality.

"Ow!" I throw it back at her.

"Remi asked you what you're wearing to the party."

I glance down at my outfit and shrug. "This?"

"Girl, you're going to be the death of me." Remi sighs and lowers her head.

"What does my outfit have to do with you?" I ask, confused.

"Ev-er-ry-thing!"

"Why aren't you grilling Lillian then?" I shift my stare across the table.

Remi interjects, "Because she's not going, duh."

"Oh, no, no, no. If I'm going to this party, and if you're dictating my wardrobe, Lillian is most definitely going."

I cross my arms and paste on my best *I'm-not-giving-in* look.

"Fine," Lillian says, puffing out an exasperated breath.

"That was intense," Cameron says while scraping the bottom of his yogurt container with a spoon.

A friend of his sits to his right. I haven't caught his name yet. The friend nods and adds, "Yeah it was. I miss the guys. Can't we go back and sit with them?"

"And miss all of *this*?" He motions to us girls.

The friend shakes his head and takes a big bite of his cheese and mushroom pizza.

Following lunch, I head to the north wing, ignoring the shadows and claiming a worthy seat in ethics. Not too far up that many people are sitting behind me, but not too far back that I can't make it around said people in case of an emergency. Always be prepared.

Sydney strides in, staring intensely at me and making his way to the opposite side of the room. *What the hell did I do to piss him off?* The energy between us flickers, and I chalk it up to another thing I need to block out to get through the day. This whole *not focusing on the weird shit around me* thing is really doing a number on my sanity. At this time yesterday, I was dreading the rest of the day, but now it's like I've shut it out enough to deal with it. Maybe I've just become immune to it—the strangeness is no longer able to drain me.

The class goes by, and I don't bat another eye at Sydney.

Whatever I did to make him hate me isn't important, and if he's going to be like that, who cares? I'm not going to play his game. I have plenty of other things to be worried about. Like getting through the next two lectures so I can see if the school has a landline phone I can call Danny from to check in. Not to mention starting my weekend and detoxing from the chaotic first couple days.

Cameron is his total charming self in psych, pulling out my chair before I sit and making me feel things I've never felt. I skipped the whole high school experience, so being courted by a guy is new territory for me. But boy am I thoroughly enjoying it. He's kind and compassionate and massively considerate despite me being *off*. His aura is fascinating, so pure and wholesome.

The exact opposite of Silas, who is shut off, distant, and cold, but with glimpses of warmth dying to show through. I'm determined to make that happen.

I half expected to see him lurking in the shadows at some point today, and I've been disappointed each time I don't catch his stare—or more like *glare*—from across the room.

After another goodbye to Cameron and a bathroom break, I head to the west wing for accounting. I walk into the room, my gaze settling on Lillian and then scanning the room—no Silas. He must be running late.

Our teacher begins attendance, and when his name is called, Silas is still nowhere to be found. So much for asking him if he'll be at the party tonight. I hope he's okay and that I didn't freak him out, given I collapsed in front of him and all. The last thing I want to do is scare him off, but maybe that's exactly what I've done.

Maybe that's a good thing.

A slight tinge of abandonment hits, and I force back the depressive feelings. Silas isn't mine to claim, and he owes nothing to me to show up to class, so why do I long for him so damn much? I push away the thoughts of him that creep in and remind myself he's not there every time my eyes wander to where he sat yesterday.

Lillian places her hand on my desk and drops a bar of chocolate without saying a word. *I love this girl*. She gets me.

"Thanks, Lillian," I say once class is dismissed and we're packing our bags.

"No worries, I thought you might need it."

"Do you prefer Lillian or Lily?"

She zips up her backpack. "Either is fine. I'm not picky."

I tilt my head in thought. "What about Lills?"

She smiles. "Lills it is. What about Wills for you?"

"We have matching nicknames, I love it."

"Are you ready for this?" Lills sighs.

"Ready for what?" I question.

"Remi and Kyra playing dress-up."

"Ohh, right. No, not really. But I'm sure there could be worse things in life."

"True." She nods, stepping into the foyer.

I point toward the indoor garden. "Isn't it so fascinating?"

Her eyes light up. "Absolutely. Have you been in there yet?"

"What? That's a thing? I had no idea."

"Yeah, there's a door. It's just glass and sort of hard to locate. It blends in well." She motions and continues, "Come this way."

We walk around the side, and she studies the enclosure intently.

"Ah, here it is. The handle is the tricky part to find."

She latches on to it and opens the door enough for us to squeeze inside. The aroma hits me immediately, scents of dirt and bark and grass and elegant floral arrangements.

"Crazy, right?" Lills asks.

I let my gaze roam, trailing the ground and up, up, up, to the glass ceiling where students on the second level walk. My heart nearly lurches out of my chest the moment our gazes lock. Silas stares down at me with his typical serious demeanor.

Lills follows my observation. "What's with you two? You don't have to tell me if you don't want to."

"I'm not sure," I mutter honestly, my eyes not leaving his.

"Have you talked to him since...well, *the thing*?"

"Nope. I was hoping to catch him in accounting."

"Maybe he'll be at the party," she offers.

"Yeah, maybe. But Cameron and Deghan are going to be there, too."

Lillian draws in a breath and exhales. "Not even a week into school and you've gotten yourself into a love square."

"A what?" I ask her.

She shrugs. "You know, like a love triangle but instead of two guys, it's three."

"I am so not in a love square." I laugh but realize she might be right.

How can I explain my immediate connection to any of them? It's like my heart—my soul—has singled them out from all the other people in this building and has determined that my sole focus should be on them. I've met other guys since I've been here, but none of them draw the same amount of attention in the slightest. I don't even find anyone else attractive. Not in a romantic way. Sure, I can acknowledge someone's good looks, but Silas, Deghan, and Cameron are otherworldly gorgeous.

Don't forget about Sydney, my gut reminds me, as if I could ever shake off the electricity that sparked between us.

He's shown zero romantic interest in me, and somehow I've already mentally upgraded the love square to a pentagon. I don't dare tell Lillian that, though, because I am well aware how irrational every single bit of this is—especially thinking I have a chance with any of them.

I wouldn't be surprised if I truly have had a psychotic break and my mind has made them up as a weird coping mechanism, and none of this is real at all.

A dull thud breaks through my rampant thoughts, and I

quickly locate the source, a disheveled Remi waving her arms for us to come on. I glance back to Silas and he's nowhere to be seen. That dismal ache fills my chest again at the longing.

"I guess there's no more putting it off. You ready?"

I shrug and we head back to the door. I have to pause and concentrate to find it. This place is like a trap if you don't know where the exit is. Sort of terrifying and wonderful if you think about it. The coldness of the glass seeps into my palm, and we step through, sluggishly making our way back to our dorm where Remi and Kyra are about to torture us.

We make it back and my eyes go wide the second I get to my bed.

"No way in hell I'm wearing that," I blurt out, gawking at the red sparkly club dress laying on top of my comforter.

"Ah, come on, Willow. You're no fun," Remi says.

"Do you want me to go?"

"Yes, of course. Why would you ask that?"

"Then choose something else. No dresses, no heels, nothing sparkly or sequin. And the same goes for Lills. I'm putting my foot down for both of us."

Remi throws her arms up, and Kyra puts a hand on her hip.

"Those are some serious demands," Remi huffs.

"Those are my terms, take it or leave it."

Remi sighs. "Fine."

Lillian winks from across the room, shoving the insane dress that the girls picked out for her to the side. "Thanks, Wills. No way in hell I was going to wear *that*."

"Wills and Lills, you two have officially ganged up on us. Not cool," Kyra replies.

"Like you two haven't ganged up on *us*?"

"No worries, Ky-bear, I got this. You start on Willow's hair. I'm going to tackle the wardrobe."

Kyra smiles devilishly and strolls across the room, pushing me onto my bed and plugging a curling iron in the closest outlet.

Is this what sisterhood is like? Sure, I had moments of this with Brooke, but not with anyone other than her. Plus, Brooke knew my limitations and almost never pushed them. These women in my dorm room don't know me as the weird girl who hid in the shadows of Harper County—the freak, the outsider. I'm just their other dormmate, and although it's terrifying, I take comfort in this fresh beginning.

A torturous yet somehow enjoyable two hours pass, and I find myself standing in front of the full-length mirror on Kyra's side of the room, gawking at my reflection.

Thick silver hair in perfect beach wave form sits gently on my shoulders. The very simple tight black tank top hugs all of my curves, shows off a few inches of my midriff, and leads down to an even tighter pair of onyx leggings. After a heated debate, I managed to convince the girls to let me wear my black boots. I take a step closer, examining my makeup in the mirror. Kyra darkened my brows and gave me smoky eyes—definitely more makeup than I'm used to wearing, but despite the drastic difference, I find myself liking what I see, even though it's only temporary.

I shove the remainder of the sandwich Lillian gave me into my mouth, then I let Kyra apply a layer of lip gloss. Immediately, I have regrets.

"This stuff is sticky. Can't I wear ChapStick?"

"You're going to ruin the entire look because of a bit of *stickiness*?'

I smile my most angelic smile and bat my eyes.

"Whatever, it's going to be dark anyway," she finally replies.

Lillian takes her place in front of the mirror, and we all beam, watching when she takes herself in. Her simple brown locks are curled elegantly and tied halfway back with two braids on both sides meeting in the middle. The deep-red tank that clings to her body leads to a pair of faded skinny jeans. To anyone else, this look might be an everyday thing, but Lills looks like a bombshell.

"You're welcome." Kyra smirks and leans into Remi, who's smiling right back.

Those two look like fashion queens, putting Lillian and me to shame. Remi sports a black crop top with silver super-snug pants and stiletto heels. Kyra has on an adorable white bodysuit with a high-waisted, hella-short, bright-pink miniskirt. Two of us might draw less attention than the other two, but together, we're bound to turn some heads and cause some trouble.

And for the first time in my life, I'm itching to let the fun begin.

CHAPTER 10

We leave the safety of our dorm room and butterflies flutter throughout my insides. Nerves settle in and dare to unravel my seams. Lillian grabs ahold of my hand, and like she's done over and over again, anchors me from floating away. In such a short period—a matter of days—these girls have become such great friends, and it's been nothing shy of wonderful. Maybe this is what being a normal person my age is supposed to be like. Classes and boys and parties and friends.

No matter how much I allow myself to enjoy my stay here, there's still always the nagging thought that I shouldn't be here. That I should be at home, caring for my mom. I should be working my part-time job to cover my expenses and making sure my mom takes her medication. I could have tried to take online college courses, but most of the schools were out of my budget, and regardless of my resistance to college in general, Danny insisted I do this.

He didn't want me to be resentful. Of him, myself, or my mom.

Danny wanted me to give college life a solid chance, especially if I'm going to take right back over when I'm finished. I'll get these few years to enjoy life before becoming a full-time mom to my mom.

At least college will help me get a better job so I can afford to find my mom better doctors to help figure out what happened to her. It was so sudden...the way her mind deteriorated and weakened. She became unable to see clearly and was often caught blinking rapidly like she was trying to wipe away sludge from her vision. I found her in the garden on many occasions, talking to her plants like they were her friends, and she told me she sent the rabbits on a mission to deliver messages to the trees.

She also told me I wasn't safe, and that scared me. Her face paled and stilled, and she'd looked me deep in the eyes and said, "They'll come for you, Willow."

I didn't really know what to make of it, being such a young age. Once, I had told social workers of her ramblings, and they threatened to take her away from me, or well, me away from her. But I couldn't have the one person I cared most about in this world taken from me, so I lied and told them I must have misunderstood what she said, and never brought it up again. The workers came to do house visits, and I made sure Mom had taken her medicine and was on her best behavior.

I fixed the problems as best as a kid could. And to this day, I focus on eliminating risks and mending problems if they arise. I try to think multiple steps ahead, like at what could go wrong, and have backup plans for the chance something does. Call it overkill, but it's been so effective when shit *does* go wrong, so I'll maintain my overanalytical mindset.

Lillian squeezes my hand, and I mirror the pressure, both of us walking behind Remi and Kyra as they lead the way to the party. In mere minutes, we arrive at the clearing. A flash of the memory of Silas standing inches away hits me, only for me to be disappointed that it was just in my head.

In the center of the clearing is a large bonfire with at least thirty students standing around, most of them holding red cups. Music plays from an unknown source, a song I'm unfamiliar with that has some people dancing in little groups. Bales of hay, or straw—I'm not really sure the difference between the two—are circled around the fire.

"This way," Kyra commands.

We follow obediently.

She leads us to a shiny contraption with a hose and a stack of cups. *This must be a keg. I've never seen one of these in person, but Brooke has told me about them from parties she's been to.* Beside the keg are two coolers, a dark-blue one and a white one.

Remi peeks inside both of them. "All right, we've got bottled water and soft drinks in the white one...and wine coolers in the blue one. Pick your poison." She grins.

"Water," I say confidently.

"I guess too much of it could be poison." She shrugs and then points to Lills.

"I'll have a Coke."

"Ohh, we're getting feisty." She hands me a water and Lillian a can of Coke.

"And for you, princess?"

"Whatever you're having," Kyra confirms with a wink.

Remi grabs two red cups and hands them to Kyra. "Here, hold these." Then she grabs the hose and holds down the little lever to fill their cups with whatever nastiness is in there.

A hand on my waist startles me almost enough to drop my water.

"You made it!" Cameron cheers.

I relax when I register it's him.

"Sorry, again with being handsy." He releases me. "But

anyway, you girls made it. And I see you found the drinks. Want to meet my friends?"

Kyra and Remi exchange a glance, raising their eyebrows at each other. *Those two.*

We follow Cameron to a group of guys, and he goes down the line, naming them all, only for me to immediately forget—except for the guy named Parker, because it made me think of Peter Parker. Now I just hope I don't mistakenly call him Peter.

Cameron nudges me as he leans in and says, "You look great tonight."

"Thanks. Not so bad yourself," I tease.

"I'm glad you didn't have a headache or anything...I was worried you might not be feeling up to coming tonight."

I take a drink of my water and put the cap back on. "I'm feeling much better, actually."

"That's great to hear."

Glancing at Remi, I see that she's made friends with one of the guys *not* named Peter—I mean Parker. Damn it, I knew I'd do that.

"We should have worn name tags. I'm never going to remember everyone's names."

I scan the crowd swiftly, hopeful to see another familiar face, but I'm met with strangers. A few minutes of casual conversation pass before a gorgeous, brown-eyed guy catches my eye.

He smirks and clears the space between us. "So, you're not a liar," he says. His gaze shifts to the rest of the group, and he smiles kindly. "Hey, everyone, I'm Deghan."

The group welcomes him warmly, and people go through and introduce themselves. I'm determined to remember more than just Peter—err—Parker's name. I can do this, one by one. Now if they can tell me their names like six more times, maybe I'll have them all straight.

For a momentary second, Cameron and Deghan have a weird standoff, but then they grip each other's hands in a firm shake and chat like old friends. It's equal parts terrifying and gratifying all at once. Maybe having more than one guy fawning over me won't be such a bad thing? Speaking of guys, I've yet to see Silas, which confirms that maybe I was right in my assumption that he wouldn't be in attendance. Perhaps he's sick, and that's why he wasn't in class today. Still, though, the desire to see him, to just be in his presence, calls to me.

I do one more scan of the crowd and notice the handsome, yet totally pissy, Sydney. He's holding a can of pop I can't seem to make out and muttering something to the two people next to him. He catches my gaze, looking me over, and then focuses back in on his friends. There's something off about him—his massive rudeness all of a sudden—like he didn't feel the power surging through our hands and into each other. Plus, he still has my pen.

An hour flies by in a rush, and somehow Remi convinces both Lills and me to dance with her and Kyra. Even though she's super outgoing, she's got liquid courage surging through her veins, so she's not half as embarrassed as me. That whole *not drawing attention to myself* thing I try to stick to isn't going over so well, but I can't be bothered right now.

New school, new me.

"Remiiiiii," Kyra slurs.

"What Ky-Ky?"

"I have to peeeee...go with meee..." she whines.

"I can't stop dancing, take someone else."

Like the natural nurturer I am, I take Kyra's hand and tell Lillian to keep an eye on Remi before leading Kyra into the forest a bit to find her a place to relieve herself.

"You're too pretty," she mutters.

"You're just drunk." I laugh. "Here, pee right here. I'll watch out for you."

She manages to take a leak easily, apparently not pee shy at all. It's impressive how, even in her drunken state, she's totally capable of not falling over into her own piss. She finishes and takes off into a sprint toward the campfire, leaving me in a trail of dust.

"Wait for m—" It's useless; she's intoxicated and gone by now.

I take a step, a whoosh of wind coming from behind, a smile creeping its way across my face before I manage to turn around. I don't know how, but I know it's him.

"You really probably shouldn't stalk drunk girls while they pee in the woods." I place my hands on my hips and watch him lean against a tree a measly few feet away.

"It's not safe out here," he says solemnly.

"I'm starting to think that's because of you...you're the only one lurking in the shadows."

I attempt to clear the space between us, but he remains stiff and matches my step one by one backward.

"You have to keep your distance," he urges.

"What if I don't want to?"

"You have to, Willow." His eyes display a sadness I can't quite comprehend.

"Okay then." I motion in front of me. "But this is acceptable?"

"This is probably a risk, too."

"A risk of what? Are you afraid of me?"

He exhales and looks down. "Something like that."

A million questions fill my head. *Why am I so drawn to you? Why are you so familiar? Why are you keeping me at a distance? What has hurt you so terribly that I can feel your aching soul? And why does my soul want to comfort yours?*

Instead, I ask, "Are you okay?"

His expression changes. "What do you mean?"

"You...you missed class today. I thought you might be sick or something."

He uncrosses his arms and wiggles a foot into the ground, almost like he's nervous.

"You were worried about me?" he questions.

I move from where I stand, and when I do, he stiffens and strides farther away.

I raise my hands in surrender. "I only want to sit down; I won't come any closer. Can we just sit and talk?"

"I'll try," he finally admits, claiming a spot on the ground, not close enough, but it'll have to do.

I slide my watchful gaze over him, sensing him tense.

He's a secret I'm dying to explore.

"Why can't we be any closer?" I hug my knees to my chest, leaning against the aging oak, a plush seat of barely-tall-enough grass beneath me, the richest scents of summer lingering.

"We can't...I can't really explain it to you. It wouldn't make sense."

I swallow. Why is he so intense? "Can you get close to other people?"

"Yes."

I frown. What did I do to be kept at a distance?

"Is it something I did?" It's hard not to feel defensive and hurt.

"Not purposely. It's...it's who you are."

"Who I am? What does that mean?"

"Can we talk about something else?" he begs.

I could ask him if I freaked him out yesterday...if I scared him away. I could pry on why we can't be any closer. But the resistance he shows worries me that I might push him away if I force it, and the thought of him disappearing again unsettles me for reasons I can't quite figure out.

"Okay then...what's your favorite color?"

Silas cracks a radiant smile. "Something simple, I can work with that. Black."

"Same." I go with something easy again. "What about favorite food?"

He hesitates before saying, "Cheesecake, for sure."

"I like cheesecake, but I love brownies." *The brownies.*

He flinches like he's waiting for me to say something about the two, but he quickly rebounds and asks, "Next?"

"What are you most afraid of?" I mutter, unsure if I'm testing the waters too much.

"Being forgotten…"

"How could you think, for one second, that anyone could ever forget you?" I almost whisper, pleading with him to comprehend how that could never happen, at least not with me. Without even really understanding it, I'm certain we've met in another lifetime.

He shakes his head but doesn't elaborate. "What about you? What are you afraid of?"

My jaw clenches reflexively like it's trying to stop the words from coming out. "Being abandoned." I pause briefly and continue, "Let's go with something easier this time. What's something you wish you knew more about?"

Without hesitating, he mutters, "You."

A moment passes, and after I let the wave of heat float by over me, I reply, "Says the guy trying to avoid me."

"You'd be surprised…what about you, though? What's your something?"

"Um, my family. I don't know much about my dad, or any of my grandparents, really. I just have my mom and my Uncle Danny."

He frowns and traces his finger along the ground, picking a blade of grass and tossing it to the side. "Maybe with time, you'll find some answers."

I mimic his movement and fidget with the ground. "Yeah…"

"I can help you," he offers.

"How can you when you won't even get near me?"

"We can do it from a distance. You deserve that."

Without thought, I blurt out, "How do you know what I deserve? I could be a horrible person for all you know."

"You're not, and you'd be lying if you said you were, Willow." His stare melts into me.

I run my finger on the ground, not saying anything, a sadness that I can't control consuming me.

"You really think the worst of yourself, don't you?"

I shrug. "What else am I supposed to think? I don't think my life is any worse than anyone else's, but the hand I've been dealt... it sucks. I've had no one to rely on other than myself, and it's fucking lonely." I can't believe the words leaving my mouth, or that I'm confessing things I've never told to another soul—and I'm confiding them in a stranger.

"I'm sorry," is all he says.

He exudes an energy so potent I can tell he means it.

"Willowwwww," one of the girls calls out, interrupting our moment. "Willow, are you out here?"

I turn toward the voice and then look back at Silas. "Will I see you again...between now and class, I mean?"

"Willow, you're freaking me out!" the voice calls, closer this time.

"I'm coming," I shout into the void, taking my eyes off him for a second to call out. When I look back, he's gone, my question lingering in the air.

CHAPTER 11

Remi all but drags me back to the party, her arm looped through mine in a loose fashion. I think this is probably the point where I cut her and Kyra off.

"Look who I founddddd," Remi calls out to the group.

Lillian and I exchange a glance like she's mentally asking me if I'm okay, and I telepathically confirm I am. At this, a bit of tension leaves her body, and she tosses me my bottle of water.

"Thanks, Lills."

Warm, large hands come at me from behind and lift me into the air, spinning me in a circle and setting me on the ground.

"Where did you run off to?" Deghan asks, his kind eyes meeting mine.

"Let's dance!" Kyra commands, extending her stance and

throwing her arms wide in a drastic attempt to get all of our attention. She's *super* drunk.

Knowing I have nowhere else to be, and although my bed and a good book are both calling my name, I decide to let loose a bit and take Kyra's hand, leading her to where other people are dancing. The rest of the gang joins us, and in a matter of minutes, we're all bumping into each other and laughing and smiling and having a wonderful time.

Even the grouch-ass from next door, Allie, doesn't make an attempt to ruin our night. She keeps her distance, still enjoying herself but not saying a single word to any of us. It's quite nice.

Deghan and Cameron take their turns vying for my attention, but their jealousy doesn't bubble over into anything out of control. And for the first time in a long time, I have one of the best nights of my life. There are moments I get to dance with Deghan, with Cameron, with the girls. The only thing missing is a broody Silas, but deep down, I have a feeling he might be prowling close by.

"This was too much fun, can we pleaseeee have a party again tomorrow night?" Remi pleads on the walk back to campus.

"Yes, yes, yes. Tomorrow!" Kyra agrees.

I glance at Deghan. "You in?"

He frowns. "Can't. I have a thing."

Cameron slurs, "Haven't you heard it's bad luck to be in the woods on a full moon?"

"Tomorrow is a full moon?" I question.

He nods. "And I've heard stories…"

"Yeah, what about?" I like a good story.

"He's drunk, I wouldn't listen to anything he has to say," Deghan interjects. "Right, bud? Let's get you back to your dorm."

The way he drags him away seems like something other than jealousy, something more like he's hiding something. Maybe he's scared of the stories of the woods during a full moon? Maybe he knows something about them? Whatever it is makes me wonder what he might be hiding. It also reminds me of how little I know about him.

"Okay, hug time," Deghan says, letting go of Cameron so he can reach out to me. "I had a wonderful evening, Miss Willow. I am forever grateful that you made it to the party."

He grabs me, reeling me in for a warm embrace. His arms wrap around me tightly, and I find comfort in the way my body presses up next to his. Everyone has their own secrets, and I shouldn't let that deter me from savoring this embrace.

He leans in close, so only I can hear, and says, "Don't forget, you still owe me a secret."

I tug him in closer, reeling in his warmth and smell—something like citrus and honey and a touch of cinnamon. I'm surprised by the contentment I discover in him, lingering for what should probably be classified as an awkward moment, but he doesn't seem to mind, and he doesn't pull away. He breathes in deep and relaxes into me.

His weight becomes heavier, and then it dawns on me. "Deghan?" I shake him a little. "Did you just fall asleep?"

He starts, his perfectly tanned cheeks showing signs of redness rising. "Shit, I'm sorry. I haven't been sleeping well." He rubs his neck. "Why are you so comfortable?" He smirks and nudges me.

"Get to bed, both of you," I command with a stern pointing of my index finger.

Cameron leans in for a chaotic hug, and even though he's much shorter than Deghan, his embrace is great, too. It's a quicker one, given Cameron didn't fall asleep on me, but enjoyable all the same, his gorgeous golden locks falling in his bloodshot eyes.

"You'll get him home safe?" I look to Deghan.

"Come on now, I'm not going to get rid of my competition by dumping him in the woods."

I slowly shake my head. "You're something else."

He reaches out and grazes my chin with his thumb and index finger. "And you love it."

Everyone exchanges pleasantries, and when we reach the center of the building, we all head our respective ways. Lillian and I hold on to Kyra and Remi, leading them to our dorm. And because Lills and I are thankful that they primped us for the party, we find their makeup remover wipes and night creams and do our best at eradicating all the crud from their faces. We take their shoes off but leave their clothes; they can deal with that in the morning.

After placing a glass of water and aspirin on both of their nightstands, Lillian and I tuck our girls into bed and stand back to admire them like the proud moms we are. Maybe not so proud that they're drunk, but proud that they're our friends and we had such a great night tonight.

"Now it's our turn," I say to Lills.

She throws me a face wipe, and I sit next to her on her bed, the exhaustion from the day finally catching up to me.

"Did you see him?" she asks.

"How did you know?" Astonishment damn well lines my face.

"You didn't seem to continue scanning the crowd for him once you came back, so I assumed he found you."

I don't want to lie to Lillian, so I tell her the truth. "Yeah, is that bad?"

"I think you should do what makes you happy. But also be careful." Such kind advice.

"That's really sweet of you." I smile. It's nice to have someone rooting for me. "Speaking of *sweet of you*, umm, who was that guy you spent most of the night dancing with?" I nudge her arm.

She turns red and averts her eyes.

"I'm sorry, I'm teasing. But really, who was that?"

"I think it was Cameron's friend, or, well, it could have been Deghan's. Either way, his name is Ethan."

"And...tell me more!"

"You're becoming just like them." She nods towards the sleeping beauties and laughs.

"Hey, you keep my secrets, and I'm forever grateful. I hope you know I'd keep yours, too." I don't know why she does this for me, but boy am I grateful.

She sighs. "Okay, okay. His name is Ethan, uh, I said that already. He's super nice. We have the class after lunch together, and he sort of asked me today if I would be going to the party. I was so nervous, and I freaked out, so I said no, and told the girls I was busy. But then you pressed, and I really did want to see him, so I caved."

"Aw, that's so exciting," I say cheerfully.

"He was so surprised when he saw me. His eyes lit up, and it really was so adorable. Part of me felt like he went just in case I did. I saw him before he saw me, and he looked so bummed, like he was forcing conversation with his friend, then he lit up when he saw me, walked right over to me, and we spent the rest of the night together. He didn't even blink an eye when I told him I don't drink. He actually dumped his beer out and started drinking a Coke. I was so mind-blown. That's never happened."

I lean in and hug her, feeling her excitement seep from her pores. "I am so unbelievably happy for you, Lills."

She hugs me back tighter than I expect, but not in a bad way, like *she* really needs it.

Moments later, I situate myself on my bed, reeling over the evening. Cameron's bright and contagious personality, Deghan's calm and cool charm, Silas's ever so serious and utterly captivating existence, and even Sydney's grouchy occasional glances.

My lips turn upward, and my eyes close, the heavy weight of them dragging me under and into a deep sleep.

A nudge interrupts me from my slumber.

"Are you okay?" Remi hovers, her brows drawn together.

"Yeah," I answer sleepily. "What's wrong?"

"It's nearly one in the afternoon. Do you usually sleep this late on the weekends? I thought you died of alcohol poisoning or something."

"I don't drink. And no, I don't usually sleep this late. Are you sure it's one?" I grab my cell from the nightstand and see it's 12:53 p.m. "Christ."

I look Remi over, not a trace of the drunken night left. "By the way, a huge thanks to whoever took my makeup off and moisturized. You are a *saint* by all accounts."

"You're so welcome," I grumble, lifting the covers back over my head. My stomach grumbles in response, and I call out, "I'm starving."

"You missed breakfast, sleepyhead," Remi chimes. "Kyra and Lillian are off doing whatever those two do, but I think Lillian brought you something. It's in the fridge."

"I need a cup of coffee. Why is it that I didn't drink but I'm the one feeling hungover?"

"No clue, girlfriend. I always make sure I alternate water between drinks so I don't feel like garbage the next day, plus it hydrates the skin, you know." She pokes at her cheekbone while inspecting it in the mirror. "But if you need coffee there's a teacher's lounge in the north wing that has an espresso machine, I've heard. They don't lock the door, so it's free game."

My mood perks up at the mention of espresso, and I make quick work of brushing my teeth in our little dorm room sink and throw on a pair of shoes. My gray sweatpants and oversized white T-shirt will have to do, I need java.

I'm jogging down the south wing stairs when it dawns on me that I have no idea which room the teacher's lounge is. I guess there are only six rooms, so it shouldn't be too hard to find. But then another realization hits me: the north wing causes me to see and feel things, and it really freaks me out. Going there alone is sort of risky, but I shouldn't have anything to worry about, right? It's a part of the school like all the other wings. I have nothing to be afraid of.

I make my way around the radiant indoor garden and

through the foyer, settling my gaze on the entrance to the north wing. No purple shadows appear, no creepy haze hovering near the doorways, just a normal hallway.

I peek into N two, no coffee maker in sight. N one and N three are also a miss. I finally hit the jackpot when I poke my head into N four, the aroma of freshly ground coffee beans filling the air. It's like I've died and gone straight to Heaven—if that sort of thing even exists, we won't get started on that one right now.

I approach the machine, scanning the buttons and contraptions, trying to figure out how to brew a slice of bliss without breaking it. The door creaks open, and I turn abruptly, like I got caught doing something wrong.

"So jumpy," he says, almost patronizing.

What the heck did I do to this guy?

His bushy eyebrows compliment those radiant green eyes that meet mine. His dark hair flows, and the sides are cut a bit shorter than the top. The sun hits it and shows a bit of golden-brown. It's strange to be so...alone with him.

I sigh. *Sydney.* The last person I was hoping would walk through that door.

CHAPTER 12

"Espresso? Latte? Americano?" he asks while strolling up next to me.

Is he really asking me drink choices right now?

"Umm..."

He points to the machine. "I've already figured it out. I practically live on coffee. What are you wanting?"

"Latte, I guess."

"Hot or cold?"

"Hot works for me."

"Vanilla, caramel, or plain?" The way he goes through the motions would make one think he'd never showed such weird animosity toward me in the past.

"Vanilla."

"What about milk choice?" He opens the small fridge and peeks inside. "Looks like there's skim, whole, and almond."

"Almond."

He pushes a few buttons, the machine rumbling to life and spewing out deliciousness.

"Why are you being nice to me?" I blurt.

He glances over his shoulder at me. "I'd really prefer you not to break the one thing keeping me sane around here."

Oh. Maybe he's stressed, and that's why he's being strange. But he also could have just noticed that I was alluding to him being mean, and he didn't deny it.

"Well, I'm sorry."

He actually looks at me this time. "Sorry for what?" He almost laughs, a bit of surprise lining his damn good-looking face.

"You said the coffee maker is the one thing keeping you sane around here. It kinda sounds like you're going through something, and I'm sorry for that. I hope it doesn't last long."

"Can I be honest with you, Willow?"

He remembers my name?

He hands me a mug of steaming happiness, and then he grabs his own mug before situating into a nearby seat.

I follow suit. Apparently this is going to be a conversational thing. Never would have expected this, especially out of him.

"You're either hiding something, or you don't know you're hiding something. And I'm not quite sure which one it is, and it's really bothering me."

At this, my eyes widen, the too-hot-to-drink latte failing to bide me time.

"Excuse me?"

"You really have no idea, do you?" He traces the rim of the cup with his finger and meets my eyes. The normally callous look is replaced by intrigue.

"Can you just tell me what it is that you think I'm hiding?" I implore.

"Technically, I can't. You have to sort of figure it out your-self." His tone is serious, but this has to be a joke.

"You're kidding. I'm being pranked or something, right? You come across all nice, then freak out when we shake hands, become an asshole, and then try to make it up to me with a fancy cup of coffee?" I swing my gaze across the room to see if anyone else bears witness to this nonsense. "I've been nothing but nice to you, and you're treating me like I'm some kind of freak." Then it hits me. "Did Allie put you up to this or something? Because of Silas?"

Sydney's brows immediately furrow. "Silas? What about Silas?" His words are short and clipped, his breath hitching.

"Well, did she? Tell me the truth."

"Silas is dangerous, Willow, you need to stay away from him."

Wow. Absolutely wow.

"I can't believe she put you up to this. What, is she putting out for you? What are you getting out of this?" I don't know why I ever got my hopes up in the first place about coming here. I always end up disappointed.

He shakes his head and puts his arms in front of him in an attempt to calm me down. "Okay, take a breather for a second. To confirm, no. No one named Allie put me up to this, I promise you that." His energy feels pure, like a cool cotton blanket.

"Oh," I say, shrinking into myself. "Sorry, I shouldn't have assumed that." Leave it to me to jump the gun about a situation I know next to nothing about. "Then what does Silas have to do with anything?"

He sighs. "He really is dangerous. And if what I think is true, you need to be extra cautious with him. His *kind*. They're dangerous."

His kind? What does that mean? What is he saying? What does he think is true? How can I be this oblivious to whatever he's alluding to?

"Can you please tell me what's going on then?" I finally lift my cup to my lips, sipping hesitantly from the very top, careful not to burn myself. A quiet moan of satisfaction escapes me.

"I wish it were that simple. And I'm surprised you don't already know. That's what makes this an incredibly bizarre situation."

"You're literally killing me here."

What's with all these guys and their fucking secrets? Is it just the guys I come into contact with or is this every single guy on the planet? This secrecy is driving me more insane than I already am.

"Okay, I'll try a different approach."

I tilt my head, waiting for him to elaborate.

"Do you ever"—he rubs his chin—"do things and you're not really sure how you were able to do them? Or see things you thought other people weren't able to see? Or maybe even *feel* things?"

I stand abruptly. What the fuck is going on? How could he...?

"I'm leaving," I say, stone-faced. Without letting him object, I continue. "Thank you for the latte."

"Wh-what? Leaving?" He stands, too, confusion racking his features.

But I see all too well what's happened here.

"I'm just trying to help." Sydney raises his hands in defense.

I force a fake smile and don't say another word, letting the door slam behind me on my way out of the lounge. I can't believe he would do such a thing. And I have no idea how he pulled it off. Unless...there's only one way he could have known the truth.

He read my fucking journal.

I burst through my dorm room door and head straight for my bed, setting the delightful, yet tainted cup on my nightstand.

"Whoa, whoa, whoa, what crawled up your ass and died?" Remi asks, bug-eyed, waiting for a response.

"I...where is it?" I mutter, wildly searching through my backpack. I slam the notebook onto the bed and rip open the pages. It's right here. How could he have read it if it's still here? He must have snuck in. Maybe while we were at the party? But he was at the party? At some point he could have left, came up here, read it, and disappeared. *Disappeared*. A chill rises up my spine.

By now, Remi has taken up perch at the end of my bed, hovering above me. "Are you okay?"

"I'm pretty sure someone read my journal. But it's been with me, minus bathroom breaks and during the party."

"Are you saying someone broke into our room?"

Lillian and Kyra appear now, arms crossed, looking a bit confused and concerned.

"I knew this thing was a bad fucking idea." I throw the notebook across the floor and into the corner.

"What's happening, Wills?" sweet Lillian coos.

Tears well, and I fight back the urge to let them loose. I will not cry, I will not cry. What is wrong with me? What is wrong with *him*? An unsettling thought creeps in, and I look at each of the girls for a brief moment. If he didn't break into the room, maybe one of them took it to him? Maybe the person I should be most skeptical of is right here in this very room? But how could that be? We've already grown so close, and they're my friends. Maybe that was a mistake.

Without saying a word, I exhale, walking over to the notebook, gripping it firmly in my hand and ignoring all of their words as I walk straight out the door.

I make it downstairs and manage to wipe away the one lone tear that makes its way down my cheek. I round the corner, head through the dining hall, and spot the exact thing I'm looking for. A random group of kids who were smoking at the party, grossing the non-smokers out.

"Hi," I say politely. "This may seem like an odd request, given we've never spoken, but do any of you have a lighter I could borrow for a few minutes?" I force a smile. "I'll bring it right back."

The group looks me over. Finally, a dark, long-haired guy

glances down at the notebook I'm white-knuckling and reaches into his pocket, revealing a navy-blue lighter.

"You are a life-saver. Thank you." I take it from him graciously.

He vaguely nods. What a lively bunch.

I continue on my journey, straight out onto the outdoor patio and toward the clearing in the woods. At least I'm familiar with that area by now, and they should have exactly what I'm looking for. A place to burn these damn pages without catching the whole place on fire.

Stopping just shy of the burnt-out firepit from last night, I kneel to the ground, opening the notebook. I rip out all of the written pages, knowing damn well I'm going to have to come up with more words for a grade or deal with an incomplete for those days. I can't risk someone else invading my privacy like Sydney did.

I run my thumb along the guard of the lighter, hitting the spark wheel and igniting the flame. I hold the paper in my other hand, letting the fire take hold, the satisfaction of destroying my evidence sinking in.

One at a time, I burn the pages. The first one didn't really need to be ripped out, given there weren't too many juicy details to be had, but the second one, well, I decided to trust in the pages and let a few things slip. *I won't make that mistake again; I should have never been that foolish.*

I skim the fiery words, and a sudden discovery startles me. I throw the paper to the ground and stomp it out before it's gone.

I allow my sight to scan the paper, and my stomach drops. I grab the rest of my papers and read through them briefly. I must have made a mistake, but how?

In my notebook, I was sure I gave away some of my deep dark secrets, but all I really alluded to was *feeling* things, and being off in some parts of the school. I said nothing about *doing* things or *seeing* things—the exact words that Sydney had used when he was interrogating me.

But, if I didn't say that in my journal, then how would Sydney have known them? And if Sydney found out some other way, he didn't read my journal at all, and he didn't sneak into my room. Not to mention, my roommates probably aren't the lying shitbags I just accused them of being in my mind.

Christ, I got this all wrong.

Maybe Sydney was right—he does know something about me that I don't. He seems to have more knowledge about me than he should, which is both terrifying and fascinating. He says I'm hiding something, but what could I possibly be hiding? And why don't I realize it?

I have to find him. I have to get answers. But first, I have to return this lighter and apologize to my friends...and confess to them that no one broke into our room. I probably freaked them out; I'm such an idiot. I don't typically jump to irrational conclusions like this, but I am all over the place this week with my emotions—they're difficult to control, like something is draining and unbalancing me.

I toss dark-haired guy his lighter.

He catches it and says, "You seem better."

"Yeah, thanks. I owe you one."

I get upstairs and hesitate at the door. I made a fool of myself earlier and I need to make this right. I turn the knob, the door opens, and the girls are right there.

"Willow, what the hell, we were so worried. Where did you go?"

Kyra glances down at my dirty soot-covered hands and notebook. "Did you catch your notebook on *fire?*"

I shrug. "Maybe," I say innocently. I walk in, closing the door behind me. "Okay, first of all. No one broke into our room."

A collective sigh.

"I'm dumb. I thought someone read my journal, and that

could have been the only way...but it turns out they didn't, and now I look like a big dumb-dumb, and I totally overreacted. I'm really sorry. This week has been an emotional roller coaster, and I'm all over the place. I totally didn't mean to freak you guys out. I'm sorry." *And I don't deserve your friendship because I'm an asshole.*

Lillian moves first, wrapping me into her arms, returning the hug I gave her last night, like she knew I'd be needing this one.

"You had us freaking. Remi was on her phone trying to order a hidden camera."

"*Trying*, but the service here is garbage. When are they going to fix the Wi-Fi?" she asks, rolling her eyes.

"Really," I resume. "I'm sorry." I shift my gaze to each of them, not a single one showing any signs of negativity toward me.

"Listen, you cleansed and hydrated my face when I was passed out drunk last night. You two are unicorn friends." Kyra beams at Lillian and me. "But what do you mean you thought someone read your journal? Whose ass do I need to kick?"

"Speaking of that, I need to go find him." I shove the notebook under my bed and make my way to the door. I turn back for a second. "Are we allowed in the boys' dorms?"

"I don't see why not," Remi ponders, looking to the rest of the girls for confirmation.

"Well, wish me luck," I say, and head out toward my next task —finding Sydney and figuring out what the hell is going on.

CHAPTER 13

I check the dining hall first, in case he might be grabbing a bite to eat. Honestly I'm just doing my best not to barge straight into the boys' dorms. No such luck in the dining hall, so I peek outside to check the patio area. Again, no Sydney. I creepily hang outside the downstairs boys' bathroom but leave after a minute of nothing. I really wish there was a paging system in the school. How are you supposed to find someone if you don't have their dorm info?

The foyer is empty aside from one lone girl sitting cross-legged and reading a book. *Atta girl.* Which reminds me, I've been here far too long, and I haven't visited the library yet. Just because I'm trying on a new version of myself doesn't mean I can't keep up with the old one, and that me, would have found the damn library by now.

Despite the growing weight of entering the north wing, I decide to check the last place I saw Sydney—the teacher's lounge. Peering into the room, I find it hopelessly vacant.

Come on, Willow, the school is only so big, just find him already.

I take a deep breath, closing my eyes and focusing on his face, the dazzling green eyes burning into my memory. My mind pulls me toward the ceiling, somehow calling me to go upstairs. *Okay, weird intuition, you want me to check dorm N four?*

I exit the north wing in a hurry, rounding the corner and taking the stairs straight up to the north wing dorms. The energy is noticeably stranger upstairs, and discomfort settles deeply into the pit of my stomach. Maybe it's simply because this is a male dorm? That must be it.

Manly figures stare at me as I make my way through the hallway, pausing in front of the room my subconscious is calling me toward.

I raise my hand to knock, not allowing pause to give myself a second to change my mind.

The door swings open, and lo and behold, Sydney's grumpy self meets me on the other side. How in the hell?

He frowns. "Come back for seconds?" He crosses his arms over his chest.

My gaze flickers to the floor and then back up at him. "Um, hi. Do you think we could maybe talk...somewhere private?" Without giving him a chance to respond, I continue, "Not, like, in your room or something, not *that* private, but you know what I mean."

His expression lightens, but he remains hesitant. "Are you going to freak out on me and leave?"

"I make no promises," I say sarcastically.

Sydney turns back to look at something inside his room. "I think it's nice outside, we could see if the courtyard is free."

"That would be great." I smirk. *Why am I suddenly so giddy?*

We walk side by side in silence down the hallway, along the stairs, and through the foyer.

It's not until we're finally outside that he breaks the quiet. "How were you able to find me?"

"I, uh...I guessed." No way I'm telling him what really happened, I don't even fully believe it myself. This must have just been pure luck.

"Mhmm," he responds. "So, what's this about?"

We sit at a far small round table with two iron chairs around it, the warm breeze hugging me gently and stuffing my lungs with a much-needed fill of nature.

"First, I guess I should say I'm sorry. You, I...I thought you had done something, and it turns out I'm not so sure that you did now, so I was hoping we could sort of start over with what we were talking about earlier. The hidden secret stuff."

He leans back on two chair legs and sizes me up, then moves back down on all fours. His stare is both intimidating and welcoming at the same time. "Okay."

"Yes."

"Yes?" he copies.

"Yes...to answer the question you asked me earlier. About doing and feeling and seeing. Yes." I swallow the lump in my throat. I haven't really openly talked about this kind of stuff with...anyone. Even Silas didn't seem to want to chat about the glowing flowers that I'm not sure really happened at all.

Sydney places his elbows on the table and crosses his arms, tilting forward. "What kind of things do you see here, at the school?"

I bite at my bottom lip. He's going to think I'm crazy. Why would I admit to him any of the stuff I've seen? Any sane person would not believe a word I have to say. But for some reason, my mouth forms words, and they fall out.

"I see...shadows."

Silence.

"You probably think I'm a freak, don't you?" I whisper.

His next words surprise me the most. "What color are the shadows?"

"Purple...but like a deep shade of purple, and sometimes black, but like, not pure black, like a black fog with a purple haze."

His eyes widen, and he lowers his head, huffing out a great deal of air.

I sit there for a minute or two, too afraid to leave and too anxious for whatever response he's going to have.

His thick hair spills over in a mess. He eventually rakes a hand through it, his eyes darkening and meeting mine. "This is impossible," he nearly whispers.

"Yeah...you're telling me."

"And you're saying you have no idea what secret I think you're hiding?"

"No, none at all. This makes no sense. Why can't you just tell me?" I urge.

"I swore an oath. I literally can't. Even this is pushing it. But I thought if I could maybe get you to figure it out yourself..."

"Well, what else could you ask to help me?"

He runs his hand through his hair again, tugging at it gently in thought. "Are you religious at all?"

"Uh, no."

"That doesn't help."

"My mom is Pagan, though. She practices Wicca, but she lost her mind many years ago, so I don't really know much about it."

"What do you mean she lost her mind?" Intrigue fills every crevice of his face.

"Like, she legit went crazy one day. Started muttering stuff about our family being cursed, how I was next, that they would be coming for me." I nervously end up talking with my hands.

"Holy shit, and let me guess, you didn't take her seriously?"

"No? I mean, at first I was really scared, but we got her on some medication that calms her down a bit, and she doesn't have the outbursts anymore, or not as often, I should say."

"That poor woman." He sighs.

"Yeah, it's really sad. I've had to care for her since I was twelve."

He pauses for a long and painful moment. "What if I told you that your mom isn't crazy?"

I let out a small chuckle. "And what if I told you pigs could fly?"

"I'm serious, Willow. What if everything your mom told you was true?"

"That my family is cursed? That *I'm* cursed? That someone is *coming* for me? That she's a witch and Grams was a witch and I'm a witch?"

With my last few words, Sydney's face nearly explodes with emotion. His wide eyes stare expectantly at me like they're pleading for me to figure it out.

"Are you saying I'm a witch?" The words come out almost silent.

"I'm not saying you aren't..." He grins triumphantly.

"If what you're saying is true, this changes everything."

And I mean, *everything.*

CHAPTER 14

I suck in a gasping breath and stand in a panic, and Sydney comes around the table to meet me.

"Hey," he says with a tone of sweetness that's unfamiliar. "Maybe you should sit down?"

"Sit down?" I call out, my entire body trembling with uncertainty. "I need to go home. I need to talk to my mom. How is this even possible? *Witch*? That's not a real thing, not in this universe." Oh God, my mom. I've accused and went along with the idea that she was crazy for over six years. I've dismissed her. I've pushed her fears aside.

But no, this can't be true. None of this makes any sense. I can't be a witch. My mom isn't a witch. We aren't cursed. I'm losing it. That's the only logical explanation.

He places his hands on my shoulders in an attempt to calm

me, but his fingers are met with a surge of power, like that day in the classroom. He flinches and draws them back, only adding to my desire to freak out.

My eyes meet his. I'm desperate to know if he felt that, too. He had to have, he pulled away like it scared him.

"What was that?" I ask, my voice hitching.

"I don't know how much I can say, not yet anyway."

"You just told me I'm a *witch*, but you can't tell me what the hell that was? That was insane, and I felt it the other day when we touched during class." I ignore the water that builds in my eyes. I refuse to cry.

"I did, too," he admits.

I nearly facepalm. "What? Why did you lie? You came across like such an asshole."

"Typically, people like us are aware of what we are...and you not being upfront about it made me think you were hiding for some unknown reason. I'm sorry." His gaze averts to the ground.

"Wait, did you say people like *us*? As in...you're a *witch*, too?" I swallow harshly. He must be lying to me. This must be some kind of sick and twisted joke.

"I'm not *not* saying that..."

"I can't...I don't...how...what...? I have so many questions."

"Let me get this straight, though, you did admission with Abigail? The wand thing, right?"

"The Wi-Fi stick? Yeah, why are you so concerned with the internet here?"

He laughs, and it soothes my nerves a bit.

"It's not really a Wi-Fi stick. It's a device to measure and determine supernatural ability. She runs them over all new students to determine where to place them. The human faction or the supernatural."

I blink at him a few times, allowing my mind to process his words.

"Did you just say *supernatural*?"

He verifies shyly, "Yeah, and apparently the oath doesn't apply to you anymore because the stipulations wouldn't have allowed me to say that to anyone else from the human faction."

"So, you can tell me what's going on now?"

"Yes and no. There's only so much I'm allowed to tell you. This sort of stuff isn't really permitted on an info-dump basis. It'll overload your servers and cause you more harm than good."

"My servers? You realize how insane that sounds. What does that even mean? Can you at least tell me what the hell the shadows are I keep seeing in the north and west wing? They're not in the other wings, and I can't make sense of it. Is it like a lighting issue or something?" I've tried to make sense of the visions to no avail, but maybe with his knowledge, I'll finally be able to comprehend what I'm seeing.

"Baby steps, okay? If you start feeling odd, tell me immediately. Like, if you have a sudden drop in energy levels."

My energy levels have been all over the place since I've been at Harper Academy, but I don't dare tell him that right now. "Okay."

"Sit down." He looks around the courtyard, and once he's satisfied, he lowers his voice and says, "Like I said, the student body is part human and part supernatural. The supes sort of blend in with the humans, and to be able to have a well-rounded learning experience, the supes have their own style of classes in addition to the traditional ones. We can't do that kind of teaching out in the open, so what you're seeing is the shadow realm the supes have their classes in. And that's why you can see it and the humans can't. It's solely meant for supernatural people to see. We call it Harper *Shadow* Academy." He finishes speaking and examines me with his steady gaze.

"I've seen people...disappearing into them," I murmur, meeting his stare.

"That was just a supe going to supe class."

I take a gigantic breath, exhaling even bigger.

"I thought my sight was messed up. I was going to schedule an eye exam with the nurse." I laugh, feeling incredibly foolish now.

"Your vision is probably fine." He smiles but it doesn't really make me feel any less crazy. If anything, I become borderline convinced I'm truly losing it for good.

"Wait, you said Abigail waved her weird little magic wand at me? Why didn't she classify me?"

"That's what I've been trying to figure out, too. The only thing I can think of is that your magic is hidden."

"Hidden magic?"

"You said you're cursed? Maybe your magic is doing a self-preservation spell to protect you. It's plausible."

"I need to go home." I shake my head. "I need to talk to my mom. If what you're saying is true, she's been medicated for six years for no good reason."

He nods quickly. "Definitely, yeah. But you shouldn't talk to anyone else about this. You really should be safe. You know you're only allowed to leave once per semester, right?

I nod, fully understanding the gravity of the situation and chalking this up to one damn good reason to use my one-time excuse.

"Is your car on campus?" Sydney asks me.

Shit, Danny dropped me off.

My shoulders slump. "No, but I could call a cab. I think they come this far." I make my way toward the building when Sydney's firm grip wraps around my forearm and stops me. The surge of energy tingles my skin, but this time, he doesn't let go. "What is that?"

"I think our magic is just getting acquainted with each other."

"That's a thing?"

The pulsing between us slows to a stop, and when it does, his eyes meet mine.

"I have a car; I can take you. But only if you want, I don't want to intrude."

How did we go from me thinking he hated me to him offering me a ride home? What other choice do I have, though—wait around on a cab for an hour or more? No, thanks.

"Really? You don't mind?" I pause and then add, "I don't want you to waste your one time on me."

"I'm a second-year student, we have more leniency. Plus, I think I owe you that after dropping that bombshell on you." He steps a bit closer.

Warmth settles through me, and I focus on his features. The gentle slope of his sun-kissed, deep-brown hair caressing his forehead, those deathly emerald eyes, the faint hint of stubble on his cheeks. *Here I go again.*

The short drive to my childhood home is quiet, minus the in-and-outs of our breaths and an occasional, "Turn there." A million questions rack my brain, but I can't seem to slow down enough to hone in on one in particular, especially if he has to be cautious with his replies.

I knew all too well what he meant about draining energy; I've felt it numerous times since I've been at Harper. That probably explains why I slept way later than usual. And why I fainted in front of Silas. Speaking of Silas—Sydney told me he's dangerous. That his *kind* is dangerous. The way he said *his* makes me think he and Sydney aren't one and the same, but if Sydney is a witch, what is Silas? And why can't Silas come near me? He made it clear he couldn't give me answers either, so maybe he's bound by the same oath Sydney is, too.

I want to ask Sydney about Silas, but given his predisposition about him, I should probably keep to myself and figure that one out on my own. I wish there were someone else I could ask. Someone that doesn't seem to hate Silas.

We pull up my drive, the gravel crumbling beneath the tires of Sydney's Toyota Corolla. He was kind enough to let me wallow with my own thoughts on the drive, and I'm incredibly appreciative of that.

"I should probably stay here," he declares while putting the car into park.

"Okay…" I say without making an attempt to leave.

He reaches over and places his hand on top of mine. "I'll be right here if you need me."

"Yeah. Okay. I can do this." I swallow and pull the handle.

I arrive on the porch, taking a glance back at the car, and then grab the hideaway key under the potted plant. I shove it into the lock, a mix of emotions consuming me as I turn it and open the door.

Danny's car isn't outside, so he must be out running errands, meaning Mom should be home alone. Errands are usually more efficient without taking her along. A sad reality, especially knowing the partial truth that I do.

This could still all be some kind of joke, I remind myself. A sick and twisted joke.

"Mom," I call out.

Rustling comes from the kitchen.

"Willow?" Surprise lingers on her tongue. "Willow, is that you?"

"Yeah, Mom." I walk towards the sound of her voice.

I find her sitting at the table, hands wrapped around a cup of coffee. The aroma is friendly and calls to me. My thoughts travel to the lone mug of heaven that Sydney made me, getting cold on my nightstand back in my dorm.

"What's wrong?" she asks.

"Mom, I need to talk to you. Is that okay?"

"Has there been an accident?" Her deep-brown hair is pulled into a tight braid that sits on her shoulder. A few wrinkles line her mouth, a tale from a time faraway when she was happy, when she laughed and smiled.

My heart tugs. "No." I shake my head. "There hasn't been an accident. Everyone is okay. I…I thought I could maybe talk to you." Tears do their best to form, but I won't let them take their journey.

"Sure, honey. What's on your mind?" Her eyes tell me a story that today has been an okay day. Not a great one, but not a hard one, just a pretty normal and good day. No signs of aggression at all, no lingering wild craze.

"Mom...if I ask you something, do you swear to tell me the truth?" I beg.

"Absolutely, I wouldn't lie to you, my sweet girl."

My heart breaks knowing—that if what I'm about to ask her is true—she's experienced the torment of dealing with this by herself for all these years.

"Mom. Am I a witch?" The words leave my mouth, and a rush of energy pulses through the room. I can't tell if it's hers or mine. The fluorescent kitchen light flickers overhead.

"Yes, I've told you this a million times before." She smiles, and it's such a *Mom* smile that I smile, and then the tears are falling, and she exhales and embraces me into a hug, and I cry silently in her arms.

"Prove it," I blurt out, desperate for her to actually show me what she's been telling me all these years.

Mom sighs and cups my cheek with her hand, her touch soft and motherly. "Sweetie, you have all the proof you need if you'd just remember." Her gaze trails mine. "Glowing flowers aren't a normal occurrence. You have powers hidden inside of you that started coming out a long time ago."

"I'm..." I sniffle. "I'm sorry. I'm so sorry I didn't believe you."

She smooths my hair with her hand and pulls away, gripping my face between her palms. "It's okay. You know now, and that's all that matters." Her expression darkens in the slightest. "But you must be careful, my Willow, magic is a dangerous thing, especially yours."

I wipe at my face. "Why mine? What's wrong with my magic?"

"Oh, nothing is *wrong* with it. But some time ago, the Oliver women's magic was suppressed with a curse. We were too power-ful, and people didn't like that. So, they cursed us to take our magic away. I've been without mine for a very long time. Once they realize you've gotten yours, there will forever be a target on your back. That's why you must be careful."

"I can be careful, I can." I grab a napkin from the holder in the middle of the table, next to the salt and pepper shakers, and blow my nose. "Does this mean you can stop taking your medicine now? You aren't crazy. I'm sorry that I ever thought you were."

She grins wide. "Oh, honey, I've been fighting you left and right with those things. Danny doesn't check like you do, and I haven't taken them since you left. Please don't stop living your life because of me. I'm sorry I've taken so much from you."

Relief floods through me, but there are still countless things unanswered.

I'm cursed? She's cursed? Who cursed us? How and why and what can I do to break it? And, like, I'm a witch? Meaning, I can do magic? What does that even entail? Sydney is a witch, too? And apparently, Silas is *something*? What about Cameron and Deghan? What about the girls? Now that I think about it, our rooms were assigned at admission, meaning Abigail waited until she sorted us to put us in our rooms, so if I had to guess, the south wing is for the human students. And given the weird vibes from the west and north wing, that's probably where the supernatural students dorm. The girls in the west wing, the boys in the north.

Holy shit, it's slowly starting to come together.

"You haven't taken anything from me at all, Mom. You've given me the world. Now I just have to piece it together and figure out what the hell is happening." I steady my sights on her. "Who's coming for me, Mom? Who placed this curse? I need you to tell me."

Her mouth opens in an attempt to speak, but she's cut off by the sound of the back door opening. Maybe Sydney got impatient or wanted to check on me?

A familiar voice fills the space. "Hello?"

"Uncle Danny, we're in here."

"You're not supposed to be home," he protests.

"I know, I know. I had to check in. The phones at school suck, it was killing me." I look to my mom, winking.

She reaches across the table and puts her hand on top of mine.

"Who's the good-looking guy waiting in the Corolla?" Danny asks when he comes into the kitchen, carrying two filled-to-the-brim brown paper sacks from the grocery store. He sets the bags onto the counter, walking over and pulling me up into a hug. "Okay, it was great seeing you, but really, you need to leave. Go be a college kid. Go to a party or something. Leave!" He literally pushes me softly but firmly through the house and toward the front door.

"Danny," I interject. I try to turn around, but he continues moving me along. At the front door, he stops, squaring his shoulders so I can't pass back through. "You're the best but somehow the worst, you know that right?"

He smirks. "And you love me all the same."

"Something like that." I shout out, "I love you, Mom! We'll talk again soon, okay?" The semester has only just begun, and I don't know when I'll be able to get back out here. Maybe I can call her from a landline, but is that the type of conversation I'm willing to have over the phone? Perhaps someone at the academy would be willing to grant me an exception if I tell them there's a family emergency. But do I really want to tell them what's going on when everything is so unclear?

She raises her hand in a wave and replies, "Love you more, sweetheart. Everything will be okay if you remember what I told you. Be careful and don't trust easily."

Uncle Danny rolls his eyes and gives me a final nudge out the door.

I'll have to get answers from her another day—today, though, Sydney will just have to do.

CHAPTER 15

Silence fills the scenic car ride back to the school until Sydney finally speaks up.

His hands grip the steering wheel firmly. "We should probably go talk to Abigail and Headmaster Walker."

"Headmaster Walker? Is he like a real, living, breathing person? I wasn't aware he had arrived at the school yet."

"Yeah," he confirms. "He hasn't been back for long, but he's back."

"That's weird. Where was he?"

"He had an *issue* to attend to," Sydney responds with tension rising slightly between us.

"Another thing you won't tell me, I assume?" I prod.

"Yep."

I stare at his profile, soaking in all the gorgeous details. Witch stuff aside, I'm totally in over my head with all these beautiful men around me. The witch stuff is more important, though, so I need to focus. I shift my gaze to anywhere but on him.

"You think they'll know what to do?" I ask.

"They sort of have to. That's their job."

He puts his car back into the same spot we found it in the school parking lot earlier. He shuts off the ignition, and I keep looking ahead, out the windshield, avoiding his attention.

"Okay," I say quietly.

Sydney continues to look in my direction, searing my skin with his piercing eyes. "We'll figure this out, okay? I'll be right there with you. I know this is more than likely super-overwhelming and we don't exactly know each other, but I'll be here for you if you need me."

I nod. "Thanks." I wrench back the handle, preparing myself for what's to come next.

We make our way inside the school, only passing a few random students on the way. Sydney stops in front of the headmaster's office and knocks on the door, whispering something under his breath. A few seconds pass, and the door opens.

For a split second, I consider running far, far away from here, but something in my gut convinces me to trust Sydney. It tells me he wouldn't steer me wrong. After all, he's the one who talked me through this entire giant revelation in the first place—why would he have done that if he wanted to hurt me?

Abigail greets us with a pen in one hand, a notepad clutched under her arm, and confusion trailing her perfectly sculpted eyebrows. "Sydney," she says while eyeing me. "And, Miss Willow Oliver. What can I do for you two?"

"Hey, Abby, do you mind if we come in? There's something rather pressing that we need to talk about."

She shifts her gaze between us and then opens the door farther, allowing us into the room, pointing for us to sit in nearby chairs.

The room is rather spacious and well-designed. A solid wood

desk adorned with intricate bronze and various succulents placed strategically around the area. Large, simple black-and-white photographs of several cities line the walls. The scent of coffee lingers.

"What's so pressing, Syd?" She stands but leans against the table, the pen pressed toward her mouth in thought, staring deeply at Sydney.

These two are on a nickname basis with each other. First Abby, now Syd. I wonder if he prefers to be called Sydney or Syd. I'll have to remember to ask him.

"You ran your *test* on Willow during admission, right?"

Her confusion turns to annoyance. "Yep, her results were conclusive, and she was assigned appropriately, why?"

"Is there any possible way that you were maybe...wrong?" Sydney cowers a bit with his last few words.

I smile a bit inside at how adorable he is.

"It's difficult to be certain of anything in this world, but historically, those results are always accurate. Can you maybe get to the point you're working toward arriving at?"

He takes a breath and blurts it out, "Willow is a witch." His eyes meet mine, and he gives me a reassuring upward turn of his cheek. "And I'm sure it sounds impossible, but I think your test may be faulty, at least on her."

She stiffens immediately at his words. "You said..."

"Right," he confirms.

"She has to be then, if you were able to say that. What else have you gotten out?" Her expression shows she's desperate for more knowledge.

"Well, she knows there are supernaturals at the school, and she's seen the shadow realm, so I explained that briefly," Sydney clarifies with a bit of excitement showing through.

She nods and pulls at her lip with her top teeth. "This has never happened."

They talk like I'm not in the room, or I am, but I'm incapable of hearing them.

"I thought you and Mr. Walker might be able to help." Sydney shifts in his seat.

"Absolutely." She bobs her head up and down again, like a constant processing of information. "And of course, we'll have to reassign her."

Finally, something to push me to speak up. "Reassign me how?"

"Your dorm." She points to me with her pen. "You'll need to change to the west wing with the other supernaturals."

"No, no, I can't. I love my dorm mates. Can't I just stay where I am? This is already a big enough adjustment," I protest.

She shrugs. "It's protocol."

My shoulders slump, and the fight leaves me, sadness consuming me. I was so stressed about starting a new life here at school, and the one thing I was able to find comfort in was my new friends, and now she's saying that's going to be stripped away. How will I explain my sudden relocation to them? I know I have more pressing concerns, but this really fucking sucks.

Sydney speaks up, "We could probably see if Mr. Walker would be willing to make an exception to the rules, right?"

She considers his declaration for a moment and says, "Yeah, it wouldn't hurt to ask."

A blast of hope immediately courses through me, and I offer Sydney a smile in return for his thoughtfulness. It's hard to imagine a few hours earlier I stormed out on him and thought he'd violated my privacy. He's not so bad after all.

"I have to ask, though, what brought you two to this conclusion?" Abigail looks back and forth between us.

I glance to Sydney, nodding for him to go ahead.

"We touched, and it basically sent a surge of energy between us. It happened the first time, and I immediately thought the worst, that she was hiding on purpose. But when it happened again, we talked things through, and Willow was unaware of her magic."

"I see, I see. And, Willow, have you noticed anything else... anything magical?"

This is absolutely bonkers. She's going along with the magical bit as though it's totally normal. I pinch my arm to see if I'll wake up from this bizarre dream.

When I remain firmly rooted in this reality, I say, "Aside from being able to see the shadow realm and students disappearing?" Like the weird shit that happened between me and Silas, the whole passing out thing.

"Mmhmm."

"Actually, yeah, I got lost in the woods behind the school on the first day of class and I had closed my eyes in frustration, only to open them and find an illuminated path of flowers leading me back to campus." The words come out, and I realize how crazy they sound. "That sounds unbelievable, right?"

"Only as unbelievable as a shadow realm," she jokes.

I let out a soft laugh in my weak attempt to mask this with sarcasm.

"So..." She flips open to a blank sheet of paper on her notebook, jotting a few things down. "Your magic reacts to nature. You could be a green witch. And you seem to have a self-preservation thing going on. What about family history? Witchcraft appears to be a surprise to you, but are you familiar with any other witches in your bloodline?"

"My mom," I say shyly.

Her eyes widen. "Your mom?" She then looks to Sydney.

I go to speak, to tell her about my mom, when the door swings open, an older gentleman walking inside.

He smiles softly. "Appears we've got a full room." He hangs his jacket on the hook near the door, strolling over to greet us. He extends his hand to me. "Headmaster Walker, and you are?" His large palm hangs in the balance, waiting for me to take it. His steel-blue eyes bore into mine. He must be in his late forties, maybe early fifties, his salt-and-pepper hair giving away a bit of his age. His cool expression leads me to believe he's a nice man, a kind one.

"Willow Oliver," I say.

His grip is firm but welcoming. A bit of energy surges between us, a light static pulsing in our grasp. Without letting go, he shifts his consideration to Abigail. "We've got a live one." He smirks.

"That's what we were discussing. You're just in time."

"Carry on, don't mind me while I settle in." Walker places his bag next to his desk, taking a few items out—among them a laptop and notepads—and lays them on his space.

Right back to business, Abigail says, "Your mother?"

"She uh, yeah, she sort of went crazy a while back, or that's what we thought. It was really sudden and unexpected...she started telling everyone she was a witch, and that the women in our family were witches, and that we were cursed.

"She had said something about *coming into* magic and that they would come for me and I had to be careful."

Like she's putting pieces of the puzzle together, Abigail speaks. "Hidden magic makes sense, but I've never seen it avoid my testing. Ancestral magic is powerful, so is green magic. Do you know anything else about this curse or your mother's magic?"

"Just that she said whoever cursed us thought we were too powerful, so they cursed us to take our power. I was young when she had her breakdown...no one took her seriously." My heart aches every time I think about what she's been through.

"Any other things that stand out that you can think of?" she questions.

I should probably tell her about Silas, but with Sydney sitting right here, I can't bring myself to do it. "I don't know if it's worth mentioning, but I can feel people's energies. Is that weird?"

She smiles compassionately. "Not weird at all, but not totally common. Another very powerful trait you possess, and I'm guessing we haven't even scratched the surface yet, given how unaware of your abilities you are."

Walker finally sits in his chair, clearing his throat and gathering the attention to him. "Willow, you claim you were oblivious of your magic until recently?"

"Yes." I swallow. "I...I just thought I was seeing stuff. I considered that maybe I was going crazy like my mom. Never would I have imagined I was actually a witch like she claimed."

"I understand," Walker says kindly. "I'll have to do a bit of research about your ancestry, but the Oliver witches seem to ring a bell somewhere in my memory."

At that, my mood perks up. "Wait, like, you know something about my heritage?"

"There aren't many witches, especially those in existence, who don't have documentation of their footprint here in this universe. I'm sure with some time we can come up with something."

This is truly insane, but in all the best ways. I mean, yeah, I have a curse, that's not good, but I've been wondering my entire life about my father and my family history. This would be life-changing to have even a tiny bit of knowledge about my past.

"That would be wonderful. Let me know what I can do to help."

His attention goes to Abigail. "Willow was assigned to the human faction?"

"Yes." She frowns.

"We'll have to change her dorm and classes to better suit her needs then." His words pierce like knives.

Sydney clears his throat and speaks up again on my behalf. "Is there any way that she can stay in her dorm? She's rather acquainted with her roommates."

Walker scratches his chin. "It's not common to have the two living side by side so closely in this environment."

"I agree, but she's already had such a shock to her system. It might disrupt her more by changing her dorms at this stage. Could she give it a trial basis to see how things go?" Sydney's posture is firm when he makes his arguing statements.

I could freaking *kiss* him right now.

Walker sighs. "On a probationary status only. But the first time I hear of any trouble, there will be an immediate dorm change. Regardless, though, classes will have to be altered."

"Absolutely," Sydney confirms.

A calming relief floods over me. Sydney just saved my ass—I was *not* ready to lose my dorm or roommates. Classes are another thing, though. What kind of changes can I even expect?

"We're going to have to go back to the basics with you, Willow, so your supernatural classes will more than likely be one-on-one for the time being, and because of the sensitivity overload, they'll be slow until you can build a tolerance. I'm not sure how much you've heard, but those classes take place in the shadow realm." He pauses, almost like he's waiting for me to confirm what I do and do *not* know.

"They didn't explain much, just that it exists. I can see it."

"That's great actually. Usually it takes several tries to properly visualize the realm. You have a natural inclination to it which should make accessing it easier on you." He then looks to Abigail. "Go ahead and note astral abilities, too, we can confirm or decline that in the future."

"Got it," she verifies.

Walker focuses back on me. "Now, the shadow realm's time passes a bit differently than ours. What are a few minutes in our world, is much longer there, therefore, you'll be able to spend more time during shadow lessons and not be missing from this world for too long. It's one of the perks that help the supernaturals blend in with the human faction."

With each word, my energy stifles the new knowledge like a pull to my core, settling itself deeply within the depths of my mind. I reposition in my seat to allow it to support me a bit more in my attempt to listen fully.

"I see this is already beginning to drain your resources, which is not at all unexpected. That will conclude our discussion for today, but before you go, you'll have to sign the oath if you wish to remain here at the academy."

The oath? That's the thing Sydney had mentioned, right?

I furrow my brows and tilt my head. "Oath?"

"Yes, of course we don't want the human faction to find out about our existence among them, so the supernatural students must sign an oath to keep their secret from the humans. You will not be permitted to discuss your abilities with human students."

"How will I know who I can or cannot talk to?" I ask, the secret I only just found out about feeling heavier and heavier by the minute.

"With time, you'll realize who you can and cannot discuss such matters with. If you were to dorm in the west wing with the other supernatural girls, you'd get familiar more quickly." He hesitates. "I would provide you with the full list but I'm afraid that sudden burst of knowledge would threaten your system."

Because there seems to be no other option, I do what I'm instructed and sign the oath stating I won't share my secret or the one hidden within Harper Academy.

Harper Shadow Academy.

CHAPTER 16

I'm not really sure what to expect when I leave the headmaster's office, but being basically freed and left to go on my own merry way was not what I had imagined. I was sworn to secrecy, so I guess they weren't really worried I'd do anything drastic, and given I have no idea how to use my magic, I'm not a threat.

I was told to report to first period on Monday ten minutes early, and at that point, I'll be instructed with what to do next. In the meantime, I've been encouraged to go about my normal life, or whatever shred of normalcy I can find. My first stop is the dining hall to scrounge for food. Perhaps that's the cause of my depleted energy levels—the fact that I haven't eaten all day, and here it is, dinnertime.

I enter the large opening, and a boisterous Remi waves me over.

"Where have you been? Did you find what you were looking for?" she asks.

I steal a fry off her plate. "Yes, and much more." A hidden string tugs at my insides, like a sudden reminder to keep my mouth shut about what I've been up to. "Be right back." I head toward the food selections, grabbing way more than I'm capable of eating. Who cares, though? I'm starving.

Kyra eyes my tray, scanning the massive sandwich, steaming fries, cup of mixed fruit, brownie, and large glass of tea. "When was the last time you ate, girl?"

"Too damn long ago," I reply, taking a bite of the BLT.

"Are you still wearing your PJs?" Lillian asks.

"Mmhmm," I mumble with a mouth full.

"Well, you need to get showered and changed, like ASAP, because we're going out," Remi commands.

I wipe my mouth, not wanting to pause between bites but wanting to ask, "Out?"

"Yeah, another party. Last night was perfect. We're all ready for round two, including Little Miss Lily."

I've been gone too long, they've corrupted Lillian.

"Again?" I say, napkin covering my sandwich-crammed face.

"Yes, get with the program, Willow," Remi teases.

I guess a party is a surefire way to keep my mind distracted for the time being.

After I've stuffed my belly and taken an extra-long and relaxing shower, I sit on my bed, covered in a towel, hair dripping wet, while I wait for the girls to torture me with yet another dress-up party.

There's no telling how many more of these days I'll have with them, so I better take full advantage of them while they last.

"Nothing fancy," I remind them. "And something comfortable, please."

"You really need to get rid of that whole *comfort* mentality." Kyra laughs.

"You really need to get rid of that whole *thinking Willow cares what she wears* mentality." I secretly loved my makeover last night, but I'd rather only do it on occasion; I still want people to be able to recognize me outside of going to parties.

The girls settle on another tight tank, this time a deep shade of purple, and they pair it with dark skinny jeans. Ultimately, if it's not an oversized tee, and it's showing some cleavage, it gets the girls' stamp of approval.

"It's all about the *curves*, Willow...you were blessed with those. Don't be afraid to show them off." Kyra motions an outline of a voluptuous body with her hands.

I roll my eyes and finish brushing out my hair. I'm going with a semi-natural look tonight—that's what Kyra told me, at least. A little bit of body and bounce. *Whatever*, as long as it doesn't involve me sitting under her while she curls my hair for an hour.

"I still can't believe this is natural. Even the shine is flawless. You have, like, metallic silver hair, girl." Remi wraps a strand of my hair around her finger, toying with it and then releasing it to fall in line with the rest.

I take a deep breath. I'm a bit apprehensive about going to yet another party, especially considering all that I found out today. My mind is still reeling over all the knowns and unknowns. But this is exactly what they advised me to do: continue on with *normal* life. And parties look like they might be part of my new normal.

Sydney will be, too.

But what about the rest of the guys?

Cameron, Deghan, and Silas.

The thought of Silas brings me back to all the things I didn't say today. Our encounter in the woods. His depth and despair... his pain that spills out like an overflowing bucket of water. Sydney told me to stay away from him, that Silas is dangerous. There's a portion of me that believes that—that Silas *is* dangerous. But aren't we all dangerous in a way? I'm a freakin' witch, for crying out loud. The extent of my powers is a mystery. What if I turn out to be the worst of us all?

Then there's Deghan, who was clearly hiding *something* last night. But again, I'm hiding something, too. Maybe what he's hiding isn't so bad at all? And there's the possibility that he could be like me, too. The realization hits that I won't see him tonight because of the *thing* he has planned. Whatever it may be, I hope I get to see him prior to classes on Monday.

Cameron will more than likely be in attendance tonight, which does wonders for my mood. He's so bright and cheerful, and his mere existence is wonderfully contagious. He did mention something about stories involving the woods under a full moon, which now that I know supernatural stuff is a real thing, I should really try to pry and see what I can get him to tell me before he drinks too much. That will be my goal for the night, have fun and dig for some dirt.

"Are you readyyyy?" Remi calls through our dorm, the high-vaulted ceilings emphasizing her voice.

We step into the hallway, and Allie and Paige pause to glare at us, then enter their room. I really don't understand their strange hatred toward us, you would think that kind of petty behavior would end in high school. Must not be true for those two.

Two by two, we lock arms and head downstairs. Lillian and me, Remi and Kyra. The invisible bonds attract us together in pairs like this. Once we're in the main foyer, Cameron and a few of his friends join us. Ethan—Lillian's crush—included.

I note the blush that crosses her cheeks when he waves to her shyly.

Cameron nudges my shoulder, and I smile up at him.

"Hey, you," he says.

"Long time no see," I answer.

"I didn't see you much today, how was your day?" He hesitantly throws his arm around my shoulders.

"It was...interesting, to say the least." Which quite literally might be all I can tell him anyway. My connection to Cameron feels powerful, but not in the bursting with magical energy way that it does with Silas, Sydney, and Deghan—leading me to believe confessing the details of today are off-limits.

"Want to talk about it?" Cameron glances down at me with those cool blue eyes of his that I absolutely adore.

"Maybe another time," I say, unsure if I'll ever get the chance to truly be open with him.

He tugs me tighter but doesn't push. "I'm here for you whenever you need me."

I smile up at him, unsure of what I did to deserve this kind of treatment from him. And even more unsure of why I'm hoping it never stops. I barely know this man, and here I am, melting into him like we're old friends, my body entirely too comfortable in his presence. How can it be wrong if it feels this right?

Our rapidly growing group stalks through the dining room, chatting with one another and gaining more people on the journey to the clearing in the woods. Once there, everyone settles into their respective places around the fire that took the guys a mere five minutes to get started. A few people haul in coolers, no keg this time, probably because tonight will be a smaller crowd. This party is much more low-key than the previous one.

I grab two bottles of water, hand one to Lills, and then open one for myself. I rip a slit into the label so I don't confuse the two. We appear to be the only ones drinking water, though, so it shouldn't be too much of a challenge to keep them straight. Music blares from someone's wireless speaker, and most of the horde moves to the beat.

Remi takes hold of Kyra, who in turn grabs Lillian, who latches on to me and drags us to the dance area. I pout for a tiny second and then let the beat flow through my body, losing myself to the music. A song or two or three passes—I can't really tell how many—and I'm dying of thirst, so I leave the girls and take a long, healthy swig of my water. It's cool and refreshing but burns on the way down, warming my chest. I ignore the sensation and continue to gulp too quickly. Water manages to go down the wrong pipe and I let out a series of strangled coughs. I rebound and catch my breath, hoping that no one saw me choke on my own water. The coast is clear, so I wiggle my way back between the girls and dance my little heart out.

Another song plays, and my head gets a bit dizzy, a mental fog settling weirdly over me. I move from the group again, getting away from the haze of the fire and loudness of the music. I need a breath of cleaner air, not the sweaty, smoky, cigarette-filled area that is the party, but that of the forest around me. I take a few steps into the bushes, blinking to clear the fuzziness. I even rub them, thinking some strange film is covering my line of sight.

My feet move me a bit farther away; I'm desperate to rid my ears of the sound of the blasting music. If I can simply clear my senses, I'll feel right. Just a little farther. But the rightness doesn't come, and the only thing I find is a growing distance between me and the party. Acid coats my mouth, and the buzzing in my head becomes heavy—like a swarm of bees has taken flight between my ears.

What the fuck is happening? What's wrong with me?

Something flashes in my vision. Maybe it's an animal in the distance. It happens again, this time a bit closer. Fear laces its way through every cell in my body, but I find myself unable to access the whole fight-or-flight thing, noting my feet as they stay planted to the ground. I should retreat, get the hell away from here, but my brain can't seem to get the rest of my body to move.

A snarl comes next. A howling in the distance. A flutter of leaves, crunching, crumbling, being swept back and forth with every trip the blur takes to and from. It's clearly trying to disorient me, and it's working. I've never felt more similar to prey being stalked by a predator in my life. Why can't I move?

My knees buckle, and my body fails, settling me into a heap of a woman on the ground. A pathetic waste of a human—err, witch. Where're my witchy abilities when I need them most? I close my eyes and will the powers to come to life like I have in the past, but when I peek through my lids, I'm left defenseless and alone. I'm supposed to be some *powerful* witch, but all I am in this moment is a weak, magicless being.

Maybe everyone was wrong about who they think I am?

I scoot myself to a tree, inches from where I fell, and curl into a ball, because that is the only thing my brain and body seem to know how to do.

Low, inhumane snarling edges closer. The noise is accompanied by footsteps.

I open my eyes, my heartbeat quadrupling when my gaze meets a large creature—lips curled over bared teeth, four gigantic paws attached to dark-brown, thick, muscular appendages. Its golden eyes melt into mine. It resembles a dog...but it's much greater in size, not cute at all but massively terrifying. The size of a wolf. Then it dawns on me, the stories of the full moon.

This isn't a wild dog, it's a fucking *werewolf*.

The wolf creeps toward me, stalking slowly like I might have a chance to get away, like it's testing to see if I'll run, and maybe that's what it wants me to do so it can have the thrill of chasing after its dinner. But I don't move, I can't, my body won't let me. Something holds its power over me, and even though I fight it, I find myself crippled. The beast pauses, its ears perking up like it's listening intently, and I think for a second that I might actually make it out of this alive.

I take in a breath, and the creature pulls its attention back onto me. It takes one more pursuing step forward, and out of nowhere, another similar being crashes into it and sends it flying into a surrounding tree. The newest addition turns toward me, and I realize this is it, he's about to consume me whole, but I'm met with these pleadingly familiar eyes—gold and honey mixed with chocolate brown. Instead of snarling, like I expect, this wolf offers me no exposed fangs, but a whip of the head, like a *get out of here* type nod. But I can't move, I'm paralyzed.

He nudges his head two more times, his gray-and-brown pelt waving wildly. Panic courses through me as the other wolf regains his composure, getting back on all furry fours, and coming back toward us. I desperately want to take the opportunity the new wolf gave me, but I have no strength left in me to move.

The wolf's eyes betray a kind of sadness as he huffs and shuffles between me and the other wolf, preparing himself to fight his kind to protect me.

CHAPTER 17

Like a coward, I close my eyes in anticipation of what is to come.

A loud crash, another thud...tree bark crumbling and limbs snapping. A fierce growl met with an opposing roar. Then hands. Hands that are cold and warm all at the same time. A deep comfort settles over me, despite me knowing damn well I might be seeing my end.

"Willow..." His voice is pure and kind and nothing like the serious and intimidating one from last night. "Willow, please, please wake up."

I squint into the night, vision blurring and making everything so damn difficult to see. A shape is beside me with calming hands and a soothing voice.

Hands wrap around my torso, lifting me, lifting me, lifting me.

The person winces at my touch, and a stabbing sadness fills me.

I don't want to hurt you, sweet person.

I settle my head into a nook under the person's chin. I breathe deeply, one of the remaining functions I can control, and savor the fresh scent that has a faint hint of gasoline. What a strange combination.

"Deghan, get that out-of-control mutt out of here," he commands loudly, but there's something pained in his voice, like he's suffering.

He repositions my frail body in his arms and he moves—walks away from the death match between the wolves and away from the party, and it seems like only seconds go by when I notice the buzzing energy of the school.

I blink my eyes open for a moment, confirming my thoughts and letting them fall back shut. A few steps later, the energy shifts, and when I look again, we're upstairs, walking through the threshold of the north wing. The *boys'* dorms. A new terror rolls in this time, and I'm unsure of this person's intentions. Maybe his façade led me to believe he was saving me from my definite death, but he has something else in mind.

A loud thud comes, like a knock on a door. Then follows the creak of said door as it opens slightly before it's rapidly pulled open.

"What the hell did you do, you vile being?" Animosity rules the space.

"Can you help her or not?" my potential savior pleads.

"Yes, of course. Bring her in. What happened? Set her here," he urges as he shoves something aside.

My body is placed on top of a warm blanket, and someone wipes a wisp of my hair out of my face.

"I...I found her like this in the forest. In the wolf's territory."

A gasp sounds.

"Deghan and one of his mutt friends were tearing each other apart. I think he attacked Willow, and Deghan was trying to protect her."

"In wolf form?" he asks cautiously, as if he doesn't quite believe what he's hearing.

"Yes."

"That's impressive." He turns in my direction. "Hey, Willow, can you open your eyes?" His words are soft, and so are the hands that follow. One on my forehead and another along my wrist. "Give me a second." A light breeze hits my exposed skin.

"Is she okay? Is she going to be okay?" my liberator asks.

"Oh, this makes sense. It's her glitch."

"Her glitch? What does that mean? Is she going to be okay or not? Should I take her to someone else?" His patience seems to be wearing thin.

"Can you back up for a second? Damn, Silas, you're making it impossible to work here."

Silas? He's the one who rescued me from the wolves? The wolves who happen to be Deghan and his friend? Did I die? Am I dreaming or something? How are they both not freaking out about all of this right now?

I feel his energy pull away, like he actually listens and takes a step back to give the other mystery person some room.

"I have to do a cleansing spell to rid whatever it was from her system." His hands graze my body, trailing up and down. He places something small but solid on my chest, muttering something I can't quite make out.

A few moments pass, and Silas finally speaks. "Is it working?"

"Shh."

A light flickering progresses through my toes, leading slowly up my calves, through my thighs, across my belly, into my chest, my arms, my neck, until suddenly, the fog that was consuming my head dissipates.

I open my eyes to have them immediately met with Sydney's. A green aura covers his body, and I find myself absolutely amazed.

He smiles weakly. "You okay?"

My mouth parts, and I'm startled by the sudden ability to form words. "Yeah."

"Damn, Willow, you reek of booze. Are you drunk?" Sydney scrunches his nose.

"Ugh, no, I don't drink."

"That probably explains what happened then. You must have drank something you shouldn't have; alcohol must be your glitch."

"What the hell is a glitch? You make it sound like I'm defective." I firmly place my hands on the bed, pushing up to the seated position. I spot Silas a few feet away.

Worry and concern trail his eyes, despite him looking hopeful I'm coherent.

"All witches have one, and they're not all the same. It's nature's balance. If we consume something that doesn't agree with us, it suppresses our magic completely and basically paralyzes us."

"That's exactly what it felt like. That was brutal." I rub my neck and remember how horrible it felt to not be able to even run away when danger presented itself. My eyes widen. "Deghan. He's still out there?" I frantically look between them.

"He'll be fine," Sydney offers, a comforting hand patting mine.

Somehow his reassurance isn't enough, but it's not like I can really go back out there and risk endangering anyone else in the process.

"Thank you," I manage, straggling my consideration to the men in front of me. "Both of you. Silas, you saved my life out there, and Sydney, you saved my life in here."

"I don't really want to give him any credit, but Deghan stopped his friend from mauling you, so it was a bit of a collective effort," Silas says, the pain of his admission showing in his jaw. "I told you it was dangerous out there."

"I know you did. I'm sorry." I shake my head. "I really am."

"You warned her?" Sydney interrupts.

"Numerous times," Silas confirms.

Sydney looks back at me. "He's not joking, Willow. Their territory is off-limits, especially on a full moon. There are many new recruits who don't have any control over their bloodlust. Did you see how there were three paths out there?"

I nod.

"The far-right is the wolf territory; the far left is witch territory. But none of us go out there on a full moon during the wolves shift. It's too dangerous."

"How did you even find me if you weren't meant to be out there tonight?"

Silas frowns, shifts his gaze to the floor, sighs, and looks me straight in the eyes. "I knew you were in trouble."

"How?" I whisper.

"I just did. I could *feel* it." He swallows, flicking his notice to Sydney for a split second.

Sydney stiffens. "What do you mean you *felt it*?" He stands, arms folding over his chest defensively.

Silas shrugs and I smirk at seeing him so...unlike himself. He's avoiding something. Hiding something. I have to admit I like seeing this side of him, though.

"It's none of your business." Silas grimaces. "So, stop pressing."

"I swear to everything, if you hurt her, I will tear you apart limb from limb." Sydney sneers at Silas.

I pause at his possessiveness, a new side of him being uncovered, too.

Silas laughs. "You could try."

Sydney uncrosses his arms, squaring up to Silas. "Don't test me, scum."

I get to my feet quickly, pleased with my body following my direction. Placing myself between the two guys, I set a hand on both of their chests in an attempt to stop them from their spat. A wicked bolt surges through my hand, and Silas flees across the room at an insane speed.

"How the...how did you get over there so fast?" I shake my head. "Are you okay? Did I hurt you?"

"You." Sydney's aggression is replaced with confusion and intrigue. "You can't touch her."

"You didn't hurt me, I'm fine." Silas's words are filled with compassion. "Let it go," he says to Sydney, replacing the care with a fiery rage.

A laugh bubbles up and out of Sydney.

"Willow, if you're well enough, I think you should probably get to your dorm and rest. You had a rough night." Silas nods toward the door, ignoring Sydney's growing hysterics.

Allowing the thought to settle, I realize I am beat and still a little bit fuzzy. "Yeah, yeah, you're probably right."

"I'll walk you to your room," he suggests.

"I bet you will," Sydney says sarcastically.

"Are you okay?" I ask him, utterly confused about what got into him.

"I'm great." He beams. "Absolutely perfect."

"Okay..." I look him over another second. "Um, thanks for fixing my glitch. Hopefully that'll be the last time that happens."

His face goes serious. "Of course, and yeah, stay clear of alcohol. The longer it's in your system, the more damage it does, and it makes it more challenging to siphon."

"Noted." I pat his shoulder, unsure if a hug would be inappropriate. He did just save my life and all. I stand there for an awkward second and he finally moves.

He lightly embraces me, and somehow, I know Silas is scowling without even looking. Either from jealousy of not being able to touch me himself, or because it's Sydney who's hugging me.

Silas turns the knob and opens the door, waiting for me to exit.

It's then that I take a fleeting moment to look around the room. Only one bed has anything around it—Sydney's. His items seem to overflow into the other spaces, but if I had to guess, Sydney has the room to himself. I don't know if I find that sad or lucky.

"After you," Silas chimes.

"Thanks, again, Sydney." I smile.

Out in the hallway, the north wing energy is thick and murky. A blanket of ease caresses me once we cross the threshold, making our way to the all-glass garden top. The view is equal parts unsettling and stunning.

Silas manages to keep a few feet between us on the short walk to my dorm in the south wing. The urge to reach out and grab his hand is strong, but without knowing the reason we can't be closer, I keep my distance.

"I'm sorry I hurt you," I murmur.

His voice cracks faintly. "You have nothing to be sorry for."

I glance over at him and quickly look back to the floor in front of me. "If we can't touch, how did you carry me out of the woods?"

His hand clenches for a second and he releases it. "It wasn't without difficulty."

My heart constricts, too. The idea of causing him pain cuts through me like a hot knife through butter.

I slow my pace as we approach the entrance to the south dorm. I desperately plead with time to slow down, to give me more with him. As daunting as the night has been, the thought of not being with him is even more upsetting.

"Silas," I say, stopping to face him.

He takes a cautious step, not letting us be too close, never close enough. His eyes are gray and violet and have a shimmering metallic tucked into one corner. They're breathtaking. The striking arch of his jaw is clenched firmly in place.

"Willow." He sighs.

"What can I do to fix this?" I don't look away.

"I don't think you can." His words slice through me worse than when I hurt him.

"There has to be a way, please. There has to be something," I beg pathetically.

He exhales, his arm moves toward me but stops dead in its tracks, leaving a space for the energy to crackle between us. "If you only knew how badly I want to touch you." His seductive gaze trails over my entire face, settling far too long on my lips.

"I don't understand, what is it? Why us?" I force my mind to comprehend the power keeping us apart but end up failing time and time again. "Will it be this way forever?"

He pushes the gap, sending sizzling energy flying, grimacing until he pulls away.

"Is it painful?" What a stupid question, he wouldn't resist if it weren't. "I can fix this somehow," I say. "Just tell me what it is... why is it happening? I'll fix it."

"Oh, Willow, there's nothing you can do. It's fate and a curse all wrapped up in one."

CHAPTER 18

After being interrupted by a loud and drunken Remi and Kyra, I painfully part from Silas and enter my room. A deep hopelessness courses through me, and I do my best to fight away the misery that creeps in, staking a home in my being.

Lillian sits next to me on my bed. "You okay?"

"Yeah," I lie.

"I was worried until Brock came back from taking a leak and said you were with Silas."

That explains why no one searched for me.

I meet her eyes and really look Lillian over, a happiness seeping from her that wasn't quite there prior.

I shift the focus to her. "How was your night with Ethan?"

"Wonderful...absolutely wonderful." She peers over her shoulder at the girls, lowering her voice. "I like him."

My heart swells for her and her newfound adoration. "That's great news! I'm so happy for you, Lills."

"He wants to get breakfast in the morning," she continues. "It's almost like a date."

"It totally is a date," I confirm. "That's so cute."

"Will you come with me?" she pleads.

"Come with you? To your date?"

"Yes, please, I'm so nervous. Cameron will be there. Will you be my wingwoman?"

I sigh, remembering I totally left Cameron hanging at the party. Not like I did it on purpose, I sort of got accidentally drunk and nearly died in more ways than one. And he thinks I ditched him for Silas, making the betrayal that much worse. If anything, I should tag along to explain to him what part of the truth I'm capable of sharing.

"I'd love to."

She squeals, grabbing me into a hug. "Thank you so, so, so much. I owe you big time."

"That's what friends are for," I say.

She practically glides to her bed, floating on a love-stricken high.

I sink into my own, not bothering to change out of my clothes, the sadness taking back over when Lillian goes to her side of the room. I pull my blanket over my head, breathing the crisp linen scent in intensely.

An eternity passes, and finally, I fall asleep.

I wake to the sound of the girls stirring. Unrested, groggy, and stiff, I finally open my eyes.

"Morning, sleepyhead," Remi teases.

Making quick work of getting ready, I swap out my clothes,

brush my teeth, and throw my hair into a low ponytail. I grab a makeup remover wipe from Kyra, and once I'm done, I splash cold water on my face to try to wake myself up. It works but not well enough. A cup of coffee might do the trick. I'd kill for Sydney to make me one, but because of Lillian pacing the space behind me, I settle on the dining hall breakfast blend.

The two of us leave the girls to finish getting ready and head to breakfast.

Lillian fidgets with her hands, her nervousness distracting me from the ever-growing pit of despair I'm being swallowed into.

I nudge her. "Hey, it's going to be okay. Other than it being daylight, this is no different than hanging out at the party. Pretend we're getting breakfast like normal, and he just happens to be there."

She bobs her head. "Yeah, good idea."

Her uneasy energy lightens a little, but not much.

I stop her at the bottom of the stairs, my hand on her forearm. "Hey," I say, looking her straight into the eyes. "Really, everything will be fine. Don't stress." I push my calming thoughts into her, willing her tension to leave.

Her shoulders wiggle, like she's shaking it away, and she smiles. "Okay."

That was easy.

And then I understand...*I just did fucking magic.*

Cameron doesn't skip a beat when his gaze lands on me. He springs from his seat, jogging the distance that separates us, and pulls me into a hug. "Hey."

"Hey, Cameron."

Ethan makes his way over to Lillian, slower than Cameron, but his growing smile gives away his excitement in seeing his girl. Stopping in front of us, he holds out his hand to me. "Not sure we've ever formally met. I'm Ethan."

We shake, and I note there are no funky blasts of energy—he must be human.

"I don't think we have either. I'm Willow. It's nice to meet you."

"Likewise." He shifts to Lillian. "You hungry?"

She nods, and they walk toward the food. Lills glances over her shoulder at me, leaving me and Cameron behind.

"Listen, Cameron," I say. "I want to apologize about last night. I didn't mean to leave you at the party like that."

He cuts me off. "What? You don't have to apologize. You're allowed to do your own thing. I was just worried about you disappearing like that until I knew you were safe."

So, he's not mad?

"I didn't want you to think I ditched you or something. Because that's definitely not what it was."

He rubs my shoulder. "Not at all. Brock said you were with Silas, which is totally fine."

"Yeah, but it wasn't like that. I accidentally drank someone's alcohol and got stupid sick. Silas was merely helping me get back to the school." It's partly true—about the only part of the truth I can give him.

His expression saddens. "Damn, Will, you okay?"

"I am now. I had to take some medicine. I'm like allergic to it or something."

"That's crazy. You'll have to pay more attention. I'll try to keep a better eye on your drink next time so this doesn't happen again." He pulls me in for a light squeeze. "I'm glad you're okay now."

"Thanks, Cameron. That's sweet of you." I nod at the new couple. "What do you make of those two?"

He side-eyes me playfully. "They're adorable. He's pretty much already in love."

I slap his arm. "No way, seriously?"

"I wouldn't be surprised." He grabs a cup of yogurt from the stand.

I eye the selection, sizing up my options. I settle for a bowl of oatmeal and a cup of fruit. Something to comfort my aching body and hopefully re-nourish my energy.

Cameron grabs a tray and holds it out for my items. He carries them to the table like a gentleman and places them in front of me.

His niceness is a bandage over my aching soul.

"Dogs or cats?" he asks me.

"Cats for sure, you?"

"Definitely cats, but I'm an equal opportunity animal lover." Cam brushes his hair out of his face. "Cats, dogs, fish, squirrels, chickens, wolves..."

I nearly choke on my drink at the last word. "Sorry." I cough to clear my throat.

He rubs soft circles on my back. "You good?"

Nodding, I pat at my lips with my napkin.

Ethan chimes in, "Willow, you come across as one of those *can't walk and chew gum at the same time* kind of people."

I chuckle. "I am a bit accident prone." My cheeks redden with embarrassment.

Cameron quickly covers with a new question. "Night owl or early bird?"

Lillian answers before I can. "If I have learned anything about this girl in the short time I've known her, it's that she loves her sleep."

"Hey now, I could be an early bird if I wanted to." I shrug. "Not that I want to."

"Fair enough," Cameron says. "I'm kind of both. I like to stay up late and get up early. Sleep and I don't really agree."

I tilt my head toward him. "That must suck."

"I'm used to it."

"Okay, my turn." I press my finger to my chin. "I got one. Would you rather have ten siblings, or be an only child?"

"Easy," Cameron blurts out without hesitation. "Only child."

Lillian and Ethan turn their attention back to themselves, talking in hushed, flirtatious whispers.

"I'm going to need you to elaborate on your insanely quick answer."

Cameron draws in a breath and his energy shifts, a sort of sadness threatening to overtake his bubbly demeanor. Immediately, I regret questioning him on such a potentially sore subject.

"Let's just say my brother and I aren't on great terms right now. And as much as I love him, sometimes..." He doesn't finish his statement, a sense of guilt filling the unspoken words.

I nudge him with my elbow. "Hey," I mutter quietly. "It's okay to think of how life would be if things were different."

"Yeah?" He glances over at me. "Do you?"

"All the time. Probably too much. It's hard not to, especially when things get rough."

"Do you have any siblings?"

I shake my head. "No, it was just me and my mom growing up."

"I guess the grass isn't greener on the other side."

"I think sometimes it's impossible for the grass to be green... no matter how much you water it."

"Thanks for not thinking poorly of me." Cameron averts his gaze temporarily.

I pinch my brows together. "Never."

Cameron is a good person. I feel it in my bones, in my soul, in my heart. His aura is pure and genuine, if not a little dark at times, his past haunting, and reminds me that no one is perfect, but damn if he isn't close to it. I see it in the way he holds open doors for strangers, listens to people share stories, nodding and smiling even when no one else is paying attention. He compliments others but not in a cheap and generic way, but in a thoughtful manner. He doesn't seem to expect anything in return and does so without recognition and gives no thought to whether anyone witnesses it.

"I'm glad you're here, Willow. I'm glad you ran into me." Cameron bumps me with his shoulder. "You're pretty cool."

"You're never going to let me live that down, are you?"

A grin spreads across his face. "Not when it was the single best thing that's ever happened to me."

"You give me way too much credit."

"And you don't give yourself enough."

I roll my eyes and lean into him, only then realizing how exhausted I still am. "You're not so bad yourself, Cameron."

I'm nearly finished with my breakfast, ready to head back to bed, when a commotion from the entrance startles me.

Deghan bolts through the doorway from the patio and hysterically searches the room until his eyes meet mine.

Not wanting to cause more disorder, I gather my trash.

"I'm not feeling so great, guys. I'm going to head back."

"Can I check on you in a few hours?" Cameron asks.

"Absolutely. Thanks, Cam."

At the sound of his nickname, he smiles a bit brighter, and it warms my tender heart.

Glancing at Lillian and Ethan, who are equally entranced in each other, I tell them, "See you guys later."

They each wave as I exit the room hastily, intercepting Deghan the second he barrels through the walkway, knowing I'm exactly who he's looking for.

With his hands on my shoulders to steady himself, he takes pause, settling his gaze over my body, head to toe. Hesitating for my response, he yanks me in for an extremely tight and welcome hug.

"Christ, Willow," he says, out of breath. "I'm so sorry. Are you okay? What the hell happened?" He pushes away again, like he may have missed something, and does another scan.

"I'm okay, I am now." I look around the area, various glances from random students meeting us. "Can we maybe go somewhere more private to talk?"

He nods. "Are you okay with my dorm?"

A few tense moments later, we step into his room. I do a swift examination and am surprised that another guy has a dorm to himself. Maybe there aren't as many supernatural students as there are humans.

"You have the room to yourself?" I question.

"For now, yeah," he says shyly.

Drawings cover an entire bed, and he does his best to shuffle them together and out of sight. He puts them into a random dresser and picks up the loose articles of clothing off the floor and tosses them into a wicker basket. He sits on his large bed and then pushes half of it away, and only then do I realize he had secured two of the beds together to make one big one. When the beds are a little over a foot apart, he pats the one opposite his and motions for me to sit.

"This blanket is cozy," I say, rubbing my hand over the dark-gray fleece.

His voice low, he asks, "What happened last night, Willow?"

I exhale, scooching back on the bed to find a more comfortable spot. "I unintentionally drank alcohol."

"So, you were drunk?" He squints like he's trying to figure out what exactly I mean.

"No, not really. Or, well, I don't know. My body reacts very badly to booze. Umm, what did Sydney call it?" I rub my chin. "Oh, he said it was my glitch."

"Your what?"

"That's what I said." I hesitate. "I'm not sure how much of this I'm allowed to say to you..." I run a loose thread through my fingers.

"Because of the oath?"

"Mmhmm."

"You can talk to me."

"Oh."

"I mean, literally, you're allowed to. It's just the other faction that we can't talk to."

Right, it said human students, not the supernatural, and I have to remember now, Deghan is supernatural. He's a werewolf. And here I am, sitting, our knees touching, alone in his bedroom.

My heart races being this close to him, not because he's a werewolf, but because he's *Deghan*. The same pull that's there with Silas is right here for him, making me even more confused than ever; how could I have possibly gone from zero potential prospects to four within a few days? Is it wrong of me to have a crush on all of them? And are all crushes *this* intense? Does this have something to do with discovering I have magical powers? Are my attractions heightened because they're supernatural? But if that's the case, why am I drawn to Cameron? If I'm not mistaken, Cameron is human, but my desire to be around him is just as strong as it is for the rest of the guys.

I swallow and stare at the gorgeous man across from me.

Deghan, the werewolf who saved me.

His aura is sincere, a fuzzy blue and warm haze radiating off his broad shoulders. His dark hair with golden hues, cascades onto his forehead, and illuminates his golden-chocolate eyes. His shirt, which happens to be inside out, hugs his chest. Deghan is a sight for sore eyes, and I am incredibly fortunate to have his interest, even putting into perspective what happened last night. The incident wasn't his fault. I shouldn't have been so reckless. I shouldn't have been on their territory. I should have been more mindful of what the hell I was drinking. If this is anyone's fault, it's mine and mine alone.

I take a breath. "A glitch is some natural balancing loophole to screw with a witch's power. Mine is alcohol. I drank someone else's drink—or maybe mine was spiked—and pretty much became paralyzed." The words come out in a rush. It feels strange and exhilarating all at once, being able to say these things out loud.

"So, you're a witch," he says.

That's what he gathered from all of that?

"Yep."

"I knew it was something, I just wasn't sure. The full moon came, and you weren't out there with us, so I eliminated wolf. Usually I can smell the vampires from a hefty distance, and you smell like honey and lavender, nothing close to a vamp. I sort of figured witch, but I could never be sure. Not without confirmation."

"Did you...did you say 'vampire'?"

My heart stutters. *Vampire*? Like, blood-sucking, garlic-fearing, sunshine-scared, turning into bats?

"Was I not supposed to say that? Shit, umm, cat's out of the bag. Surprise! Vampires roam the earth." He tries to play it off jokingly.

For some reason, this revelation startles me the most. Especially putting the other things together. Sydney, a witch, loathes Silas and his *kind*. Said he was vile and threatened him about my safety. Silas, on the other hand, is stiff and fast and massively serious about keeping his distance. Plus, the wickedly sharp incisors I caught a glance of the other day.

This all seems to make sense.

Sydney is a witch.

Deghan is a werewolf.

Cameron is a human.

Silas...Silas is a vampire.

And I have intense feelings for each one of them.

CHAPTER 19

At the mere thought of all of this new information, a weighty exhaustion hits me like a ton of bricks. How is it possible that I have romantic feelings for four guys, three of them being supernatural? That's what this is, right? I have nothing to compare it to other than the few fictional crushes I've had throughout my semi-pathetic adolescence. Maybe I'm blowing all of this out of proportion, and this is how people my age feel about each other on a normal basis. Maybe I'm exaggerating the strange simmering of emotions that stir every time I'm with them. Maybe I truly have lost my mind.

It's only been a day since even finding out my own truth, that I'm a witch, and now this? So much for flying under the radar, blending in, and enjoying a normal college experience. Maybe, though, this is the exact change that I needed in my life. Now I have to figure out how to keep learning about my true self and the ones I care for without depleting my energy sources left and right.

I yawn widely, and my eyes water.

Deghan smirks. "Me, too."

"I'm so tired. Is this normal?"

"Yep, you're processing excess amounts of new info, stuff that has been hidden from the world. It's strenuous to consume. Eventually you'll build up a tolerance, and it'll get easier."

Without much thought, I lean my body sideways, head resting on the pillow next to me. My legs still hanging off the bed,

I just awkwardly lie to the side. I inhale deeply. This must be Deghan's pillow. It smells of him. Warm and earthy. I settle my face on it.

Deghan reacts by reaching down. One hand on my shoe, he says, "May I?"

I murmur an "Mmhm."

He pulls one foot free, then the other, lifting the bottom of my legs and gently placing them onto the bed. He wiggles the comforter out from under my body, tenderly covering me with it. His feet shuffle across the room, and the light flips off. He's back and relaxing onto his other bed within seconds.

Every touch sends another shock through me, but not in a jarring way. No, his touch is warm and cool all at once, and I desperately want it to consume me. If I weren't so exhausted, I might actually be brave or foolish enough to press the matter.

A very small part of me thinks I should leave, that it's dangerous or wrong to stay, but Deghan saved my life last night, so if anything, I should accept the safety he provides. And that's exactly what I'm going to do.

Easier than I expected, I get pulled under, only waking once when my hand falls off the bed. Being too tired to move it, seconds later, I'm glad I don't. Warm fingers meet mine and they weave their way together. Butterflies erupt in my body, but in a gentle fluttering manner, not a spike of overly anxious nerves. I'm unsure if he does it on purpose or in a hazy sleep state, but either way, it doesn't matter, I welcome it all the same.

Monday morning, I do as I'm told and show up early to my first period class. North wing, fifth room. The one with the oversized window that in a simpler time, I'd love to curl up on and read a book, letting the natural light bathe me while I explored fictional worlds.

I expect a professor, someone I haven't met yet, and am surprised to catch a glimpse of Headmaster Walker strolling down the hall toward me.

He nods and smiles at passing students.

"Good morning, Willow." He hands me a steaming cup. "You can thank Sydney."

I take it gratefully, smiling, and smelling the heavenly goodness. "Morning, thank you."

"Today we're going to take things fairly slow and work on accessing the shadow realm and going over a few basics. I imagine this will take a toll on you, so we're going to be cautious with how much we do too soon. Over time, this will all become much easier to process."

I nod. "Okay."

"Now, tell me if you notice anything." He mutters toward the doorway.

Immediately, the purple haze appears, and I flinch at the closeness of it. "Um, yeah, I can see that." The vivid colors weave through with a saturated darkness. It's mesmerizing. The colors form to make a shape, like a silhouette of the doorway.

"That's great, do you see the entrance?"

"Yes," I whisper, completely unsure of myself and the magical forcefield I'm gawking at.

"I'm going to ask you to take my hand, and then say the words, *infito grantum modem*, and then we're going to step through the threshold together. There will be no pain. Everyone experiences it a bit differently, but the general consensus is a momentary tingling sensation."

"Okay." I hold out my hand, ready to see what this shadow realm is about, not afraid or intimidated, more curious than anything.

He takes my hand, and we say the words together. They're solid and smooth on my tongue, rolling off with natural ease. We cross over, and for a second, I swim in the purple haze, and then I land on the other side in an identical classroom. No tingles, no shocks or startling bolts of energy.

I frown and look up to Walker. "Did I do something wrong?"

He chuckles. "No, you did everything right. This is it, the shadow realm."

I allow my eyes to adjust, scanning the room. It appears to be exactly like the other, but upon further examination, the seams of the room are a bit fuzzy with dark-violet hues trailing.

"This is incredible." I gawk.

He releases my hand and walks to a desk, sitting on top and watching while I inspect the space. "The first time is usually much more challenging than that, Willow. You have a natural predisposition that is remarkable. Trained witches sometimes struggle on their first attempt."

"Is that bad? That I didn't have an issue with it?" I take a long look around and then meet his gaze. "I have no idea what to expect."

Walker shakes his head. "Not bad at all, but a bit unexpected, given the circumstances." He sniffs and readjusts, his tone changing. "I was able to find a little bit of information about your heritage."

I swallow and take a seat a desk away from him, anxious anticipation coursing through me. "You were?"

"Willow, you're descended from a line of incredibly powerful witches. With that power comes danger, though. I could only find bits and pieces of it but, your lineage's magic was suppressed sometime in the past, basically making the Oliver name and history fizzle out centuries ago."

"But I have power, right? Does that mean the curse is broken?" I don't understand, not this, not any of it, really.

"I don't think it's broken at all; I just don't think it's taken its hold on you yet."

I allow a small gasp, letting his declaration sink in.

"You're in the best place for this, though, Willow. Harper Shadow Academy can aid in giving you the knowledge you need to grow, prosper, and protect yourself. And we're prepared to help you every step of the way. We preserve all things good, and we're willing to fight this battle with you."

"But why?" I mutter.

"We stand firm in the sanctuary and education of the supernatural. We don't want there to be death and destruction because of misinformation or limited resources. We want to better those blessed with their gifts. Being different than the rest of the earth's population is a lonely enough thing, that's why we band together to help the ones that we can."

"How do you even find people like me?"

"We can scan and locate supernatural adolescents. Sometimes we can establish a relationship early on and encourage their attendance. Your case is a bit different. From what I'm told, your magic is hidden, untraceable by our methods. Which is great because if you have a target on your back, that makes it that much harder for them to locate you. The school is under protection, too, doubling that barrier."

"This is all a lot to take in," I admit.

"That's understandable. Are you experiencing fatigue right now?" His brows shrink together in concern.

"No, I meant in general, it's a lot. I feel surprisingly great right now."

"I'm not surprised." He huffs. "Because I don't want to force things too quickly, that will be it for now, to see how you handle traveling to and from, but if you're up for it, you can continue lessons following your lunch period. Pending no major side effects, that is. I believe you're due in the north wing again, am I correct?"

"Yes, ethics, N six."

"Great. I'll make arrangements." He takes a long swig of his coffee.

Only then do I remember the cup in my hand. Apparently, coffee can travel to the shadow realm, too.

"I must warn you, Willow. You must not access the realms alone. Make sure you always have an experienced traveler with you. Eventually, you will be able to have more control, but for now, you must not take that risk."

What would happen if I did? Would I get stuck?

"Okay, I won't." I wouldn't be stupid enough to find out, anyway.

"You may experience a negative surge in energy when we return to the proper realm. Each time you use the portal, you leave a small portion of your magic behind. Of course, it will replenish itself without you knowing, but I wanted to warn you in case you feel any adverse reaction." He stands, motioning toward the way we just came. "You ready?"

That was a quick lesson, but in the real world, I definitely would be late for first period.

"This time the incantation will be *infito grantum hodem*." He holds out his hand.

We step back through, the shadow hugging me midway but not making any noticeable impact on my body. No strange feeling, nothing.

On the other side, Deghan is leaning up against the opposite room's doorframe. He smiles, like he was waiting for me.

"Morning," Deghan says.

Walker nods to him, then focuses back to me. "Let me know if anything changes between now and lunch. Otherwise, same thing, ten minutes prior."

"I will, thank you. And please let me know if you find anything else about what we were discussing."

Walker offers a sad smile. "We'll get it figured out. Don't you worry." He turns on his heel and strides down the hallway, disappearing from my line of sight.

Bug-eyed, Deghan asks, "Soooo...how did it go?" He clasps a hand onto my shoulder and nudges me into the classroom.

"Surprisingly well." Minus the whole being cursed a long-ass time ago thing that is ultimately going to find and rob me of the powers I newly discovered.

"I partially shifted my first time," he whispers into my ear.

"No way," I blurt. "That sucks!"

"You're telling me. I got so nervous and freaked out at the whole idea, my body was like nuh-ugh and tried to only send one portion of myself. Talk about embarrassing."

"I didn't think it was that bad. I mean, not to make you feel inferior about yours. I expected it to like hurt or *something*, but I just said the words and bam, there we were."

The room fills with students, and our conversation comes to a halt.

"Hey," he says quietly, pulling a notebook out of his backpack.

"Yeah?"

"I know it's early and all...but if you're not doing anything after school today, you should come over for a nap."

I fight back a growing smile. "A nap?"

"I slept better than I ever have yesterday. We can stay in separate beds. I'm not trying to force myself on you or anything, I swear."

I laugh a little. His words ring true for me, too. I slept wonderfully in his room, his presence lulling me to a blissful slumber. I thought maybe that would never happen again, but here he is, asking for it right now.

"I'd love to."

He blushes and turns away, giving the teacher attention when class starts.

A calming warmth settles over me. Even with all the terrible news, there's still wondrous things happening, like funny moments with Cameron, intense ones with Silas, mind-changing ones with Sydney, and comforting ones with Deghan. My new friends are a blessing, too. One of the greatest breakthroughs of all is the solace in knowing the truth about my mom and being able to breathe a little easier knowing I didn't totally abandon her, that she's going to be fine without me there around the clock.

As big and heavy as all of this is, I'm surrounded by the people who are going to help me get through this. I just have to figure out where to start, and when lunch is over, I hope to uncover more about how to make it through this new life I've found myself living.

But for now, I have to get through this math lecture.

CHAPTER 20

"Willow," Abigail calls to me while walking down the north wing corridor, meeting me at the entrance of room six. "It's you and me this time." A large bag hangs over her left shoulder. "You ready?"

I nod, and she takes my hand into hers.

"*Infito grantum modem*," we say in unison.

The shadow realm continues to leave no lasting imprint of the journey. I don't know whether that's a good or bad thing. I glance up to the walls, checking the space for the hazy violet seams to confirm I'm in the right place.

"Go ahead and take a seat," she commands politely, pulling books out and onto the table in front of me. "We're going to go over some witch basics today to fill you in on some history and give you a better understanding."

"Okay." I look at my backpack. "Should I take notes?"

"Not now, no. We prefer you to retain the information without documenting it on paper." She opens a sizable volume, scanning her finger over the first few pages, then flipping about a quarter of the way in. "This may come as a surprise, but there are endless *types* of witches. You've got cosmic witches, who deal with celestial things. Then there's divination, who focus on predictions. We have green, who use nature, like you. There's also sea witches...you can probably guess they deal with bodies of water.

"Witches who practice alone, we call them solitary. There are eclectic ones who use various power sources, and then the more traditional ones who access old grimoires. Some are born into their magic. Hedge witches can do astral travel. The possibilities are endless."

"Yeah..." I manage to mutter. "I'd say so."

"There are witches who dabble or even fully partake in dark magic, too. They use their power for evil and coincide with the demon realm."

At her last statement, I pause. "Demon realm?"

She nods. "We are fortunate enough to access the shadow realm, a mere blip on the other side of our realm. It takes minimal magic to access and is so close to our own plane, that we can access it with ease, especially on ancient grounds like where Harper is located." Abigail takes a breath. "With greater access to magic, there are other realms, some of which are incredibly dangerous and off-limits. And when I say that, I mean one hundred percent off-limits. Demons lay waiting for unsuspecting—or sometimes suspecting—witches to cross into their realm, allowing them access to our territory. They take up space in multiple realms. Not all of them are bad—the realms, I mean—but they're so few and far between that we no longer explore to find the non-threatening ones."

"Demons?"

"Yeah, like flesh-eating, eyes bulging from their hands, gaping mouths, will tear you apart type of demons. They come in all shapes and sizes, but let me tell you this, they are bad news. So please, if you gain the power and knowledge to do so, don't ever cross into a demon realm."

I glance around the room, looking for cracks in the seams. How can she be so sure we aren't taking that risk now?

"I know what you're thinking, but the shadow realm we've tapped into is safe. We've taken drastic measures to ensure this and are constantly on top of any change in the structure. None of those wretched creatures are here. They wouldn't have the power to be, especially without a willing witch opening the portal from our side."

Her words don't put me at ease; instead, they make me wary of this place.

"Anyway, over the next few sessions, I'll be doing my best to explain these types of witches in more detail. My goal is to help you discover your abilities. Then we'll get into more advanced things, and yes, before you ask, we'll touch base on demons and the demon realm."

"That's good."

"Mhmm," she says while going through a few pages. "Now, I don't want you to think I'm going to be teaching you spells in the sense of words and flicks of the wrist; that type of magic comes from within. The magic you harness is self-tapped, and for the most part, a simple act of willing it in your thoughts is enough to make it happen. But there will be certain elements you can draw from, like crystals, the weather, ancestral powers...things like that.

"It will take time to gather the control you need, but that's what we're hoping to help you accomplish, along with informing you of history and various other things. Speaking of history, I took it upon myself to do a little research about your curse. I was able to find something cryptic regarding *love*. Does that ring a bell to you?"

"Um, no. Not that I can think of," I reply, unsure.

"In very old text, I found a passage about the Oliver witches, that they were fueled partially by *love*, and in order to suppress them of their powers, their *love* was taken away, rendering them defenseless."

Jesus Christ. If that's true, I hope like hell there's some way to break it.

My mom mentioned that her magic was taken from her by the curse long ago. Did that mean that her *love* was taken, too? If that's true, that would explain the lack of a father figure in my life. I always thought he was some lowlife nobody who wanted nothing to do with my mom once he found out she was pregnant with me. What if he was actually forced away, or worse, killed? Mom was always too sad to talk about my father, so at a young age, I started to pretend I never had a dad, and that it was only ever me and mom. It was another one of those things I resolved myself that I would never know the truth to.

But what if the truth was that it was a curse that rid him of our lives?

How could I be fated to such a horrible thing?

Fate.

A curse and fate, all wrapped into one.

"Do you know anything about Silas?" I blurt out.

She tilts her head. "Silas Harlow, vampire. Super grouchy, endless good looks, and cold exterior?"

"Yep, that Silas." I laugh. "Do you know about his ancestry?"

"Not much, no."

I frown. I was really hoping she would have known something about what he meant.

"Although, Harlow, that rings a bell now. If I'm not mistaken, they are fated to one true love, which is incredibly sad, considering they're immortal. Most of them go decades and decades without finding their person, while others are fated to a mortal, merely to get a short glimpse at happiness."

Fated—to one true love. Was that what Silas was referring to?

His words burn into my memory. *I've been waiting on you for an eternity.*

But no, that couldn't be it, could it?

He was fated to have one true love, and I was cursed to have no love at all?

Could it be that we're a match made in Hell? The perfect storm.

And if that's the case, there must be some way to fix this, and I'm determined to figure it out.

"Are there any texts about the Harlow family I can borrow?"

Abigail laughs. "First day of magic school and you're already taking on a personal assignment."

"Yeah, I guess so."

"I can give you what I have on the Oliver family, too. But because you're still dorming in the human faction, you'll have to reserve your research time to when you're here in the shadow realm. I can try to move the schedule around to give you a bit more supervised free time, and I can help, if you'd like, too."

"Yeah, that would be great. Thanks, Abigail."

"Absolutely. I'm a hopeless romantic, so if there's anything I can do, just let me know."

"I appreciate it, truly." I add Abigail to the list of good people that I've met here at the academy so far. Aside from Allie and her occasional irrational mean girl tendencies, everyone has been surprisingly nice. If I knew the real world wasn't this bad, I may have considered joining it a long time ago. But I'm well aware that good things don't last, and sooner or later, the rug will get swept out from under me.

"Back to magic, let's talk about yours," she says, her hands resting in the book and her attention focused on me.

"Uh, okay, yeah."

"Where in your body do you feel it most?"

I avert my gaze, blink a few times, and look back up at her. "I don't understand the question."

She smiles softly. "That's okay." Abigail holds her hand out. "Let's do an exercise together."

I bob my head up and down, a willing participant in whatever she has in store.

"Focus your attention into your palm, to your fingertips..."

Turning my hand over, I stare into my palm, examining every little line and groove.

"Now your forearm, your biceps, into your chest. Close your eyes if it helps you visualize."

Without hesitation, my lids flutter closed.

"Good." She continues, "Pay special attention to every part of your body. The top of your head...your mouth..." Abigail exhales quietly. "All the way to your feet. Repeat this as many times as you need to, until one spot feels more alive than the rest."

I do exactly what she says, forcing myself to stop at every square inch of my body, none of the spots any different than the next. At least a minute or two go by, my cheeks flushing with nothing other than embarrassment at failing such a simple task.

How am I supposed to use my magic if I can't even locate it?

Am I defective? Why did I think this was going to be easy?

Maybe my magic is only strong enough to make a few flowers glow and alter the occasional person's mood. Maybe I'm not the powerful Oliver descendant people think I am. Maybe all I'm capable of is disappointing those around me.

"I'm sorry," I blurt out. "I'm wasting your time."

Abigail shakes her head, and her brows pinch together. "Oh, no, sweet girl. Don't you dare apologize. I'm here to help guide you through this, no matter how many times we have to try. You shouldn't expect any of this to come without great effort. You've gone your whole life without knowing you're a witch, Willow. And if I'm being completely truthful with you, I'm baffled by the progress you've already made, given those circumstances. This is uncharted territory for all of us, and we're prepared for this to take as long as it needs to get you familiar with your magic."

Tears well in my eyes but I do everything I can to keep them from going anywhere else.

"Hey." Abigail closes the textbook and sets it aside. "Let's go again, okay?"

I swallow the lump in my throat and nod stiffly. "Yeah."

And so we do, for the next hour, we repeat the same exercise, moving to different parts of the room. I sit, stand, kneel, lie down —anything she suggests that might help access my power, until finally, I nearly fall over in exhaustion.

"Willow," she says while reaching out to steady me. "I think that's enough for today."

"No," I tell her. "I can go again."

Abigail sighs. "It's there, I promise, just right under the surface waiting for you to find it. But it'll be no use to you if you're completely worn out. If we're going to do this, we have to do it right, and you'll have to trust me to guide you."

A heavy wave of defeat washes over me.

"Let's keep to two-a-days this week to see how your energy levels bounce back. We don't want to do too much too soon and have you crash on us. Meet me here prior to your first class tomorrow, and we'll try after lunch, too. Sound good?"

"Yeah." I chew at the inside of my lip. "Thank you."

"Don't give up on me, because I'm not giving up on you." Abigail latches onto the book she was going over with me earlier. "Deal?"

"Deal." I join her near the door and force a smile, grabbing her hand and muttering the words that send us back to the real world.

This time, Sydney is waiting for me on the other side. He and Abigail exchange pleasantries, and then we make our way to ethics.

"Did everything go okay?" he asks with a hint of concern remaining.

"It went great," I lie. "I'm ready for tomorrow already."

And more so than that, I'm eager for those texts on the Harlow and Oliver families so I can get cracking on figuring out whatever the hell is causing Silas to be in pain when he touches me.

I'm also growing impatient on last period coming so I can see

Silas and tell him I've made a tiny bit of progress on our issue. I've never felt such a strong determination to solve a problem.

Sydney's eyes lighten, flecks of green catching my attention. "That's so good to hear. I wasn't sure what to expect. I'm glad you're not feeling the effects of the glitch anymore."

"Not at all; I can't thank you enough for helping me through that. You're a life-saver."

If I'm not mistaken, Sydney blushes.

"Anything for you," he confesses. "I'm sorry we got off to such a rocky start."

"Me, too."

Sydney reaches forward and tucks a loose strand of my hair behind my ear, my heart skipping a beat with his touch. His fingers trace my flesh and send a wave of heat straight between my legs.

Oh my god, what is happening to me?

I stare at him, completely dumbfounded, noting the way his cheeks turn up slightly and his gaze lingers from my eyes to my lips.

He pulls away slowly, and somehow, it's still too fast.

If I were a witch capable of freezing time, I would have done it so I could have felt his hand on me at least a millisecond longer.

He shifts to face the front of the room, and I stare at the base of his neck, the trail of dark hair covering the hem of his shirt.

My hand twitches like it's trying to act on its own, pleading with me to reach forward and run my fingers through his hair. In the blink of an eye, I imagine rising from my desk, walking the few inches that separate us, and climbing onto his lap. I'd take his face into my hands and stare into his emerald eyes before what I could only hope would be our first kiss.

But that will never happen, because I'm not that brave, and things are already complicated enough; I don't need to make them worse by borderline assaulting him in the middle of our ethics class.

If only he knew how important he already is to me, though. Regardless of my attraction for him, he's changed my life permanently.

If it weren't for Sydney, none of this would be possible. I probably never would have acknowledged my magic; I wouldn't have known to go to Abigail or Walker for help. I would have been too overwhelmed and shut off and in denial of the current of power running through my body. He sparked it to life with his touch, and then again and again. He awakened me, enlightened me, and he showed me the way.

I will be forever grateful for his role in helping me uncover my true identity. The label of a *freak* no longer, I am an Oliver witch. A powerful one. Err—well, I will be, once I figure out how to locate and tap into my magic.

You better believe the first thing I'm going to do is figure out how to break this wretched curse Silas and I have been wrapped up in.

Even if the curse is mine, and mine alone, I will break it and free all of those who came before me, and all that come after. Silas just gives me that extra push to make it happen.

Fated to one true love.

Is it really possible that that's true? I'm his one true love?

My memory flashes to the crackling between us, his face when he pushed it momentarily a little farther. His strength faltered, and it was heartbreaking to watch him struggle so immensely. His pain becomes mine, and the pain only fuels the desire to break the curse that much more.

My heart stutters as I think about my experience with Silas. The familiarity in his presence, the fierce pull we have. The urge to be near him, pressed against him. I need to know everything about him but somehow feel like I already know all there is to know. His gray-violet eyes tell a story of soul-crushing longing and sadness. But maybe it's that he really has been waiting a very, very long time for me to cross his path. If I'm fated to him, is he fated to me?

Here I am, lusting after the man sitting in front of me and thinking I might be fated to another. How could things be any more messed up? And what does that mean for Cameron and Deghan?

CHAPTER 21

The phone rings three times before the answering machine picks up. My mom's voice greets me on the other end of the line with the standard message she recorded years ago. It's strange to hear it now, knowing what I do. She was right all along.

"Hey, mom, it's me," I say through the static of my barely functioning cell phone. "I was hoping we could talk soon. Can you call me back when you get a minute? If it goes straight to voicemail, leave me a message so I know you called. The service is spotty here, but I'll get back to you as soon as I can. Or you can send me a text." I pause and add, "No, never mind. That's probably not a good idea. Anyway, call me back. Tell Uncle Danny I said hi. I miss you. Love you."

I sigh and stare out the window of my empty dorm and decide

that if I'm going to have this time alone, I better utilize it properly.

Dialing another number, I catch myself holding my breath in anticipation for it to connect.

"Oh. My. God. Look who it is," Brooke blurts out.

"Hush, it hasn't been that long."

"Too long if you ask me." She exhales dramatically. "I thought you were breaking up with me."

"Never."

"Okay, so spill, tell me all the tea."

I laugh and lean against the windowsill. "You know I'm too boring for tea."

"Bullshit."

Not to mention, most of the exciting things going on here at Harper Academy are secrets I'm not allowed to share with her.

"Fine, make me pry it out of you," she continues. "Tell me about your roommates. Are they weird? Do they smell? Any strange habits? What are they like?"

"Not any weirder than me," I tell her. "But honestly, they're really nice. Very pretty. Kind. Funny. I enjoy being around them."

"Okay, okay, so I have some competition."

"You know it's not like that."

"I know I'm irreplaceable," she teases. "I'm glad they're not creeps, I was worried."

"Yeah, I had no idea what to expect, especially with the stories we've heard of this place. It's actually super nice though. Very mysterious, up-scale, kinda gothic vibes. Think Hogwarts if it weren't on steroids."

I pinch my lips together, realizing I should not have said that, and hoping like hell she doesn't read into it.

"Aw, my little Hufflepuff finally got her acceptance letter."

"I am so not a Hufflepuff."

"Uh huh, whatever you say."

"You're just mad because you want to be a Slytherin and you're not."

Brooke takes a deep breath in. "I am far too cunning to be a Gryffindor. You know it. I know it. But that generic online test does not. Anyway, I must know, are the guys there Harry Potter or Cedric Diggory level hot?"

"I was always more of a young Tom Riddle kind of girl, remember?"

She laughs loudly but it crackles through the unstable service of my cell phone. "Before or after he lost his nose?"

"After, obviously, who needs a nose to get in the way."

"You're disgusting." She chuckles again. "Gosh, I missed this, Wills. I missed you. But stop distracting me, I need to know about the guys."

"Okay, fine. The guys." I reposition the phone and consider just how much I'm willing to confess. "They're much more attractive than I think you or I ever imagined they would be."

"You little vixen. Spill!"

"So get this, the first day I'm here, I literally had just stepped foot into the building, and I nearly knocked down this guy named Cameron. Total hunk. Baby blue eyes. This sweet and innocent vibe to him."

"Is he tall? How old is he? What's his last name? Where did he go to high school? What does he smell like? Spare no detail, Wills."

"Why are you so obsessed with how people smell? And while we're at it, would you like his social security number, too?"

"Actually yeah, it would be much easier to do a background check on him."

"You've lost your mind," I tell her.

"I can't believe you would deprive me of such information. What are best friends for?"

"How about this to satisfy your friendship quota...after I got my schedule and dorm assignment, I ran face first into this other guy. Tall, broad shoulders, tan skin, dark hair, dark eyes, a smile to freaking die for."

"Wait," Brooke blurts out. "Am I hearing this correctly? My

lifelong best friend, who has had zero interest in men, to the point I seriously questioned whether you even liked them, has not one, but *two* guys that have caught her attention?"

"So, like, this is the part where I really blow your mind."

"If you tell me you had a threesome, I hope you know you have to give me *every single* detail. There is no such thing as too much information."

"Brooke!" I shout into the phone. "You really have lost it." I lower my voice. "I did not have a threesome." Although, I'd be lying if I said I don't think the idea of it is extremely hot, but I don't dare confess that to her.

"Okay, well, I mean, don't take it off the table. You're a college woman now, Wills, live life on the wild side. But seriously, what is it? You're killing me."

"You are the most impatient person I have ever met." I drag out the wait even more just to fuck with her.

"Don't think I'm not aware of this slow, torturous thing you're doing right now. I had no idea my best friend was so evil. Spill or I'm going to get in a taxi and find out what I'm missing at Harper Academy."

"If you'd be quiet for more than half a second, maybe I'd get a chance to spit it out."

Silence falls upon the receiver, and I pull my phone away to check that she didn't hang up on me. Once I confirm the call is still connected, I let out a breath. "I already told you about Cameron, guy number one. And guy number two is Deghan. Both total sweethearts." I leave out the tiny detail of Deghan being a werewolf for multiple reasons. "Then, there's this other guy. We sort of had a rocky start but have grown close. And because I know you—he's got this dark and mysterious thing going on. Long-ish, sorta curly hair. Completely mesmerizing green eyes, like get lost in them if you're not careful. He's smart, serious, stoic." My voice trails off as I lose myself in the daydream I'm having of Sydney.

"Should I take the silence as confirmation that you have the hots for *three* different men?" Brooke says into the receiver.

"Four," I tell her, because why stop now?

"You're on a roll, how about one for each day of the week?"

"I'm going to punch you in the boob."

"I wish you would, right after you confess every single thing about guy number four."

Steadying a breath, I recall his intense features. "He's not like the other guys..."

"What does that even mean?"

"I don't know, B. Things with him are different. It's like I knew him in a past life or something. I get how stupid that sounds, but he's...he's familiar, and when I'm around him, it's strange and exhilarating and comfortable and terrifying all at the same time."

"He sounds like a Leo."

"You *would* chalk this up to astrology."

"I'm serious." She laughs. "But for real, I'm happy for you, I just want you to be careful. This is a lot of men to juggle. What if they get mad? Or jealous? Or have some battle over who gets you?"

"I'm not some prize to win," I say with a hint of defensiveness in my tone.

"You're the ultimate prize, Willow. They don't know how lucky they are to have you in their life." She pauses and then adds, "But wait, you didn't mention the names of guy number three or four."

"Sydney and Silas."

"Oh, sexy. Okay, so we've got Cameron the goodie boy. Deghan the sweetheart. Sydney the smart one. And Silas the... twin flame. Did I get that right?"

I roll my eyes even though she can't see it. "Mmhm."

"So, what are you going to do? Who are you going to choose? Polyamory is always an option."

My heart skips a beat at the idea of being with all four of

them. Is that really an option, especially when two of them don't exactly like each other? How would that be fair of me to expect that of them? Not to mention, none of them have *technically* confessed their feelings for me, so I could be massively reading way too far into this.

"Sydney and Silas don't really get along."

"That's a bummer."

A knock sounds on my door, leading me to believe it's someone other than the girls, because they would have simply entered the room.

"Hold on, B." I cover the bottom of the phone and tilt it away from my face. "Come in," I call out toward the door.

Deghan pokes his beautiful head inside. "Hey, you busy?"

I shake my head despite my best friend whisper-shouting into my ear.

"Who is that?" she asks.

"It's Deghan. I'll call you back later, okay? Bye."

"Oh! Mister tall dark and handsome—"

I disconnect the line before she can blurt out anything else he might overhear.

Deghan grins widely. "You told someone about me?" He steps in, partially closing the door behind him and leans his back against the wall.

Leaving my phone behind on my bedside table, I make my way over to him. "My best friend, actually."

He clutches his hand to his chest. "I'm honored."

I pause in front of him, my arms crossing and my sight desperate to take in every bit of him it can. "What's up?"

Deghan's tan cheeks flush and he scratches at his chin. "I was wondering if...I don't know, maybe you wanted to watch the sunset with me?"

My face takes its turn reddening. "Really?" Why am I this giddy about an attractive man asking me out on *kind of* a date?

Deghan shrugs. "I mean, you don't have to if you don't want to, or if you have other plans, I just thought—"

I step toward him and daringly press my hand to his shoulder. "I'd love to."

"Perfect." He reaches up and cups his big palm around my hand, enveloping it in an ocean of warmth.

For a long moment, our eyes meet, his lingering down to my lips and then back up. "You have no idea how badly I want to kiss you right now," he mutters.

I inch closer to him, my body having a mind of its own. "I think I do."

With his hand still holding onto mine, he places the other on my hip, gripping me tightly and guiding me closer.

Time slows and I want nothing more than to make this moment last.

He continues, pulling me into him and leaning down all at the same time. "Willow," he whispers, his lips just a breath away from my own.

I swallow—the realness sinking in at what is about to happen.

But the sheer moment my eyes shut in preparation for what comes next, the door to our dorm bursts open and Remi and Kyra dart through, breaking whatever divine timing apart, ripping the endless what-ifs completely to shreds.

"Oh shit," Remi blurts out as I step back from Deghan, the blood pooling in my cheeks more than it had a few minutes ago.

"We were just—" I point to the door. "Leaving."

Not wanting to hear a single word from either of the girls about what they think they just saw, I latch onto Deghan and drag his bulky frame through the door and yank it shut behind me.

"I am so sorry." I release him and continue down the hall, my hand growing cold with the absence of his touch.

Deghan throws his arm around my shoulder and pulls me toward him. "You have nothing to be sorry for Lil' W."

I laugh at his nickname. "Am I supposed to call you Big D?" It's then that I realize how incredibly wrong that sounded once it left my mouth. "Oh my God. I am not calling you that."

Deghan's beautiful eyes go wide, and he covers his mouth as he chuckles. "You said it, not me."

"I have a feeling I'll never live that one down."

"You'd be surprised how forgiving I am." He glances over and winks at me. "Plus, I'm like sixty percent sure you were going to kiss me back there, and I'm kind of on cloud nine about that."

I tilt my head toward him and pinch my brows. "What about the other forty?"

"You could have had to sneeze or something."

"Yeah, that's it. I definitely had to sneeze." I poke him in the ribs. "Sorry to disappoint."

"Man, Lil' W, you're just out here breaking hearts." Deghan guides us down the stairs and into the dining hall, his arm never leaving my shoulder.

"Hey," Cameron calls out as he approaches.

Instinctually, my whole body tenses not knowing how this interaction makes him, or Deghan feel.

"What's up, Cam?" Deghan releases me to slap hands with Cameron like they're old friends. "We were just going out to watch the sunset, want to join us?"

I unclench my jaw, my mouth nearly dropping over at how *easy* this is between them.

"Yeah, man. I'd love to." Cameron turns his focus toward me. "Actually, I was going to come find you, Willow." He extends a small, covered plate that's in his other hand. "I made you something, and I want you to try them."

Raising an eyebrow at him, I say, "You *made* me something?"

"What is it?" Deghan asks, his nostrils twitching as he sniffs the air. "Smells pretty damn good."

"Come on." Cameron grins, nodding his head toward the door.

The three of us walk the rest of the way outside and onto the patio behind the academy.

"Over here." Cameron strolls past the few people who are sitting at tables on the deck and settles on a spot in the far left corner, the same spot I had seen Silas in that very first day when I lost my phone out the window. Cam props the plate up onto the railing and peels the foil off the top, revealing what I can only assume are brownies.

"You made those for me?" I eye him and the brownies, then Deghan, who is basically salivating at the decadence in front of him.

Deghan leans against the railing and narrows his gaze on me. "You're going to share, right?"

I laugh and shake my head. "With you? Never."

Deghan feigns sadness, only, it's entirely plausible that he really is sad about thinking he might not get a brownie.

"That is so sweet of you, Cameron." I chew at the inside of my lip, wondering what I ever could have done to deserve such a thoughtful gesture. "I had no idea you could cook."

Cameron lifts his shoulder. "Technically, it's baking, but yeah, I love to cook. It's relaxing." He holds the plate toward me. "Here, try one."

I snatch the biggest piece I can find, only to offer it to Deghan.

"I knew you cared about me." Deghan takes it without question, his smile warming my heart.

Grabbing another piece, I bite into it while Cameron watches me like his whole life revolves around whether I enjoy his creation.

My eyes flutter shut momentarily, a moan escaping me. "This is fucking delicious," I mumble with a mouthful.

Cameron's eyes twinkle, and I consider for a split second that I may have died and gone to Heaven.

Between the happiness written all over his face, Deghan's, and no doubt mine, I can't imagine things could get much better.

Well, maybe if Sydney and Silas were here, too.

That's a long shot, though, and I should be content enough that Cameron and Deghan get along the way they do.

"Dude," Deghan says to Cameron. "I think I'm in love with you."

Cameron laughs and rocks his head back and forth. "You'd eat anything."

"Did you try one?" I ask Cameron. "They're amazing, seriously. Here." I all but shove the rest of the brownie in my hand into his mouth, grazing his bottom lip and wishing I could run my tongue over it instead.

"Can I have another one?" Deghan points to the plate, completely missing the intense stare down between me and Cameron.

"What do you think, Cam? Can he have another?" I cross my arms, my finger rubbing my thumb where Cameron's lip just was.

He winks at me and then turns his attention to Deghan, nudging the plate toward him.

And for a few moments, I forget there's an entire world I know next to nothing about, that I'm cursed, and that there's this nagging thought that things are about to get much worse.

CHAPTER 22

"Are you sure we should be doing this?" I ask Sydney while standing near the door on the inside of his dorm. "What if we get caught?"

He grins and runs his hand through his dark hair. "People perform magic all the time, Willow, the humans are just oblivious to it. It'll be fine."

"But Abigail said—"

"What she said was a precaution. As long as we're careful, there's no reason we can't attempt to tap into your power." Sydney steps away from his desk. "Not by yourself, obviously. But with me." He comes a little closer and lowers his voice. "You're safe with me."

I swallow harshly and stare into his deep green eyes, wondering if I'm a complete fool for trusting him. I barely know this man, and here I am, alone in his room and considering letting down my defenses enough to locate my power. I've tried it with Abigail numerous times, but I end up frustrated and questioning whether we have this all wrong.

Am I defective? Why is this simple for everyone else except for me? Supposedly this is so basic that it's not even taught. Like a baby taking its first breath, they recognize immediately the source of their magic.

"Will you show me yours?" I take a sip of the latte he made me.

"My magic?"

I nod. Was that too intimate of a request?

Sydney doesn't hesitate, instead, he extends his hand, leaving his open palm exposed, and within a split second, a shimmery haze of green appears.

I quietly gasp and clutch my chest. "It's beautiful."

He cups his palm, putting the other hand on top, and creates a ball of power. Hovering just along its edges, he molds and shapes it with ease, the bright light never once flickering. Faint green trails up his arms, cascading along his skin and illuminating him in such a miraculous way.

My breath hitches in anticipation of what he might do next.

How magnificent that he's able to call his magic to the surface and maintain complete control over it.

But before he can continue, the door to his room opens and draws both of our attention toward it.

"Angels," Sydney blurts out. "Do you knock?" The soft smile that was just kissing his cheeks leaves his face as Silas enters the room, his heady presence taking up residence in my chest, tugging me toward him in a way that makes no sense at all.

Silas, with his jaw tense and his black leather jacket, stares between Sydney and I, his gaze flickering on me momentarily and locking onto Sydney. "What do you think you're doing?"

I step into his line of sight, and immediately, his resolve softens.

He blinks a few times. "I got worried when you didn't show."

I glance at my wrist, only then realizing I'm not wearing my watch. This whole not having a phone on me makes me completely lose track of time, not to mention the bizarre time difference when we visit the shadow realm.

"I'm so sorry," I tell him. "I..." I shoot a look at Sydney over my shoulder. "I told Silas I'd study with him."

Sydney crosses his arms and shrugs. "I guess I'll see you later then."

I let out a small breath, hopefully not noticeable to either of them. "You can come with us, if you want. We're just going out on the patio."

"It's fine," Sydney says while shooting daggers out of his eyes at Silas. Only a fool would be blind to their animosity. "I have other things to do anyway."

"Oh, okay." I have a feeling he's not telling me the truth, but we don't exactly know each other well enough for me to press the issue. Regardless, I walk over to him and extend my arms, wrapping them around him for a quick embrace. "Thanks for your help," I whisper into his ear and then release him.

His tension seems to melt away, and that alone leaves me much more content with going away with Silas like planned.

Taking my latte, I exit Sydney's room with Silas, but I keep a bit of space between us. My fingers itch to reach out and touch his shoulder, his back, heck, maybe even be bold enough to hold onto his hand. But I don't. Not just because I'm not that bold, but because I know it would cause him a great deal of pain. Still, the desire to touch this man lingers long after the initial thought.

We walk silently, with Silas just barely behind me, down the supernatural guys' dorm hallway, and down the stairs to the main level of the academy. Once we're through the dining hall and onto the patio, I finally break the silence.

"What's with you two?" I ask him while leaning against the table we've spent the last few days at.

"What do you mean?" Silas places his satchel down and pulls

out two old grimoires that have some kind of cloaking spell that prevent the human students from noticing they look different than normal books.

To me, they appear the way they're supposed to, so it's hard for me to determine whether the spell works or not, but according to Abigail, it does, and is the only way we're allowed to take certain texts out of the hidden parts of the academy. Some of the books yield far too much magic to disguise them, but the ones Silas has suggested we go through pass Abigail's rigorous tests.

"I mean, you two are always at each other's throats." I finger the thicker of the books and glance up at him.

"I think you'd know it if I was at his throat." He flashes me a seductive grin, exposing one of his fangs.

"How do you have so much self-control?" I sometimes forget that he's a vampire, that I'm a witch, that any of us have magical powers. It's fleeting, especially considering my mind has been a whirlwind ever since I found out, but at times, my mind likes to play pretend that we're all just normal college students.

"Years of practice."

"How old are you?" I ask him.

Silas locks his gaze onto mine. "Twenty-three."

That's only three years older than me...until I realize...

"How long have you been twenty-three?"

"A while," is all he says and I can tell he isn't quite ready to tell me the truth.

It's strange how I can sense these limits to him, like I feel an internal push back, and I get the sinking feeling that if I pry too much, I'll blink and he'll disappear.

I rub at my shoulders, suddenly regretting not wearing at least a long sleeved shirt or bringing a sweater.

But as if he can read my mind, Silas reaches into his bag and tugs out a black sweatshirt. He shoves it toward me. "Here."

I clear my throat and hesitantly reach for his offering. "You don't need it?"

He shakes his head stiffly. "I brought it for you."

"You did?"

"You got cold yesterday and wouldn't take my jacket. I came prepared this time."

My heart flutters at such a small but thoughtful gesture. He's a difficult man to read. Sometimes he's lurking in the shadows, other times saving me from near death. And here he is lately, volunteering to spend countless hours with me, scouring the same texts multiple times to see if we can figure anything out about my past.

We've had no such luck, but I'm not giving up hope, not yet.

"Put it on before you catch a chill," Silas says.

I drag it over my head, immediately breathing in deeply and savoring the scent left behind of him. Pulling the sweatshirt down, I smooth out the sides and lower the hood, freeing my hair from its confines.

"This smells like you." I bring the fabric to my face and inhale again, not caring that the man it belongs to is standing right in front of me. If I can't be near him, maybe this will have to be enough.

Silas reaches toward me, his hand hovering just an inch from my face, but he stops, not moving it any closer. The sizzle of power crackles quietly between us, an invisible barrier separating my skin from his.

"You have no idea how badly I want to tuck your hair behind your ear." His voice breaks a bit, no doubt caused by the pain of being this close.

I sink back, adding to the distance between us, even though I want nothing more than to close that gap. Hurting him hurts me, though, and I won't do that to him.

There must be a way I can fix whatever is preventing us from touching.

But how can I do that when I can't even figure out how to access my freaking powers?

CHAPTER 23

"Go again," Abigail tells me. "We're not giving up. It's close."

I draw in a breath through my nose, clench my jaw, and exhale. "Okay." Pinching my eyes together, I try not to let the frustration set in yet again.

"Think about something that makes you feel safe." Abigail keeps a cool and soft tone like she's navigating a bomb that might explode.

Safe? When have I ever felt safe? I grew up in a house where the only parental figure I had was going through her own issues, causing me to fend for myself—and take care of her. I realize now why she was the way she was, but that doesn't change what I went through.

I was the person who provided my safety. Emotionally and physically.

None of that really gives me the warm fuzzies.

And to know that I have some kind of ancestral curse, I'm not the poster child for safety.

But here at Harper Academy, I've never felt more seen. In a short period, I've learned more about myself than I ever bargained for. I've made friends, I've laughed, I've experienced moments of what might actually be happiness.

"That's it, Willow. Keep going," Abigail quietly cheers me on.

My chest stirs with emotion as I continue to think of the people I've met here.

Cameron, the first person I ran into. He's been nothing but a sweetheart to me, showing me more kindness than I ever imagined. Deghan, with a smile so contagious, who gives the best hugs in the entire universe. Sydney, the man who challenges and pushes me to do better, be better, to learn and grow. And Silas, my broody protector with a haunted past and a connection to me that I'm not sure I'll ever understand.

They make me feel safe. They make me feel loved.

A gentle hum fills my ears, and I catch a faint gasp leave Abigail.

Opening my eyes, my heart lurches at the flickering pink kissing my skin.

My arms, from shoulders to the tips of my fingers, radiate a glowing energy that I wasn't quite sure would ever rise to the surface. I move them slowly and admire the magnificent display, my gaze flitting to Abigail as she watches with a triumphant smile on her freckled face.

"You did it, Willow."

I nod my head in mild disbelief. "I did it."

The power surges through me, igniting my core and simmering something deeply inside me that I think was always there. It's familiar, immense, and only just the beginning.

And damn am I excited to find out what happens next.

"Remember that moment, whatever it was that you were thinking about," Abigail guides me. "When you're having trouble accessing your magic, that will be there to help you pull it out until you can do it without hesitation."

Love, I was thinking about love.

My arms shine brighter, the magic pulsing at the mere recollection of how I brought it to the surface.

"Like that." Abigail clasps her hands together and hugs them close to her chest. "I'm so proud of you, Willow."

I turn my arm over and bask in the glow. "I think I'm proud of me, too." I chuckle and the magic falters, dimming slightly before disappearing completely.

"That's normal," Abigail says immediately. She reaches out and places her hands on my shoulders, looking me directly in the eyes. "You've done the hard part, Willow. Now we can move onto the fun stuff."

"The fun stuff?" I raise a brow at her.

Abigail grins and bobs her head up and down. "Oh yeah. The *fun* stuff. I'm going to mold you into one hell of a witch. When this is all said and done, you're going to walk out of Harper Shadow Academy a new woman."

And even though she's only been in my life a short while, there's a part of me that completely believes that from this day forward, nothing will be the same.

Here's to hoping that isn't a bad thing.

CHAPTER 24

The next few weeks quickly fly by.

I'm able to build my tolerance to have a shadow realm session three times per school day. Abigail and Walker are impressed with my ability to retain knowledge and have been confident with divulging more and more information about the supernatural world. Things come much easier now that I've broken the initial barrier that was hiding my magic.

Abigail brings me old grimoires and spends extra time allowing me to scour the aging text once we've finished our lessons. I've made tiny progress but progress all the same.

Sydney has made sure I've had my morning latte without skipping a beat. He's always there to greet me prior to ethics and is my go-to guru for all things witchy *not* related to Silas.

Deghan adorably walks me to my second class nearly every

day, and we have our post-school naps a couple times a week. He hasn't tried to kiss me, and I've been too nervous to make the move myself. I'm okay with taking things slow, though. He insists I attend every party and always save him a dance.

Cameron never fails to make me smile and is true to his word on keeping an eye on my drink. He's proven to be reliable, hilarious, kind, super-hot, romantic, and such a great friend.

Silas is great at keeping his distance despite the insane pull between us. Most days, the only time I get to see him is during last period. On occasion, he'll meet me on the outdoor patio with an old family grimoire to help me with my research. More frequently, though, I'll feel his presence lurking in the shadows, watching me always, a deep longing filling the void.

The girls are great. Lillian and Ethan spend most of their free time together, which is incredibly cute. Kyra and Remi have a few guys on their radar but haven't managed to call dibs just yet.

Brooke and I managed to spend an hour on the phone a couple times, and damn was it great to hear her voice and finally catch up—what I'm allowed to fill her in on, that is.

I still haven't had the chance to talk to my mom, but that isn't all that surprising. She never was much for returning phone calls, and since I can't leave the school, I'll have to wait until a more appropriate time to return home and resume our long overdue conversation. I feel better knowing the truth about her, and I take comfort in how much better she was when I was able to sneak out of the academy with Sydney to see her.

Allie continues to give me dirty looks every chance she gets, only shying away when Kyra scowls. It's equal parts hilarious and embarrassing. She clearly dislikes me because of the Silas thing. I've witnessed her attempt to talk to him, but he walks away or barely says anything in response. I don't know why she's so hell-bent on going after a guy who clearly isn't interested. Remi told me it's the appeal of wanting something you can't have, but to me, that just sounds like torture.

Either way, according to fate, she never really stood a chance.

And according to the curse, I may not either.

"Um, Willow," Abigail remarks, her tone alarming.

My heart speeds up. I stand from my desk and make my way to her swiftly, checking the ceiling reflexively to make sure the seams of the shadow realm are intact.

"You're going to want to sit down," she cautions.

I swallow the fear that rises and plant my butt firmly on the edge of the chair across from her. "Please tell me already, what is it?" My hands shake in my lap.

She bites her lip and abruptly closes the text she had her hand rested on. "Actually, never mind."

"No, no, no, no. Open it back up. Tell me what you found." A ringing fills my ears, and a dull ache forms in my chest. "Abigail, please."

She inhales through her nose and right back out through clenched teeth. "The text said, *quo facinore mori manibus amori vacare.*"

I tilt my head. "Translation? What does that even mean?"

She lowers her head. "It basically means, *love must die at the cursed hands in order to be free.*"

"At the...cursed hands. My hands...I must...I must *kill* the one I love to break the curse? That's...no, no that can't...can it?" The words tumble out of my mouth, and I desperately try to decipher and make sense of this new information. To free the past and future Oliver witches, I have to kill someone. Someone I love. Someone who loves me. I shake my head. No. This can't be.

Tears threaten to fall down my cheeks.

"Willow, we'll keep researching. This isn't solid, we don't know for sure."

She might be right, but without fully understanding it, I know, somehow, deep down, these are the cards I was dealt. The curse is solid and heady in my core, and I recognize it to be true; I feel it in my soul.

If someone has to die at my hands to break the curse, someone I love, I'll make damn sure it'll never happen. I won't love. I won't let anyone love me. I won't feed the curse my power if I don't allow it the opportunity to take it.

I shove my things back into my backpack and hastily walk toward the entrance. I turn back. "I'm going to cut out early. I'm sorry." Without allowing her to protest, I mutter the incantation and head back to the regular realm early, knowing Sydney won't be there yet.

Instead of waiting for him or heading to ethics, I skip the rest of my classes for the day and go straight to the headmaster's office.

A knock later, Walker answers the door. "Come on in, Willow. What can I help you with?"

"I'd like to transfer to the supernatural dorm." I pause. "And if it's possible, can we rearrange my schedule?"

He takes a breath. "Perhaps you should sleep on this decision? It seems rather sudden?"

"No," I say, stone-faced, knowing I must do this now before I change my mind. "Effective immediately would be preferred."

"Okay then. You're a bright young lady, and I trust you've thought this through. Your schedule will take a bit to work out, and I'll need to have the specifics of your request, but..." He opens up a folder, glancing it over, and says, "Dorm W five is available."

"Thank you, sir."

The words exit my mouth, and the door opens, Abigail filing into the room. She catches my eye, and I half expect her to be mad, but she shows no signs of disapproval.

Walker speaks. "Willow here wants to switch her classes and dorm. Think that's something you can help her with?"

"Absolutely," she confirms, not questioning whatsoever.

"W five is still open, correct?" he asks her.

"Yep, all good." She turns her attention to me. "You've had a rather *rough* day. Why don't you go ahead and take your last few classes off?" She looks to Walker. "Is that okay with you?"

He nods. "I'm aware all of this has been a lot on you, Willow. We've put a lot of pressure on you in a short amount of time.

Take the rest of the day. I can have one of the teacher assistants bring you dinner if you'd like."

Why are they being so accepting of my demands? Whatever the reason, I'm glad I didn't have to put up too much of an argument. I'm nearly bursting with emotion and need to be alone.

"That would be great, thanks." I smile weakly.

"I can help you get your things from your dorm," Abigail offers.

"That won't be necessary, I don't have much. Thank you, though."

"I'll drop your finalized schedule off when I make the changes."

"Okay," I mutter, walking to the door and leaving, not wanting to stay any longer and risk breaking down in front of them. I head straight up the stairs, thanking the universe that none of the girls are randomly in our room between classes. I grab my suitcase and duffel, ramming every stitch of my belongings inside hastily. It takes a few moments to shove everything in enough to transport them to the west wing.

I pause, soaking in the room and racking my brain on how I'm going to tell the girls about this sudden change. Only then do I remember I won't have to. A spell I had read about floats to the surface of my mind, almost like a gift from the universe.

Stepping away from my bag, I raise my hand and walk toward Lillian's bed. "*Moma prote forgodum,*" I whisper and then head to Remi's and Kyra's sleeping areas. I don't erase myself completely, just the bits and pieces that would cause them to ask questions. Alone, I'll retain everything we had, everything we were. They can't be hurt by the things they don't know, and they won't miss what they don't remember.

It'll be better this way.

I can protect them this way.

Leaving my old dorm without another thought, I head straight to the west wing, reeling in the shift in energy along the corridor. I arrive at W five and find the door unlocked, so I step inside. To my surprise, the room is completely bare, minus the standard-issue beds and dressers. No decorations. No comforters or clothes strewn about. No sign of life whatsoever.

I take a further look around, stepping inside and shutting the door behind me. Exhaling, I stop and lock my eyes onto the massively breathtaking curved window, then it dawns on me—all of the room number *fives* have this gorgeousness in common.

I drop my bags where I stand and drag myself to the windowsill seat. The area is cushy and has a built-in padded sitting area, perfect for reading or simply sightseeing. I plop down and bask in the natural light. No longer able to fight back my emotions, I choke back a sob, and the tears finally make their way down.

I cover my mouth to hide my hysterics, unsure of why since I'm painfully alone. A sad reality I'll have to come to terms with. I've always been afraid of this, but I never thought it would be because of my doing. Maybe my fear of abandonment was so deep-seated because subconsciously I knew I'd end up this way. I was cursed to this solitary life, and my fear was just to prepare me for what was to come.

A light knock startles me. I wipe furiously at my face and walk to the door.

"It's me, Abigail. Can I come in?" Her tone is sympathetic and respectful.

I turn the handle and let her pass.

She breathes in the room and settles her look on me. "We're going to figure this out, okay?"

My bottom lip quivers in response, and I bite the inside of my cheek to fend off more waterworks.

"Here's your new schedule." She holds out a paper. "And here is this." She places a pen in my hand.

"A pen?" I say, confused.

"I spelled it with a cloaking spell. Just click the top"—she motions to the lever—"and you'll be cloaked. I figured you'd want to dodge the people you're trying to avoid between classes as well as during them. But make sure you do it in a private place, we don't need to freak people out with disappearing acts."

"You've thought of everything." I hold the pen, turning it around and examining it. It's merely a standard clickable pen, nothing special about it, except the magical cloaking spell.

"Our schedule doesn't change, just where we're meeting, so look that over and make sure to adjust where you meet me. We still have work to do, don't forget that." She clutches the bag that's hanging over her shoulder and hands it to me. "And here's this. Now that your dorm has changed, you can keep these here for your reference. Some of the texts have to stay in the shadow realm, though, so not everything is in there."

I sniffle and take the bag, muttering, "Thanks."

"Willow, please don't give up. I get that this is all a bunch of shit, but you're going to get through it—we're going to get through it together."

Her words are soft and generous but do nothing to soothe the gaping hole daring to consume me from within.

"Okay. I'll go, but please reach out if you need me. Otherwise, I'll see you prior to first Monday morning. Take the weekend for yourself. I'll have food sent up." She motions toward a corner in the room. "You have a full bathroom in here, too. Not sure if you've seen that."

My eyes widen. This room is perfect, and given any other instance, I'd be completely and absolutely giddy, but all I can really feel is grateful that I won't be forced to leave my room for the next three days.

Abigail leaves and I grab my pillow and blanket from my suitcase and trail over to the oversized window again. I place them haphazardly and climb onto the seat, letting the warmth of my blanket do what it can to comfort me while I eye the seemingly endless forest in my line of sight, forcing away every last thought that comes to mind until everything finally fades away.

CHAPTER 25

Although I manage to sleep away the rest of my Friday and most of my Saturday, I finally decide to get up and do something. I take a long, hot shower, cleansing away the remnants of tears left behind. Once dressed, I scan the food selections that have been brought up and settle on a salad. The taste is bland and boring and purely reminds me of how down I am. How can a bowl of lettuce and toppings cause someone to feel so *blch*?

I scan the few books that Abigail brought me, pulling them onto my lap and examining their covers. I'm disappointed to not see the one she had recited the passage from; the one that created all this chaos in my mind. It must be one of the texts that had to stay behind in the shadow realm.

I'll have to make sure I spend my extra time there studying the contents to see if I can figure out another way to break the curse. A way other than killing someone I love.

A migraine creeps its way in like it's my body's way of reminding me of the caffeine I've forgotten today. Risking being seen on a coffee crusade is not in the picture, though.

But with Abigail's spelled pen, I don't have to risk someone potentially spotting me.

I press the button, per her instructions, and my entire body is suddenly invisible. It's fucking spooky but so damn cool. I push it again, and my body comes back into vision.

I throw on an oversized gray sweater and pair of slippers, clicking one more time to cloak myself, and slowly open my dorm room door. I peer outside to make sure the coast is clear, quietly shutting the door behind me and making my way down the hall. Up ahead, a few students hang around the lounge area in the center of the building. I hold my breath in anticipation, but when I walk in their line of sight, not a single one of them glances in my direction.

Thank you, Abigail.

I shuffle my way down the stairs, sure to not make any noise in the process.

I'm about to make my trek through the foyer but stop dead in my tracks, my eyes locking on to Silas. He's sitting firmly in place in one of the leather lounge seats. His head rises, and I'm almost certain he's spotted me, but he never quite latches on to my gaze.

I stand, not daring to move, watching for his reaction.

A few moments pass and his shoulders lower, and he resolves back into his seat. He appears like he's waiting for something... maybe me. My heart breaks, but I know this is what I have to do, at least until I find a better solution. I won't let anyone get hurt on my watch. If I could take all of the pain for myself, I'd do it in a heartbeat.

My head throbs, reminding me of my mission. I close the space to the north wing, peeking through the teacher's lounge door to confirm it's empty, and then step inside. Even though I only did bookkeeping at the local coffee shop, I still made myself familiar with the machines, at least enough to make my own, so with that experience and Sydney's help the last few weeks, I feel pretty confident in which buttons to push without him here. A few moments later, I have my delicious cup of coffee. The sweet and roasted scents are familiar and tug at my chest as memories of making coffee with Sydney play in my mind.

Mug in hand, I make my way toward the door only to be startled by oncoming traffic. *Shit.* I didn't expect my cup to be visible, but because I cloaked myself prior to making it, it's not hidden with me. Hastily, I set it on a nearby table and freeze as the door to the room opens.

Slowly, I step backward, matching the strides of the newest members, Abigail and Headmaster Walker. Right when I'm about to alert them of my presence, they start speaking, so I hesitate.

"I can't quite make sense of it," he says.

"And you're sure the hole keeps reopening?" Concern lines Abigail's face.

"It's like it's being fueled somehow. Some unknown source is giving it power, enough to keep breaking open. No matter how many times I seal it off, it happens again." Walker looks tired and desperately stressed, the wrinkles more prominent on his brow, dark rings around his eyes like he hasn't been sleeping well.

Abigail grabs two cups and brews their coffees. Simple, black coffee—Walker's with an extra shot of espresso and two heaps of sugar.

"I keep repairing it, every time making sure it's rock-solid, only to find it broken back open. Luckily, it hasn't been large or there long enough for something to come through."

Did he just say *something to come through?*

She shakes her head. "I'll continue with my research for something more concrete to keep it closed. I'll pull my resources."

He takes the coffee she holds out to him, and they exit the room, leaving me with my thoughts and my own drink.

What keeps opening? Clearly, they're referring to something

supernatural. Are they talking about the shadow realm? Cracks in the seams? The same seams I check every single time I enter out of the fear instilled by Abigail about the demon realm? I could offer my help, but how would I do that without letting them know I eavesdropped on their conversation? I'll have to wait until one of them says something and then I can speak up. In the meantime, I'll stay focused on my own problems.

I grab my drink, uncloaking and recloaking myself swiftly to include the cup, and head out of the room. Stealth game strong. Upon exiting the hallway, I spot Silas again. This time he's joined by Sydney.

"You're telling me you haven't seen her?" Sydney urges.

Silas shakes his head. "No. Abigail said she needed some space. Have you talked to Deghan?"

"Deghan hasn't heard from her either. And he asked Cameron, but he hasn't either."

Sydney lowers his shoulders. "I'm worried about her."

"Did you ask the girls?" Silas questions.

"They act like they have no idea what I'm talking about. Remi's exact words were: *Why would we know where Willow is*? It's like she's done a memory spell on them to forget her. I just don't understand why. Why would she leave us all like this?" Sydney's hair is disheveled, and a frantic look stretches out on his face.

It's strange to see the two of them communicating like this.

I reach my free hand toward them, desperately wanting to click the pen and show myself to them to ease their pain, but knowing damn well that the main thing I'd be doing is prolonging the inevitable.

It's better this way, I remind myself. It has to be.

"It's beyond me, but I'm sure she had her reasons," Silas finally admits.

Not being able to take the sorrow flowing through the space, I turn, walking straight past the garden and up the stairs, leaving no trace of myself behind.

Inside my room, I breathe a little sigh of relief, watching my body take shape into the world again with a simple click of the magical pen. I resolve into my lone window seat, coffee in hand, watching as the sun disappears. My gaze flickers to something lower, on the ground.

Crossing his arms over his chest, he solemnly studies the same burning sky.

Deghan. He never misses a sunset.

If I can't be near him, at least I can enjoy the view with him, even if he has no idea. I close my eyes, thinking deeply of him, willing him to know he's not alone, that I'm right here, I still care. I care so goddamn much.

I open them back up and a faint, radiating pinkish orb flows from my chest, through the glass, gliding its way directly to him. It perches on him and soaks into his body. Somehow, the tension in his shoulders relaxes a bit, and he rubs his arms, glancing left then right, then, surprisingly behind him and up toward my window. His gaze scans the building, and before he can see me, I cloak myself from sight. His striking deep golden eyes pierce through my window. Deghan runs a hand through his hair, sighing and turning back toward the sky.

Maybe I'll tell them about the sacrifice I made for them eventually, but not now, not while it's all so fresh and raw. I'll sink into the shadows and do my best to disappear from their lives. It's a pain so deep and sharp and wide and haunting, to be so close to having so much, only to be left with nothing at all. To taste such bittersweet happiness and lose it in the blink of an eye.

No longer able to sit back and do nothing, I grab the books from the bag and arrange them on my bed, desperate to come up with something, anything. The texts are old, covered in layers of dust and decay, and a great deal of them are illegible, some foreign languages I can't seem to translate. I stay up most of the night scouring them, and at some point, the bright sky and howling in the distance reminds me that it's a full moon, and the woods are a dangerous place for anyone who's not a werewolf.

My heart aches again at the thought of Deghan watching the sunset alone, not a clue as to why I left without a trace. To Sydney resorting to talking to one of his least favorite people in an attempt to find me, desperation obvious in his features as he nearly begged for any type of answer. To Silas, hopelessly waiting in the most central of locations in the school for a whiff of my existence, and even when he found it, I was too much of a coward to let him confirm his suspicions. And to Cameron, who has the least answers of all. At least Silas, Deghan, and Sydney can assume it's something supernaturally related. Cameron probably thinks I've up and vanished for no reason, and no one can offer him any explanations, including the girls.

I wouldn't know what to say if I tried.

Ugh, hey, guys, I sort of have feelings for all of you, and I'm cursed to kill someone I love to break the curse, so I have to say goodbye so I don't have to murder any of you. Sorry, it was fun while it lasted. Oh, and according to what I recently discovered, you'll all be driven madly away from me at some point, so if we continued on the path we were on, we would have had that to look forward to. At least like this, we can just use our imaginations with what we thought our futures together might have been like.

And maybe eventually, this won't hurt so bad. Maybe we'll be able to pass each other in the hall with a kind smile as we think of what could have been, them never really knowing why it couldn't have worked, but blissfully happy that we got the time together that we did.

If anything, I'll be forever grateful for the moments I shared with each of them, and now, I'll continue to care for them from a distance while I watch them slowly forget about me.

CHAPTER 26

Time passes—first the long, agonizing minutes, the empty hours, lonely days, depressing weeks. It blurs together, fades into nothing, just like I do.

I cloak myself every chance I get, and Abigail has started to warn that if I don't talk to the guys soon, she's going to take my pen away. I avoid them like the plague. The plague that consumes my soul and leaves me a blubbering mess most nights.

It's pathetic, really. The way this entire situation has taken hold and made me so fucking miserable. I've become so obsessed over figuring this out that I've started going to the shadow realm to study by myself when school isn't in session. It's the easiest way to sneak around and have the time alone to think and process the texts.

Abigail has been kind and given me extra time during our

sessions, but it's never enough, and the daunting seconds that pass are a reminder that I need more—more knowledge, more time, more answers.

So that's what I've found. Well, the time part, anyway.

I thought by now the guys would have tried to move on, but each time I silently pass them in the hall, their desperate energy clings on to me and threatens to shatter me into a million pieces. It only fuels me more to figure this out, but each time I try, I come up empty-handed.

I can't figure out who cursed the Oliver family, it's been written out of the history books. I can't figure out why, other than we were too powerful. Someone was jealous of the sheer mass of our magic and found a way to steal it, to harness it for themselves. They've been exploiting the Oliver witch energy sources for far too long, and now, it seems nearly impossible to break the curse. It's a short matter of time before they locate my magic and come for me, too.

"I'm telling you," Abigail insists, her friendly demeanor dissipating. "Either give it here or go talk to them. They're literally driving me insane. Every single time I walk through a hallway in this building, one of them stops to see if there are any updates. You're like a missing freaking person to them. They need answers, and it's not my place to give them the answers they're looking for."

She's become my closest friend these past few weeks, and the only person I've really talked to. I show up for my normal classes but stay as hidden and out of sight as much as possible, getting my work done, turning in my assignments on time, and cloaking myself to and from class. It's not always easy, but I manage.

I'm not sure if it's my inhibitions lacking or the need to soothe their pain, but I say, "Okay."

Her eyes widen. "*Okay* like you'll talk to them or *okay* like you're giving the pen back?"

"I'll talk to them." I swallow and comprehend, deep down, that it's the right thing to do, it always has been. I was wrong for leaving them behind like this, but at the time, I thought it was the right thing to do. I thought it would make it easier on all of us, but watching the time go by and not seeing any of us getting any better, I realize it was a mistake, at least in the way I did it.

"Damn, that's great." She pauses. "You mean soon, though, right?"

"Where's Sydney?"

She closes her eyes, breathing in deeply, concentrating fiercely. "His dorm."

Her magic gives her the ability to do a mental locator spell. It's absolutely mind-blowing. Most witches have to have a personal item or some DNA to do a locator spell, but Abigail can simply focus on them intently and find where they are.

"I'll see you in the morning," I say, shoving my notebooks into my bag and swinging it over my shoulder. "Wish me luck."

She smiles kindly. "You've got this."

I head back into the school's realm, cloaking myself so rapidly you'd never have noticed my presence. I round the corner and enter the north dorm's hallway, immediately feeling both Sydney's and Deghan's energies.

Not giving myself the chance to change my mind, I gently knock on Sydney's door. My heart seems to beat out of my chest, and I fight back the urge to cry, something I've been so damn afraid of encountering any of them.

The door swings open, a look of hopefulness fleetingly lost when he finds the hallway empty. He steps into the space, and I sidestep around him, not to bump into him. Being this close to him sends shivers down my spine.

He frowns, slowly retreating and shutting the door behind him. I watch him meander back to his bed, sitting and throwing himself onto his back with a sigh.

I clear my throat, making my company known, and then uncloak myself.

He's on his feet so fast, he's a blur rushing toward me. He

stops only inches from my face, taking me in and scanning me for any harm.

"Hey," I say, not able to meet his eyes.

He grabs his chest. "Willow," he breathes. "Are you...are you okay?"

I nod. "I'm okay."

Extending his hand, he hesitates.

I die for him to complete his task, to pull me in, but I don't dare deserve the physical comfort. I don't deserve the sheer concern spilling out of him in heaps.

"Where have you been, sweet girl?" His hand brushes against my face.

I close my eyes in response, a single tear tumbling down my cheek. At this, he gives in, tugging me into him, and I die a million deaths in his embrace.

"I'm sorry, Syd...I'm so sorry."

"No, no, no. Shh, it's okay. You're okay." He presses closer, holding me tight and patting my hair. "Here," he says, leading me a few steps away from where I appeared, motioning for me to sit.

I sigh. "Listen, I can't stay. I just wanted to tell you it's okay to stop looking for me. I'm sorry I left the way I did, but it's for the best. There are things out of my control, out of all of our control, and it has to be this way."

"What do you mean? You can't be serious."

"I need more time..."

His expression changes. "Is this about the curse? We can figure this out, Willow. You don't have to do this on your own."

"I do, though, to an extent. I can't risk you getting hurt, any of you. I'd never be able to live with myself if I knew I harmed you and could have done something to prevent it. I'm sorry this has been hard on you, but you need to know, it's okay to move on, to stop looking. Please, do it for me." The words come out along with more tears. I hate myself for breaking down but know there's no other way.

I stand, taking Sydney's face into my hands and place a soft kiss onto his forehead, and back away, going invisible with a click.

He shakes his head. "You don't have to do this, Willow. Let me help you, please, I'm begging you."

I open his door, and he rushes forward, but anticipating him following me, I spell his door temporarily shut, leaving myself enough time to take a couple of steps down the hall, wipe my eyes, and knock on another door.

It's like a bandage, ripping it all in one swift motion, the pain immediate and intense, but soon enough it will ease, right?

A beautiful face greets me, and I uncloak myself, watching his eyes brighten and sadden all at once. He pulls me in without another thought, and I'm wrapped in his musky, earthy scent, and I'm reminded all over again of our times together. I missed him so much, just as much as I missed Sydney, too. It's another painful, gaping wound I've tried so desperately to mend with no success.

"Willow, God, Willow, where have—I don't care anymore, you're here, you're here now. Christ, I was so worried." He pushes back, scanning me over like he did that day in the foyer, following the night in the woods the time his friend nearly killed me.

I don't protest his hold, even though he's partially cutting off my oxygen supply. I smile into him, closing my eyes at the same time more tears make their way down my cheeks.

It's like the more I told myself to stop caring for them, the more innate that feeling became, like it weaved its way into every fiber of my being. Caring for them is a part of who I am now, and there's nothing I can do to shut it off.

"I came to tell you I'm okay, and you can stop contacting Abigail and Walker for information." The words come out harsher than I anticipated.

He frowns. "You're leaving me again?"

His words break me.

"I have to," I whisper.

Deghan shakes his head. "No, Willow, you don't. What's wrong? Tell me so I can help you fix it."

"You don't understand, you can't. It's not something *you* can fix...I don't know if it's something I can fix. But to keep you safe, it has to be this way."

He huffs. "You're worried about *my* safety?"

I nod. "I get that it doesn't seem like a big deal to you, but your well-being is one of my greatest concerns. This *thing* I'm up against, it threatens that. It threatens all of you. And I'm sorry that it has to be this way." I rake my hands through my hair and pull. "I wish it didn't have to be this way, but it does, and you have no idea how sorry I am for that."

Almost like I did in the prior room, I take Deghan's face into mine, this time placing a kiss on his cheek, and back away, going invisible again.

"I'm sorry, Deghan."

I open the door and repeat the spell, sealing his door shut.

He grabs on to it, yanking and pounding. "Willow, don't do this. Please."

My heart continues to throb, but I hold it together, knowing I have one more stop. One more person to find. I don't have any answers for Cameron, not today, and regardless of how painful that may be, I say the few goodbyes I'm able to force.

I walk invisibly down the north wing hall, focusing my thoughts on finding him. My body finds its way down the stairs, through the foyer, past the garden, into the dining hall where I catch a glimpse of friends who have long forgotten me, and out onto the patio.

I don't know *how* I knew he was here, but settling my gaze onto him, I confirm I was correct. I stop abruptly, scanning his body when he shifts toward me.

Can he feel me? Does he realize I'm here?

I step forward, cautiously watching him move.

He stands and, turning on his heel, he walks away, only briefly glancing over his shoulder, like an invitation to follow.

I do what my instincts command and trail behind him into the forest where it all began.

He approaches the clearing and stops sharply. "I know you're there," he offers.

Not needing to hide any longer, I change into my visible self and wait for his reaction. Seconds go by excruciatingly slow.

"There hasn't been a day that I haven't felt your presence, and your absence. It's been unbearable." He doesn't turn, maintaining his back toward me, unwilling to face me.

I don't blame him. I wouldn't face me either, not after betraying and abandoning him, and everyone, like I did.

At this, he decisively moves, his eyes revealing infinite sorrow.

"I'm sorry I ever kept my distance from you," he admits. "This"—he nods to the space between us—"has been torturous."

I step forward, and for once, he doesn't attempt to go back.

"I can't stay."

This time, he attempts to close the gap.

"You can't leave. Not yet." His eyes are pleading.

"I came to tell you…" I fight the tears that no matter what, I cannot overcome.

"You came to tell me goodbye?" He advances again, and this time he's so, so close, inches away, his breath on my cheek.

"Yes." I swallow. Why is this so fucking difficult?

"If this is goodbye, and you're telling me I have to experience a more brutal pain than this…" He inches his hand forward, sparks crackling the moment he breaks the barrier between us. "Then please, give me one thing. I'm begging you."

His hand cups my face, and he guides me in, disregarding the surging power threatening him away.

I summon every ounce of strength I have and will the force to stop, to give him a moment without the insane agony, and somehow, it works. For the briefest moment, there are no flashes, no sputtering energy disallowing him entry.

He seizes the moment, bridging the gap, leaning down, pressing his warm lips to mine, breathing me in and kissing me like there is no tomorrow, because for us, there might not be, and right now, I'm okay with that.

I swim in his touch, his soft, subtle mouth, curving perfectly into mine. He tastes like sunshine and darkness and a freshness so sweet. He's like heaven, despite being wrapped up in this hell on earth.

All too soon, I pull away, knowing I can't fight the forces battling us much longer.

He leans back in and leaves the gentlest kiss on my lips, and a wash of fear consumes me at the realization that *that* might be all that we'll ever be.

"I'm sorry," I say.

Silas trails his hand down my cheek, and the second he tugs at my bottom lip with his thumb, the energy reignites, and he flinches in response.

I click the pen in my pocket, going back to being cloaked.

His hand lowers to his side at the same time his face droops.

"Losing you," he whispers, "is more painful than that will ever be."

I bite my lip so hard as tears cascade down my cheeks. I back away until he's just a blur in my vision, and I'm all alone once again.

CHAPTER 27

I will not break.

I will not break.

I will not break.

The heartbreak that rips me apart is so intense, I'm not sure I'll make it back to my dorm to fall apart safely. I blink and find myself in the dining hall. *Okay, good, now just get through here and turn left.* I blink again, my body showing me the way, on autopilot for the rest of the trek to my room.

I cross the threshold and click myself back into existence, collapsing into a heap on the floor, bawling so uncontrollably that I don't even recognize the sounds or emotions leaving my body anymore.

Who am I?

What have I become?

Why am I so weak?

So much self-doubt fills me and creates drastic internal chaos.

At some point, the cries turn into sniffles that eventually lull me to sleep.

When I wake, I have no idea how much time has passed, but glancing at the window, I see that the sun has already gone down. A sharp determination forces its way to the forefront, and I no longer allow myself the privilege of wallowing in self-pity.

I am an Oliver witch, and I will fight this.

I have to.

Not bothering to cloak myself, I grab my backpack and leave the room, ignoring the look from the short, dark-haired girl walking into the dorm next to mine. I've seen her going to and from her room since I've been dorming here, but she hasn't seen me. I'll have to introduce myself some other time—right now, I'm on a mission.

No matter how long it takes, I will scour every inch of the text back in the shadow realm, until I figure out some fucking way to break this curse. I have to. Seeing the pain and confusion, *feeling* their grief—it was enough to wreck me time and time again.

I take the steps two by two, jumping down the last few onto the landing below. I jog past the garden, not bothering to peep in the foyer, my eyes straight ahead. I'm focused solely on the room Abigail and I have been using for our extended study sessions; the place she leaves the ancient books.

Upon me muttering the words, the same familiar purple shadow appears, and I step through. Only this time, I'm absolutely baffled at what's on the other side.

"Cameron?" I say in a rush.

"Willow?" He looks to me, so scared, so frantic, shuffling to his feet.

"Cam, how...how did you get in here?" I stutter the words. This is impossible.

He shakes his head. "I don't know. It feels like I've been here forever." His eyes lock on mine. "Are you okay?"

I nod. "I'm so sorry, Cam. I'm so sorry I left you."

"It's okay, here, come here." He holds out his arms, and alongside his fearful energy, he's oozing with pure happiness. He pulls me in and holds me tight.

I don't deserve the comfort he gives, not after leaving him like I did.

"You pathetic human," a voice breaks the silence.

I back away, shifting my attention around the room, desperate to locate the source. I shove Cameron behind me despite his best attempt to do the opposite.

"Trust me," I command, turning around and firmly gripping his shoulders.

I locate a flaw in the seam, something I've been so fucking afraid of since I first stepped foot in the shadow realm. It continues to break and fissure, a complete blackness on the other side.

"I do thank you, though. Your weak attempts have only given me the power I need." The voice cracks and echoes.

Cameron shivers from behind me. "What the fuck is that? Where are we?"

I can't answer his questions, not even if I wanted to, but that doesn't stop me from asking my own.

"Who are you?" I ask the mystery voice.

"You mustn't need my name, for it would make no difference."

The barrier between this world and the next continues to break, and I do the one thing that comes to mind.

I grab Cameron's hand, rushing to the entrance, muttering the words that have never once failed to get me out of here, unfortunately this time, they do exactly that—fail.

"Oh, you thought it would be that simple, Miss Oliver?" His laughter bellows.

"Cameron," I urge, gripping his hands in mine. "I want you to go over there, stay in the corner, do not come out. Do you hear me?"

"What is happening, Willow?" He's so afraid.

And it only continues to tear me apart.

The wall crumbles, darkness consuming the entire right side of the room.

"Now!" I yell. Not breaking my concentration from Cam, I summon my strength and focus it solely on him. "*Protecum morkai.*" Thankfully Abigail and I have maintained some level of magical training despite the other pressing issues in my life.

"A protection spell, how cute." The voice appears closer, a sludge of a shape creeping into the shadow realm.

"What do you want?" I say, the surge of my magic gushing through me more profoundly than I've ever known.

"Well, you have something that belongs to me, and I'm here to claim what's rightfully mine." The shape forms a figure so tall their body is curved by the ceiling, like a Christmas tree that doesn't quite fit, although this sight is massively more terrifying than a too-big pine.

"And what's that?" I know damn well what his answer will be.

The creature laughs again, and I'm unable to decipher where his face begins and ends. There is no distinguishable head, only tiny pinpricks that glow where eyes might be. All he seems to be is a mass of black, surrounded by a gloomy shadow that's so straining on the eyes it's difficult to stare for too long.

"Give me what is mine," he says, despite having no mouth, "and I will let your pitiful human live."

"I don't know what you want from me."

"Your magic, deary." Another sadistic laugh follows.

You can do this, Willow.

Without allowing another second to pass, I beckon my magic, but not to give it to this disgusting creature.

"*Fotum brunai,*" I whisper, feeling the surge and looking down to watch it take shape on the outside of my body. A beautiful shade of electric pink, starting from my shoulders and making its way down onto my hands, sizzles to life. Raising one hand slowly, I whip it forward and send the demon straggling back a few feet.

Holy shit, this is it, I'm going head-to-head with a fucking demon.

"Nice try," the demon teases and flips what I think is an arm, sending a force so sudden that I'm also thrown back and slammed into the wall.

I wince at the immediate pain in my shoulder, and judging by the way my arm is hanging, it's dislocated. A sudden sense of déjà vu hits me, bringing me back to the nightmare I had the first week of school.

A low, guttural growl fills the space, like in the dream, and I assume that this is it, I'm going to be torn to shreds, the same thought I had then.

I close my eyes and urge every bit of me to find its strength, afraid that when I open them, I'll find the same fate from my dream, but when I do, a small halo of light appears, and I realize it's coming from me, from my radiating magic.

I force another blow to the demon, sending the mass shooting to the other side of the room in retreat.

"You cannot beat me," it growls out, firing another blow in my direction.

Anticipating its move, I surge my energy forward, blocking the attempt. This time the laugh comes from my own body. *I just blocked a shot from a demon.*

Cameron gasps, and I take a split second to look over my shoulder and make sure he's okay.

The demon, seeing my weakness, fires another, and before I can fully jump out of sight, the blow lances my injured shoulder.

Fireballs of heat course through my body. Pure, wholesome pain rips through me, and I know for sure there is serious damage done to my shoulder. I pull my arm to my chest, shielding the rest of my body and focusing all of my magic to rush to my uninjured arm.

The demon advances on me, and my chest tightens at the

reality that I'm no match for whatever he might be. I've only done basic training with Abigail and Walker, and even though they've told me of my potential, it hasn't been recognized yet, and it's only a matter of time before the demon overpowers and consumes me. My only regret is not being able to get Cameron out of here.

Tears well in my eyes, and I know that I can't go down without a fight. I've been through too much to allow defeat to take me so easily.

I focus my attention to my hand, forcing the energy to build and build, waiting for the opportune moment to strike—if there even is one in this losing battle. I'm about to unleash what might be my final move, when the energy of the room changes and someone appears in my peripheral.

Shit. I thought I might be able to hold off this demon, but there's no way I can handle more than one assailant at once. I go to retreat, and my gaze finally settles on the newest member.

It's not a demon at all.

It's Silas.

He flashes toward me, using whatever super vampire speed he has, and steps in front of me, standing between me and the demon.

"Willow, you're injured," he blurts out, but I cut him off before he can continue.

"I'm fine, but we're screwed. The portal is locked from the inside, there's no way out. We have to take him out first."

"Ahh, this continues to grow more interesting, my dear," the demon taunts, floating around the entrance to his home realm.

Silas peers over his shoulder and whispers so only I can hear, "Sydney was right behind me, he shouldn't be long."

I nod, glancing at Cameron and turning back to the demon, a small amount of hope filling me at the possibility that the people who I've pushed away might be my saving grace after all.

"On three," Silas mutters. "One... two..."

On command, we both split. I throw a massive ball of fire that I had no idea I was capable of conjuring up, and Silas slams into the demon from the opposite direction. I didn't know he could manifest his power that way, but damn if it isn't a beautiful sight. Light violet and gray orbs pulse from his fists, landing a few blows on the demon and then using his speed to get away.

The demon twirls around from the impact, and as he rights himself, he throws two balls of power toward Silas and me. We both jump out of the way, but the residual energy gets too close for comfort to Cameron. I watch the darkness hit the protective dome surrounding him, threatening to break through with no success.

Silas and I exchange a glance again and throw another set of blows toward the demon. We go on like this for what seems like eons, until finally, Sydney bursts through the realm, only to stop dead in his tracks and then fall to the floor the moment Deghan follows him through.

"What the f—?" one of them says.

"A little help!" Silas shouts.

Sydney quickly shakes his head, resolving to not ask questions as he powers himself up, the green magic flowing almost immediately. It's hard not to notice how magnificent he is, how magnificent all of them are with their abilities on display.

Deghan partially shifts, wolf fangs and claws exposed on his human body, his golden eyes glowing with a rage so ferocious.

Cameron's helpless energy pulses from behind me, and I desperately send him a ball of relief to ease him. It penetrates the barrier, and he resolves a little.

Thank God for my ability to calm people. Especially considering how dangerous it is for me that their nervous energy becomes mine—it's nice to nip it and do what I can to eradicate it.

"Good, this is great. I can eliminate all of you in one fell swoop. If anything, I should thank you," the demon taunts, and then dives down, heading toward Deghan.

Sydney throws two green balls of power toward the demon,

who misses his target, and Deghan takes the opportunity to pierce the demon's borderline translucent body with his talons.

Silas and Sydney exchange nods, somehow telepathically strategizing their next move.

Never in a million years did I expect to see Silas and Sydney working together, but here I am, witnessing them fight perilously side by side to protect me. At all costs.

A strange ooze falls from the demon's wound and sizzles on its way down. Gross.

"Enough!" the demon screams. Immediately, his body widens and stretches, and a boisterous power soars from him, blasting Deghan, Sydney, and Silas away from me and to the floor.

I shift my focus around to all of them and revel at the anger that consumes me.

The demon settles his attention directly on me, and with the burning rage from within, I blast off my power, crashing it into him, and somehow, he deflects most of the hit and forces it onto the closest target—Silas.

Silas's body is thrown violently across the room, slamming into a wall, bones snapping from the impact.

My heart fucking breaks. I never meant to hurt him; I meant to hit the demon.

I rush to Silas's side, drawing his head into my hands, his lifeless body falling limp in response. My soul aches, desperate for him to open his eyes, to deny what just happened.

Please, Silas, just wake up. Please, it can't end like this.

The demon takes the moment to advance on me, creeping closer, daring to steal what he thinks is his.

A force so intense, one I can't explain, bubbles up within me, and without even really knowing why or how, I scream.

I scream so loud that I lose track of where my voice ends and the ringing in my ears stops.

I scream until blood pools from my nose, my ears, my eyes.

I scream and build a magical strength that is so vast it consumes me whole.

I scream until there is no light at all within the room—until every bit of illumination is trapped within my diaphragm, and I scream...scream until I release it all back out into the world, into the shadow realm, into the demon hovering in front of me that's terrorizing me and the ones I care for.

I scream until the demon disintegrates into nothing but dust floating through the air like debris from a burning building.

I scream until hands find their way on my shoulders, rubbing and stroking and quieting the seemingly endless supply of rage overwhelming me.

CHAPTER 28

I stop screaming, but it's like there's this other version of me inside of my head not letting up.

Silas's head is still tucked in my lap; tears roll down my cheeks.

My vision goes blank, other than the sight of him, limp, unmoving...gone.

At my doing.

I go numb along with him.

A conversation appears in my senses.

"Is she okay?" one person says.

"Can you grab her?" another directs.

"You, take him. We have to get out of here."

"Silas," I whisper when his body is torn from mine, the pull on my heart that much more.

One by one, the sound and touch of Sydney, Deghan, and even Cameron, reassure me that they're okay, that at least they are safe. But the one voice I'm the most concerned about doesn't respond and is the epitome of silence. It's deafening.

Exhaustion consumes me. Energy levels at an all-time low. I'm not really sure I could move if I actually wanted to. Existing feels like a burden more difficult than I'm capable of.

I'm carried for a little while, through long walkways, upstairs, more hallways, until I'm eventually placed on a soft, warm surface—a bed. I breathe deeply, not daring to open my eyes. I don't recognize the space I'm in, its energy different than mine and Sydney's and Deghan's room. I'd only been in Cameron's dorm a few times, but we're not there either.

I'm no longer able to process my whereabouts. Fear and misery roll back in, taking their turns assaulting me.

This is your fault, Willow.

You did this, Willow.

You are a freak, Willow.

You never deserved a single one of them, Willow.

I suppress a sob, curling myself into the fetal position.

"I think she's in shock," a voice says...Deghan's.

"I've never seen that kind of magic, the sheer volume of it was insane."

Sydney.

A clearing of a throat, "Uh...yeah, me neither."

Cameron.

How is he still in here? How is this not breaking the oath?

"Obviously," Deghan replies sarcastically.

A warm body appears beside me; I'd be able to identify it anywhere—Deghan. We've spent so many afternoons napping together that, even at a distance, I memorized the feeling of his presence over and over. He rubs my back, his energy pooling into me.

Cameron's familiar hand finds its way onto mine as he cups

my palm with his. He's scared, but I can identify the worry is more for me than anything else.

"Here, hold this," Sydney tells one of them.

Deghan shifts.

A strange whooshing emerges, and then a light wind, kind and delicate, traces my skin, but from the inside of my body. Pain consumes me, and without anyone touching me, my shoulder snaps back into place. I bite down a scream, my throat too sore to make another sound. The physical agony subsides, and within seconds, my energy increases a bit, like I'm being plugged in and recharged.

When I'm finally able, I open my eyes, soaking in all of the beautiful faces around me, all except one. My gut wrenches, and the pain of my reality slices through me. I start to cry again.

"Shh, it's okay," Sydney tries to comfort me. "You did so well, Willow."

I did well? Silas is *dead* because of me.

I shake my head and scan the room.

Deghan, sitting to my right, gorgeous as ever, staring intently, rubs circles and then grabs my free hand.

Cameron sits to my left, his kind eyes meeting mine, a type of understanding hidden within them, like he knows now why I did what I did, at least partly.

Sydney, planted below Deghan on the bed, holds a giant clear crystal in his lap, his hand on my leg, firm and accepting.

I meet each gaze before shifting my concern to the last remaining member of the room.

Silas.

His body remains still, lying on a nearby bed. So motionless.

What have I done?

I'm on my feet, scooting to the edge of the bed I was gently placed upon. I'm surprised at the strength returning to my body, the energy renewing.

"Let her go," Sydney whispers.

I crouch next to the bed, taking Silas's hand into mine,

holding it to my face, against my cheek. *I'm so sorry.* There are no cracks, no fizzling energy pulsing between us. No sign of pain on his face from my touch, and that's how I know for sure, I did something awful.

I did the thing I was so terrified of doing, and now, now it can't be undone. I forced them away so none of them would get hurt, and here I am, staring the inevitable in the face.

I close my eyes, pressing his palm against my face, relishing the last remaining moments with him I have.

Bodies stir across the room, a signal that they'll be prying me from him soon, that my time is limited that much more.

"I'm so sorry," I say, this time out loud.

"How...how are you doing that?" Silas's voice cracks, sending shockwaves through my body.

I open my eyes and nearly stumble back, only barely regaining my composure.

His eyes blink to life, along with my heart and soul.

"Do it again," he pleads.

Without question, I take his extended hand, placing it to my face. No sparks. No wincing in pain. No restraints.

"I...I killed you."

He smirks. "I'm immortal, Willow. I've died more times than I can count."

"I killed you." I laugh. "I broke the curse because I killed you." I blubber the words, the realization overwhelming me.

More tears fall, and I'm unable to stop them as all of my warring emotions flood into one gigantic mess.

I broke the curse.

Silas shifts his body, using both arms to lift me off the floor and into his arms. His embrace is like a waterfall, so peaceful and serene but absolutely magnificent, and capable of wrecking me.

"I'm hugging you," I say. "And you're not in pain?"

"No," he mutters beside my ear, breathing in deeply, savoring this moment.

A knock at the door resonates, and I don't dare let go, not yet.

"I thought you were gone," I admit.

He tightens his embrace. "You can't get rid of me that easily."

The door swings open. Abigail, Walker, and another professor, I'm unsure of his name, step into the room.

"I see that you're all safe and sound," Walker speaks with authority. "We've managed to reattach and repair what we can of the shadow realm, eliminating the remains of the fallen demon." He pauses. "I can't thank you enough for what you did, although I'm not sure why you were there in the first place. That'll be a conversation for another day."

I finally force my attention away from Silas, only to turn around and face the headmaster, my body still pressed against Silas, not wanting to miss a beat of this newfound unrestrained distance between us. I'm close enough to Deghan to touch, so I reach out and grab his free hand, cupping it into mine.

"Cameron, these instances are rare, and there is a specific protocol we must follow."

My body goes rigid. *Protocol.*

Walker raises a hand in my direction. "But, given the circumstances, I would like to offer you a choice."

"A choice?" Cameron asks, his voice uncertain.

"Mmhm. It seems this *group* is rather fond of each other, and given the drastic majority being what they are, I'd like to offer you the ability to keep your memories or have them erased. Now, before you answer, I must warn that you will be forbidden from discussing any of these matters with another human student, and if you decide to agree, you will have to sign a magical oath that will disallow you from doing so. This is a very serious matter, so please use caution in your decision."

Cameron's attention shifts from Deghan to Sydney, to Silas, and then falls on me.

I nod, giving him what I can of an approval and secretly begging him to say yes without using my magic to convince him to do so. Having Cameron knowledgeable would only make our lives that much easier, considering we wouldn't be hiding something as big as *this* from him, but knowing these things puts Cameron at risk, too. Had he known, though, maybe he wouldn't have been lured into the shadow realm, and maybe that knowledge would have kept him safe. I hope like hell it will aid in his safety, if he chooses that option.

He swallows deep, the sound apparent even at a few feet apart. "I'd like to keep them, sir."

My heart swells, and I break contact from Silas and Deghan to grab Cameron and bring him in for a hug. Everyone must think I'm crazy, but the thought of losing him, or having him forget me, is almost too much to handle.

His energy is content and relieved.

"I thought you might opt for that." At this, Walker then mumbles something to Abigail.

She reaches into her bag, exposing the same scroll and pen I signed my name to what feels like a lifetime ago. "Cameron, if you'd come over here so we can go over some details."

He obliges, stepping away from my embrace, leaving me cold and alone.

Walker points to me. "You need to rest. The destruction you caused was immense and had to have taken plenty of your resources. I'm surprised to see you standing."

"It's not without challenge," I admit.

"We will discuss matters more in depth come morning, in the meantime, I assure you that our perimeter is secure."

"How can you be so sure?" I ask, not wanting to question his authority but not totally sold on his declaration.

"We have disabled the shadow realm." His face is solid and serious.

I gaze at the man standing next to Walker, who hasn't said a word since his arrival.

"You two haven't met. This is Professor Tremont. He was able to provide his assistance in deactivating the realm."

Tremont extends his hand, and when we touch, his energy is

all over the place. He locks his eyes with mine. "It's lovely to meet the infamous Willow Oliver."

I chuckle, unsure of how to accept that response.

Walker clears his throat. "Now that Cameron has vowed his secrecy and we have exchanged formalities, we shall leave you for the night. Please," he scans the room, meeting all of our eyes, "get some rest. We have a big morning ahead of us."

Abigail winks in my direction, and I offer a small smile in return.

They clear out of the room, and a silence falls upon us—one I know is my responsibility to break.

"I'm sorry, to all of you," I start, meeting the stares of the guys. "I never meant to put any of you in danger." I sigh. "I owe you all an explanation. A few weeks ago, I found out some details that, long story short, put all of you at risk. My ancestral curse states: *love must die at the hands of the cursed in order to be free*. I thought the only way to protect all of you was to push you away, to force you to go on with your lives without me in hopes that you would all eventually move on, and I would deal with things on my own...alone." I shake my head. "Watching each one of you from a distance, realizing you weren't getting over my absence...it tore me apart. There was never a day when I wasn't there, you just couldn't see me. But don't for a minute think I wasn't wrecked about this, it was the hardest thing I've done.

"I knew it was wrong, though, and that I needed to say good-bye, to actually give you a bit of closure, but seeing how devastating that was, and how badly it pained me to feel your anguish, it was my undoing. I literally bawled myself to sleep only to wake up knowing I had to figure out some fucking way to break the curse. That's when I went back to the shadow realm on my own to find answers, but instead found you." I point to Cameron. "I knew something even more terrible had happened, because never in a million years should you have been there. Everything else sort of becomes a blur, but my point is and was, I'm sorry. I never meant for any of this. I'm sure this apology will more than likely mean nothing compared to what I've put you through, but I need you to know I only wanted the best for all of you, and I knew with me in the picture, I'd only hinder that from happening."

I stop speaking, and my chest is heavy as I wait in anticipation for any type of response. I understand I don't deserve anything from them, but the uncertainty drives me insane.

Cameron speaks first. "When did you get your hair done?"

"Rude." I frown.

"No, I'm serious." He points toward my head.

I walk to the mirror and gasp in shock. A thick lock of my forever silver hair is dark, like, jet-black dark. How is that possible?

Deghan walks up behind me, placing his hand on one shoulder. "I'm not mad at you, Willow, let me make that clear. I was worried. I was afraid. I hated not knowing why you left the way you did."

Sydney approaches next. "I had a feeling it was something to do with the curse, but I never expected you to deal with it on your own. And knowing what I do now, I have no reservations about wanting to stay by your side."

Cameron continues, "I'm not mad, either. Honestly, I'm fucking surprised...at all of this. But I mean, it makes sense, too. I'm just glad you're okay." He shrugs. "Promise you won't leave us like that again?"

Warm tears well. I expected them to shove me out the door and never speak to me again. *That* type of response is what I deserve.

Silas rubs his neck. "Tell me next time you need to kill someone. I'm glad to be of assistance."

I chuckle, waterworks bubbling over at their honesty.

They all reach in, grasping me for a big-ass group hug. I've never felt such an enormous and endless loving energy. It's fucking bliss.

"I can't believe any of you like me, especially after this."

"I don't know about all of you, but I'm beat," Deghan confesses.

A few of the group let out tired murmurs, and I yawn in response.

"Hold that thought," Deghan says, opening the door and walking out.

A scratching sound fills the hallway, followed by him carrying a bed in sideways.

"What're you doing?" Cameron asks.

"Slumber party, duh," Deghan answers. He sets the bed on the floor and then grabs the others, arranging them in a circle around the room.

Sydney and Cameron help him position the beds, and Silas stands back, looking grumpy that they're in his space but not uttering a word in objection. It's then that I realize we're in Silas's bedroom.

Once the beds are in place, we all grab one and settle in under the covers.

"Goodnight," I murmur.

A collective, "Goodnight" follows.

A hand appears from my left, resting gently next to me. I take it, swimming in the ability to be able to touch him without fear of hurting him. Another moment passes, and Deghan reaches from the other side, and I place my hand on top of his.

I breathe in deeply, a calmness taking hold in their company, and somehow, despite the insane day, it pacifies me to sleep.

There's still so much left to figure out, but for now, I must rest.

The following morning, I wake first and sneak out of Silas's room, but not without pausing to look at each and every one of the men who saved me, from the demon, and from myself.

I'm just passing through the garden area when a figure appears in front of me.

"Is this another one of your disappearing acts?" Silas says, arms crossed, leaning against the wall.

"Believe it or not, a girl's gotta shower, especially after getting demon guts all over myself. You should probably wash those sheets by the way." I point my thumb over my shoulder toward his dorm.

"Only as long as you're not really leaving for good again." His eyes are sad, and I'll do anything to erase his pain.

I reach forward, resting my hand on his arm. The pulsing energy that exists between us now is something out of this world. "I'm sorry for leaving you."

He grazes my cheek with his hand. "Go shower, I'll be here when you're done."

Once I've cleaned the dirt and debris away, thrown on fresh, clean clothes, and braided my still-damp hair, I walk back out into the hallway, uncertain of where exactly I'm supposed to go. Do I head to Walker's office? Silas's room? Deghan's? Cameron's? Sydney's?

I let my stride take me down the hall, and when I enter the big opening in the center of the building, my heart happily pulses in response to what I see in front of me.

Sydney, holding a steaming cup of coffee. Deghan and Cameron chatting like best buds, and Silas, looking sullen and so like himself. It's truly a magnificent sight.

Handing me my drink, Sydney says, "You ready to go have the *talk*?"

"The *talk*?" I question.

"With Walker—he's expecting us," he confirms.

"Oh, right. Yeah. Thanks for waiting for me."

We head downstairs, Abigail greeting us in the lobby upon our arrival.

"You all look great and somehow very well-rested." She beams.

Funneling into Walker's office, we each find a place to sit. Silas manages to grab the spot to my right, and Cameron to my left— Deghan and Sydney are on the side next to Cam, like they're avoiding being near Silas.

Walker clears his throat. "Good morning, group. I wanted to have this little meeting to fill you in on what happened." He looks to Cameron. "I trust this is all in confidence, correct?"

It must be a rhetorical question, considering Cameron signed the oath of silence last night.

Cameron responds, "Yes, yes."

"Some of you may be aware that the shadow realm was able to maintain its power from the remnants of power left behind during each visit. While this is common and we frequently do routine maintenance to preserve any cracks that may develop, there became a point in which Willow's energy reserves were so great that the shadow realm took more than what was necessary. And because she increased her visits, the realm got an abundance of power that essentially opened up a portal to a demon realm. We're still trying to piece together exactly what happened, but that's the gist of what we've gathered.

"The demon targeted you specifically, Willow, luring Cameron in and trying to attack you, sealing you in from the inside. You are fortunate these young men followed you in, otherwise, I'm not sure how you would have fared alone. Not that you can't hold your own, but fighting demons is uncharted territory for most."

Silas interrupts, "She handled herself quite well."

"She actually blew a burst of magic so massive that it obliterated the demon and then shattered the entrance. That's how we were able to escape," Sydney confirms.

"Ahh," Walker says. "That answers one of the questions I had." He pauses. "The realm was nearly destroyed by the time we got there, hence disabling it. It will take some time to repair, especially taking into consideration the recent vulnerabilities."

I had no idea I blew the shadow realm apart. I really don't even know much of what happened between thinking I killed Silas and him waking back up; it's all sort of foggy.

"With that being said, I applaud each of you for overcoming such a situation. It truly is a wonder that you all made it out of this unscathed. I'd like to offer my deepest apologies for allowing this to happen. I was naïve in thinking I had the condition of the realm in manageable order."

Trying to pay courtesy to the words Headmaster Walker is saying, I find myself focusing on the energy around the room, teetering onto each of my guys and soaking it in. I find myself in shock when I meet Silas's gaze, the unbelievability of last night still remaining.

"Willow," Walker says loudly.

I snap my head his direction. "Yes, sir?"

"I'd like a moment alone, if you don't mind."

I stand to leave, and he continues, "With you, that is."

"Oh, yeah, right. Absolutely." I give a weak smile to the group.

They clear out, leaving Walker, Abigail, and me in the large office. Anxious energy fills me.

"It's come to our attention that your behavior may have been a bit reckless, Willow." He massages one of his hands into the other. "And it should go without saying, but you broke an important rule by visiting the shadow realm unattended. But, in doing so, you shed light on an incredibly weak spot that was an oversight on our behalf, and because of this, you will not be reprimanded for your insubordination."

I let out a small sigh in relief.

"We'd also like to offer you the ability to assist in the rebuild of the realm. Like I said to the group, supernatural classes in the traditional sense will be on hold until we can come up with a better resolution, and with your newfound strength, you would be a great asset to the team."

He's proposing that I *help* them?

"Yes, whatever I can do to be of assistance," I say in disbelief.

He grins. "That would be wonderful." He looks to Abigail. "Now, I believe Abigail had some things to discuss with you as well."

I shift my focus to her.

"You broke your curse," she declares.

Instinctually, I smile and then frown. "Accidentally, but yes." It's such a bittersweet thing to have thought I killed Silas. On one hand, it's terrifying and rips my soul apart, but on the other, it freed me from a horrible fate. And if I'm not mistaken, it unchained the other Oliver witches, too.

Abigail fidgets with the zipper on her sweater.

Her nervous energy pools into me, confirming that whatever comes next will not be good.

"I haven't had the chance to tell you this yet, Willow, but your curse, it has fail-safes. It's uncertain how many are put into place, but this is just the beginning. You've broken through one obstacle, but there are more to come if you want to defeat the people who have a hold on the Oliver magical lineage."

A new fracture rattles my core, threatening to destroy me from the inside out. Fail-safes? More curses? One of many obstacles? How can this be possible?

"We're determined to do what we can to help you, Willow. You're not alone. You don't have to do this on your own. Now that you've put one curse behind you, it's important to see that you are capable of great things, that you can overcome this," she says with a sad kindness.

I bite my lip, shifting my gaze across the room as I think about her words.

"I know this is a lot to process. All of this is. But whenever you're ready, I've secured part of the library for you."

"Library?" I blurt out. I guess I *knew* there was one, I've just never come across it in all the time I've spent at Harper Academy. How could something that I once prioritized have fallen so far behind on the list?

"Yes, the library." She smiles. "It's a bit off the beaten path. It's below the main floor of the school. There is an access point near the east wing stairwell."

A place I've never needed to visit, so it's no wonder I never saw it.

"I can take you there, if you'd like. When you're willing, I can show you around and let you explore the space I've obtained for you."

"That would be great. How about tomorrow?"

"Tomorrow sounds wonderful. But it's okay if you need more time. I don't expect you to rush matters like this."

"What better time than now? I'd just like the day to get things in order and breathe a bit before jumping right back in."

"That is understandable."

"Well then," Walker breaks in. "It's nice to see we're on the same page here."

"Could I ask a favor?" I ask, unsure of how they're going to react.

"I'd say you've earned yourself a favor. What is it?" he questions.

"I sort of...erased some of the memories from my old roommates when I switched dorms. I thought it would be easier for everyone to forget me instead of trying to explain what was happening. Is there maybe a way I could return their memories but have some sort of explanation for why things are the way they are? I already have a spell that I could do to give them back, but it's the justification part that I'm unsure of."

I'm sure this is a long shot, but it's worth a try. I miss the girls something fierce, and I'd do just about anything to have them back in my life.

"Hmm," Walker says, rubbing his chin.

"What about dorm distribution?" Abigail offers. "We could say we had to equal out the students and Willow got relocated because of that."

I rejoice at the idea, turning to Walker for his reaction.

"I don't see any issue with that. It's not completely a lie. The west dorm is severely lacking in occupants," he adds.

"I could write something up today," Abigail verifies.

"That would mean the world to me. Thank you, both of you." Despite hearing that I'm still cursed, the knowledge that I might have my friends back in the near future does wonders for my mood.

"Thank *you*, Willow. You are a brilliant addition to the academy," Walker declares.

I stand and shake both of their hands, then walk out of the

room. A heaviness weighs on my chest, but I fight it. I'll deal with it tomorrow.

There, waiting for me in the foyer, are my four guys. The charismatic Deghan, the romantic Cameron, the intelligent Sydney, and the protective Silas. Looking at them, I can't help but wonder how I got so damn lucky.

Luck or not, I need to come clean with what I was just told. At first, my knee-jerk reaction to finding out I was still cursed was to run far away, push everyone out, and deal with this on my own. But Abigail and the guys were right—I don't have to do this by myself anymore. I have a team of gracious people willing to help me overcome what life throws at me. I don't deserve any of them, but somehow, they're still here, standing in front of me, willing to do what it takes to protect me.

"You guys up for food?" Deghan breaks the silence.

After a few shrugs and nods, we head toward the dining hall together.

I hang toward the back with Sydney. "Think you can help me put up a sound barrier?"

He side-eyes me. "Yeah, definitely. But why?" Concern lines his voice.

"I have something I need to tell you guys, sort of for our ears only type of thing."

Once we grab some grub, we walk out onto the patio, pulling two tables together to fit all of us comfortably. The late morning air is crisp and warm, perfect for breakfast outside. Sydney holds true to his word and helps me put up a spell to block our conversation. Even though there aren't many people outside with us, it's better to be safe than sorry with these types of exchanges.

I take a long drink of my coffee before speaking. "Abigail informed me that she uncovered a bit more about my past than I was aware of." I steal a glance at the guys. "She said there were fail-safes put into place. That I didn't *just* have the one curse, and there are many others to fall back on if it was broken." I pause and look at them. "I'm telling you all this because…the last time I found out about my curse, I chose the flight option without telling any of you. This is me being transparent and telling you upfront that the curse didn't end there, and that I understand if any of you choose to walk away. But this is me saying I'm not walking away, not this time, I'm choosing to fight."

"Damn, Willow," Deghan says. "You have some shit luck, girl." He wipes at his mouth with his napkin.

Cameron laughs. "No kidding."

Sydney squares his shoulders. "I'm not speaking for the group, just for myself, but I'm not going anywhere. Especially not now." He places his hand on my shoulder, meeting my eyes, his emerald energy beating into mine.

"You really think we're going to up and abandon you?" Deghan asks. "You're crazy. Syd's not, I'm not, I know damn well Mister Grump Ass over there isn't. What about you, Cam? You with us?"

"There's no backing out now," Cameron confirms.

My heart swells, growing infinitely larger in size, so full it could damn well explode with love. Never in a million years could I have anticipated that *this* is what I'd find at Harper Academy.

My true self.

My powerful magic.

Great friends.

Four amazing guys.

A seemingly endless curse.

Harper Shadow Academy has been full of surprises, and I can't imagine it will stop here.

But for now, I can breathe easier knowing that soon, I'll hopefully have my friends back, and not a single one of the guys sitting right here with me is going to abandon me, despite all I've put them through.

Tomorrow, I'll start the next adventure. I'll explore the library with Abigail and learn more about the safeguards trying to steal my power. I'll go home and visit my mom. I'll tell her all the things that happened here, and maybe she can help me uncover our past and the monsters that threaten to destroy us.

But I'll be doing it with the knowledge that I'm not alone.

That I am a force to be reckoned with.

I slayed a demon; I broke a curse.

I am an Oliver witch, and I will use my hidden magic to defeat what is to come.

Even if it kills me.

Read on to find out what happens next to Willow and her men in *Cursed Magic*, book two in the *Harper Shadow Academy* series.

Acknowledgments

Bringing **Hidden Magic** to life was a new and wild adventure for me, and there are a select few people I have to thank for supporting me along the way. Without each one of them, this book would not have taken shape and become what it is today.

My tiny human—for making sure I have quiet time to hit my word counts & for always being so excited to share my successes. One day, you'll find your passion and I look forward to watching you shine.

The wonderful folks who support my journey on Patreon: Clayton, James, Victoria, and Tyler Bunn.

Tiffany, my incredible assistant, who I could not survive without.

Michelle, your support keeps me going!

The RHRA Facebook group. You all have given me some of the most invaluable feedback and support and this book would never have been possible without that.

And to you, the reader, for sharing your time with me and letting me take you on a trip inside my mind. Thank you from the bottom of my heart. <3

Also by Luna Pierce

The Harper Shadow Academy Series

(Paranormal academy reverse harem)

Hidden Magic

Cursed Magic

Wicked Magic

Ancient Magic

Sacred Magic

Harper Shadow Academy: Complete Box Set

Falling for the Enemy Series

(Paranormal reverse harem)

Stolen by Monsters

Fighting for Monsters

Fated to Monsters

Sinners and Angels Universe

Broken Like You (Standalone)

Untamed Vixen (Part One)

Villain Era (Part Two)

Wings of a Devil (Standalone novella)

Ruin My Life (Standalone)

London & Archer's Story (Standalone)

About the Author

Luna Pierce is a paranormal and contemporary romance author who loves getting lost in her stories. She brings you tough characters that love fiercely and fight for what's right. Luna loves all things gritty, and even supernatural, especially: witches, vampires, and werewolves.

Join Luna's newsletter to receive updates at:
    www.lunapierce.com/subscribe

If you enjoy my books, please consider leaving a review on Amazon, Goodreads, or Bookbub.

Want to chat about the book and tell me the things you liked and disliked about **Hidden Magic**? I'd love to hear from you!

Join the exclusive reader group — Luna Pierce's Gritty Romance Squad